Subtle Felonies

by

Austin S. Camacho

ISBN: 979-8988533306 – Trade Paperback
ISBN: 979-8988533313 – Epub

Cover Design by GinnefineArt

Published by:
Intrigue Publishing
10200 Twisted Stalk Ct
Upper Marlboro, MD 20772

Subtle Felonies

CHAPTER 1

"Wow."

Hannibal actually said it aloud. He stepped out of the black Mercedes-Maybach sedan in front of a house that filled his view. He had to swivel his head left to right a full 180 degrees to see the entire building. Then he looked back inside to make eye contact with the driver.

"Yeah," the driver said with a grin, nodding his understanding. Hannibal closed the door and felt the car ease away behind him. His clientele had included some wealthy men, but he had never been called to an actual mansion before. He knew a lot of people who thought anyone who owned a house like this couldn't have real problems.

Hannibal knew that when you reached this level, the only kind of problems you had were gigantic.

The wooden double doors in the center of the stone monolith beckoned him. Local wild birds tried to warn him off, but he moved up the five steps to the entrance, his mind slipping back through the morning that brought him here.

His office phone rang at exactly nine o'clock that Monday morning, the start of his office hours. She introduced herself as Charlotte Brown, wife of Alexander Brown, as if she expected him to recognize the names. Her voice was South Baltimore, smoothed a little by Northern Virginia. She had a big problem that called for discretion. A previous client, Ben Blair, had referred her to him. Blair was a tech millionaire who had hired Hannibal to find a man who had stolen from his maid. A good man, and Hannibal would take any client referred by him.

Hannibal agreed to meet with her but when he asked for an address, she said she would send a car to pick him up. He preferred to drive but she was adamant, so he agreed and in less than half an hour he was riding to McLean, not a town but just an area of Northern Virginia, home to diplomats, Congressmen, and other high ranking government types. And the CIA.

Hannibal soon understood why it was easier for his new client to send a driver than give directions. After a couple of turns off the beltway they made a sharp turn into a hidden entrance onto a one lane road he would have probably missed more than once. The long, winding private road led them to the tall iron gate that protected the mansion he was about to enter.

As he reached for the doorknob the door swung inward. A trim blonde woman in a black double-breasted dress with white collar and cuffs waved him inside.

"You must be Mr. Jones," she said in an accent-free voice. "Mrs. Brown will see you in the sitting room."

She turned and led him across dark hardwood floors, past white pillars beside tall arches, past a winding wooden staircase, and around a round glass-topped table that seemed to serve no purpose except to be in the way, maybe to stop anyone from running down the hall. She deposited him at the entrance to a hexagonal room scented by big white lilies that stood proudly, maybe arrogantly, on the mantle of a fireplace at the bottom of a stone column that rose, it seemed, to the clouds. In this house even the flowers looked down on him.

Panning left from the fireplace his eyes slid over a grand piano, three tall multi-pane windows, an overstuffed sofa covered with enough pillows to leave no space to sit, a framed painting whose pastoral scene fell short of the actual view through the windows, and two chairs that matched the sofa. Instead of pillows, one chair held a woman. Her skin was polished ebony. Light brown eyes flashed above high, Nubian cheekbones. Hannibal hated the fact that he was surprised. She wore a white, form-fitting sweater dress and a warm but formal smile. She waited for Hannibal's gaze to reach her before she stood and extended a hand.

"Charlotte Brown. Thank you for coming on such short notice, Mr. Jones. Please, have a seat."

Hannibal accepted the handshake, turned to the empty chair and tentatively lifted one of the three pillows.

"Oh, throw those on the floor," Charlotte said.

Hannibal carefully placed two of the pillows beside the chair and perched on the edge of the cushion. "On the phone you said you had a problem I could help you with. Why don't you tell me what that is?"

Charlotte took a deep breath while examining Hannibal. Her eyes scanned him top to bottom. He felt the way he did in the airport when they put him in the chamber and told him to raise his arms overhead. Was she staring into his eyes, or wondering about his dark glasses? Were his black suit and white shirt inappropriate for the season?

"Ben told me that you were very good at finding people," Charlotte said. "And that you were trustworthy and above all discreet."

"Yeah, and he probably figured you'd be more comfortable with a black investigator."

She grinned. "Yes, there is that. You wear those shades all the time?"

"Unless I'm asked not to."

"Well then, would you mind?" She leaned in. He removed his sunglasses and slipped them into his suit jacket pocket. She leaned even closer.

"Blue? No, I think hazel eyes," she said. "Where'd you get them?"

"You'd have to talk to my parents about that. Now, who's missing?"

A brief smile touched her lips, and she relaxed a degree. "It's my husband. I need you to find him and bring him home."

"I see. How long has he been missing?"

"He left Friday afternoon. Since then, not a phone call or text or anything."

"So, a long weekend. I assume you tried to call and text him."

"Of course," Charlotte said, her voice rising. "Repeatedly. Over and over. He's just not responding. It's not like him. I mean, he was a real party animal in the early days, but since he retired, he's calmed down a lot."

Or he's learned how to be discreet too, Hannibal thought. Aloud he said, "Retired from what?"

Charlotte blinked in apparent disbelief. "Excuse me?"

"You said your husband was retired. What was his occupation?"

Charlotte shook her head. "My husband is Alexander Brown. THE Alexander Brown. He was the star forward of the Wizards for almost a decade."

"Sorry, I don't follow basketball."

After a pause she said, "He's been out of the game I guess eight years now, but with all the endorsements I'd think…well, I guess I don't have to worry about you being star struck."

After his Secret Service time on the president's security detail Hannibal felt pretty much immune to stars but knew not everyone was. "I'm sorry to ask but is there any chance he's just lost track of time with some eager fans, or…"

"Or some groupie? Not a chance in hell," Charlotte said, with as much confidence as any married woman could show. "That's not his weakness, Mr. Jones. He's much more likely to get sucked in by some shady businessman. He's got a soft heart. It's easy for him to give his money away, and con men find it easy to take it."

Hannibal nodded. It was good to know what she was really afraid of. She could deal with her man having a lost weekend with some young girl, but if he was a target for swindlers, that was unacceptable.

"Can you find him?" Charlotte's voice said this wasn't really about the money. She was worried about her man.

"I can only promise to try my best," Hannibal said. "Did he say where he was going? That's always a good place to start."

"You should ask Darrell," she said. "The driver that brought you here. He drove Zander out of here Friday." She gave no hint that there was anything unusual about her husband leaving without telling her where he was going, which struck him as odd but not at all unique in his cases. A truly worried woman who took the time to apply makeup correctly, that was unusual. Appearances seemed way too important to her. Her gaze rose over Hannibal's head. He looked over his shoulder to find the housekeeper in the archway. Charlotte stood.

"Lunch is up." Was Charlotte like his German mother? If the plumber was working in their house at noon his mother would make him lunch. It was an oddly old school attitude toward visitors, even if they were workmen.

"Actually, I'd like to start with a look in your bedroom. There's a lot I could learn about your husband…"

"Oh, come join us," she said. "You can look up there later. Besides, you said you wanted to know where Zander was going Friday. At lunch you'll be able to talk to Darrell."

"He eats with you?" Hannibal asked.

"He lives here," Charlotte said. "Well, in one of the guest houses."

Wondering if the offered meal was a deflection to avoid more questions, Hannibal slid his glasses back into place and followed Charlotte through a side entrance to a covered outdoor area that looked at first like a galley kitchen with seating for five along one side. He spotted two smokers, double burners, a refrigerator, and, yes, a television. The young black man busying himself at the stove wore a jacket similar to the housekeeper's dress. Must be the staff uniform. Two people in swimwear sat at one end of the sideboard, chatting. Or more accurately, the man was chatting at the woman.

The woman turned toward him holding a frozen smile. She was a time-lapse younger copy of Charlotte, her hair in long braids. A black one-piece swimsuit showed off her bountiful figure to best advantage.

Charlotte stopped between them. "Mr. Jones, this is my daughter Francine. Dear, this is Hannibal Jones, the man who's going to help us find your father."

To Hannibal she said, "Frankie, please." Then to her mother, "Mama, why don't you just call the police for God's sake?"

"You know why, dear. We don't need any more headlines and reporters snooping around here. And Mr. Jones, you've already met Darrell."

The driver slid off his stool and held out his hand for a solid shake. "I go by Cawfee. Good to really meet you."

"Coffee, like the drink?" Hannibal asked.

"Yeah, but I spell it C-a-w-f-e-e. From back in my DJ days."

"You were on the radio?" Hannibal asked.

"No man, like an MC, you know? I spun the tracks and did the mix behind rappers on stage. They used to compare me to DJ Jazzy Jeff." Cawfee had a warm, ready smile but he was built like Mike Tyson in his prime. A whole lot of man for a chauffeur. Hannibal figured he also served as a bodyguard.

Charlotte looked at Hannibal, patted the seat next to Cawfee and seated herself one stool away. As Hannibal slid into the empty seat the cook pushed plates in front of them all, followed by bowls.

"Soup and sandwiches," Charlotte said. "I still love a simple meal."

Simple, Hannibal thought. But the vegetable soup was cold. Still, he had to admit it was accompanied by a perfect grilled cheese sandwich. When it was half gone, he decided to get back to business.

"So, Cawfee, where did you take Mr. Brown Friday afternoon?"

Cawfee turned from Frankie long enough to say, "He was meeting some friends up in Baltimore. Can we talk about all that after lunch? I can give you a tour of the grounds and whatnot."

Hannibal nodded. It seemed he would get more useful information about the missing man's coming and going from the chauffeur than the wife, and he wondered why that might be.

CHAPTER 2

After their meal the ladies went into the house and Hannibal walked with Cawfee past the swimming pool down a path toward an open green space. The driver needed no prompts to start talking.

"Man, I never thought I'd live in a place like this. Look at those shrubs and all the bushes, trimmed just right. The garage at that end holds eight cars. Four of them go up on lifts. This one over here where I park, hold the two we drive most. They all luxury cars. You ever ride in a Maybach before?

"Well…not in the back seat," Hannibal said. Misleading, but true. "So, you live in the mansion with the family?"

"Naw, Jack. I got my own place. Right over there." Cawfee pointed at one of the two guest houses. "But I'm like family. I got the run of the place. Swim when I want. Use the gym, upstairs over the main garage and it's got everything. And I'm getting paid to hang out with my main man."

"Yep, sounds like you're living the dream," Hannibal said. "But you're not with your man today. Where'd you take Mr. Brown?"

Cawfee stopped to open a small shed that faced an open green space. "Zander wanted to go to this exclusive club up in Baltimore. The Statuz Club, with a Z. Not the kind of place he'd want the Mrs. to know about. That's why I wanted to get away from the women. Here." He handed Hannibal a golf club. "This here's his own private driving range. It's like, four acres so you don't have to worry about hitting nobody."

"So, you're not worried at all?"

"About Zander?" Cawfee asked. "Nah. He's partying somewhere. He'll come home when he's ready."

"Did he have a suitcase with him? Overnight bag maybe?"

"Nah, nothing like that," Cawfee said. "But he's a spontaneous kind of guy." He set a bucket of balls down between them and planted one on a tee.

"Golf's not my sport," Hannibal said. "Didn't know it was Mr. Brown's. I'd expect a basketball court."

Cawfee chuckled. "Zander, he figured he was as good as he wanted to be on the court. But rich folks play golf and since he's rich folk now he wanted to master this game."

"Right," Hannibal said. "So, you dropped him at the Statuz Club. Were you supposed to go back and pick him up?"

Cawfee wound up and drove a ball down the fairway. The impact of the shot sounded to Hannibal just like a man getting hit in the head with a club. "Naw I come home. When he goes there, he spends the evening, sometimes the night. He calls me when he's ready for a pickup."

"You saw him go in?"

"Yep." Cawfee hit another ball. It sliced off to the right. "He's got a regular girl he sees up there. I heard him call from the back seat, making sure she was there that night."

"Catch her name?"

"Something weird, start with a Z I think." Cawfee took a few seconds, then swung again, hard. It was an impressive drive right down the middle. He smiled into the sky. "Yeah, I remember him telling me she was a tall, black haired Spanish girl. He said she knew some tricks that could give you the bends."

"Eloquent," Hannibal said. "Sounds like she was the last one to see him. A good place to start looking."

"I can drive you up there. Nothing else happening today."

"Good. You have a girl there?"

"No." Cawfee's smile dimmed a bit. "Like I said, it's an exclusive club. Guys like me, they don't get to be members."

Hannibal nodded. "Mrs. Brown might not know about this club or this girl, but she doesn't seem stupid to me. Think she's scared of some young thing snatching her man away?"

Cawfee held his hand out to accept the club Hannibal wasn't using. "Naw, she knows he's coming home. Trust me, I was there when they met, when they married, when he adopted her little girl. Trust me, she got his heart locked up. Twelve good years, them two. Solid. What she scared of is, he's going to give it all away to some slick talker with a get-even-richer-quick scheme. Or that she'll lose him to the drugs."

"He got a drug problem?"

"Had," Cawfee said, moving slowly toward the house. "Got loose from the pills a couple years ago. But she's scared he could get hooked again. I'm telling you, that's the real reason she's worried when he only been gone a couple days."

"And what about the money angle. Who has he given a pile of money to lately?"

"I can't help you with that one," Cawfee said. "Me and Zander, we don't talk money. But I can hook you up with Gene, Zander's money man. You know, when you got real money, you get to pay somebody else to handle it."

CHAPTER 3

"You sure this is cool?" Hannibal asked from the back seat as the black Mercedes turned onto Dolley Madison Blvd.

"We good, man," Cawfee said. "Charlotte told me take you wherever you wanted to go. You got me until we got Zander back. Gene's office is only about ten minutes away in Tysons and you'd have to go there anyway."

That much was true. Charlotte said Gene Young would handle his contract, pay him and take care of any expenses. Hannibal pulled out his phone and did a quick search. Zander Brown's family saw him as a celebrity, so Hannibal had not asked for a photo, like he would in any normal missing person's case.

In seconds he had Brown on his screen. A handsome man with bright eyes and a sincere looking smile. He was popular with the fans, known for his flashy style of play. One reporter said he would pass up the three-pointer for a shot at making the slam dunk. And he liked to party, able to go clubbing all night and still turn in a peak performance on the court the next day. At least that's how he was described until he married and, four years later, retired. What must that feel like, to be retired with a family and a fortune at age 32? Some men in that position would be overwhelmed by arrogance and ego. But every reference Hannibal found described Brown as well liked, respected, and generous to charities. Overall, a good man worth finding.

Hannibal pulled black driving gloves out of an inside jacket pocket and pulled them on. It was a ritual for him, putting him into the on-the-job mindset. "Been with the Browns a while I take it?"

"Hell, yeah. Me and Zander been tight since college. I was already in his posse when he went pro. I was there the night he met Charlotte. Best man at the wedding." His voice lowered a bit. "Got to admit, at first I thought she was a gold digger, you know? A waitress with an eleven-year-old daughter. But she been nothing but good to him. And good for him."

Hannibal hopped out in front of the office building on Tyson Blvd and rode up five flights. The gold plaque beside the double glass doors held only two lines. Eugene Young. Wealth Management. Hannibal liked a man who kept it simple. He stepped inside to face a perky young secretary dressed for church. Blonde over blue, she belonged in a Crest commercial.

"Good morning, sir," she said. "How may we serve you today?"

Too perky by half. But he smiled, gave her his name and offered his card.

"Oh, yes! Mr. Young is expecting you. Please follow me."

She hopped up and sashayed down a short hall to stop at the second door on the left, which Hannibal could probably have found on his own. She tapped twice and eased the door open a couple inches. "Mr. Young? Mr. Jones is here to see you." Then she pushed the door wider, stepped back and assumed a modified parade rest stance. Hannibal stifled a laugh and walked in.

The office was large and over-furnished. The walls were covered with plaques, certificates and photos of houses, boats, cars and wine bottles. The slender man who rose and walked around from behind the mahogany desk stood three inches shorter than Hannibal's six feet but offered a surprisingly strong handshake. Hannibal guessed he was the kind of man who used a variety of products on his almond-colored face.

"So happy to meet you Mr. Jones. Mrs. Brown called to say you'd be stopping by, so I cleared my calendar. Is it true that Zander has gone missing?"

Young waved Hannibal to a comfortable chair beside a round glass table and settled into the chair on the other side.

"Apparently," Hannibal said, "But I've just begun my investigation so it's too soon to get worried."

"Well, Mrs. Brown told me to take care of the business with you. I'll have your fee direct deposited into your account every day, and I'll make sure we cover any expenses you encounter. Now tell me, how else can I help?" Young asked, twisting a ring on his right hand. Was he that worried about losing a client?

"The family thinks Brown might have spent his lost weekend with somebody who was suckering him out of a lot of money. Is he the kind of guy who…"

"Absolutely!" Young said, eyes rolling skyward. "I have spent countless hours pleading and cajoling him to not sink thousands into this or that shady enterprise." Hannibal thought Young must charge by the hour. The seventy-dollar haircut, thousand-dollar suit and Gucci loafers said that handling other people's money was mighty good for his own wallet.

"Sounds like you know Brown's business pretty well."

"Well, it's not just business," Young said, leaning back with hands wide. "I'm a close family friend. I met Zander and Charlotte back when I was selling life insurance. I grew my business and when I finally got my CFP he was my first client. Kind of built my practice on him, and I feel very protective of him. But there are always parasites looking to suck the blood out of men like him."

"It sounds like one possibility is, he's on a cruise with one of those parasites and lost track of time," Hannibal said, "or just lost his phone. Can you tell me anything about the last couple of hustlers who went after him?"

"Of course. I vet these people thoroughly, although often it does no good. Just in the last month there was a treasure hunter who needed a stake to find a gold-filled Spanish ship off the coast of Florida, and the guy with the high-tech, next-level virtual reality gizmo. Then there's that company that makes high performance socks."

"Seriously? Socks?"

"Brother, they have me shaking my damn head," Young said. "Tell you what. Why don't I put together a portfolio of each of those last three shady deals and I can bring it over to Zander's place this afternoon?"

"That'll work," Hannibal said. "I'll probably be back there later today after I check some other things out."

CHAPTER 4

Embedded in a row of warehouses, the Statuz Club looked just like all of its neighbors. If not for the large colorful sign over the door it would be easy to miss. Hannibal suspected that was no mistake. A low-key location like this would appeal to party people who leaned toward alternate ideas of fun. He got out of the car and took a few steps toward the door before he noticed that Cawfee had also gotten out.

"Hey, you can wait here if you want," Hannibal said.

Cawfee grinned. "What do you go, maybe a buck eighty soaking wet? I'm thinking you might need some backup. And I might get fired if I let you get hurt."

Hannibal shrugged. Cawfee followed him up the five concrete steps. He pressed the door buzzer and waited, thinking this place probably got very few afternoon visitors. This was an after-dark place, and no place he'd ever bring Cindy. The thought took him back to his conversation with her in the car on the way to Baltimore.

"Hey, honey," Cindy said after the secretary put him through. "Nice to hear from you, as always. You on a case today?"

"Yeah, and it raised a couple questions you might be able to answer."

"Is this legal stuff?" Cindy asked. "You know there's a charge for my…legal stuff." Even over the phone Hannibal thought he could see the twinkle in his woman's eyes.

"Uh-huh. Anyway, what's a CFP?"

"CFP?" she repeated. "Like, Certified Financial Planner?"

"That's got to be it," Hannibal said. "Would a guy like that put together portfolios on possible investments and take them to a client's house?"

"Sounds like something his staff would do," Cindy said. "And he'd have clients come to his office. Your new client an accountant or something?"

"No, that guy works for the client, or actually works for the missing person the client is paying me to find. He's a retired basketball player. Alexander Brown."

Hannibal heard a rolling chair shoved back telling him Cindy had jerked to her feet. "What? Zander Brown? From the Wizards? That's who you're looking for. Damn, babe. You hit the big time now."

"So, you've heard of him."

"Everybody knows Zander Brown," Cindy said. "What happened to him? Got any good leads?"

"How about we discuss it over dinner? I've got a bunch of other calls to make."

Hannibal spent the rest of the ride to Baltimore doing the unrewarding legwork that came with any missing persons case. He was on the phone to hospitals in Fairfax and Baltimore Counties and the District of Columbia. Twenty-six short conversations turned up no unidentified admissions. Three more calls to police connections revealed no unidentified DOA's.

All of which had brought him here, standing at the door of a closed nightclub. He rang a second time, and a third.

"Maybe nobody here during the day," Cawfee said.

"No, this is when a club is setting up. They serve liquor?"

"Of course," Cawfee said.

"Then they take deliveries during the day." Hannibal brushed past Cawfee and walked around to the side of the building. He hopped up onto the loading dock and pushed through the wide plastic strips hanging over the entrance to keep the heat out. Cawfee followed him through the storage area and into the main room. Steps led up to a second level where more private entertainment would surely take place. Aside from a sitting area with couches and love seats Hannibal didn't recognize most of the furnishings. He saw benches people might kneel at, a wooden X in one corner, and a tall framework with various ropes hanging from it. But a regular bar stood in the far corner. A buxom brunette stood behind it, scanning bottles, maybe doing inventory.

Hannibal took three steps toward the bar before a linebacker type in a skintight black tee shirt and a kilt appeared in front of him. His red hair hung in a thick braid from the back of his head.

"The hell you doing here?" the redhead asked, flashing his teeth.

"Just need to speak to the manager," Hannibal said in his calm-them-down voice.

"Don't open until seven," the redhead said. "You breaking and entering."

"Breaking?" Hannibal asked. "The door's wide open. Not looking for trouble just need to…"

"What you need to do is get the fuck out of here."

Behind Hannibal, Cawfee said, "Want me to move this mother fucker?"

The woman behind the bar looked up. "What's going on over there, Ginger?"

"Nothing I can't handle," the red head said. He swung a hard right cross, which Hannibal easily side-stepped. He grabbed the braid with his left and, with a quick foot sweep, put the man on his back.

"Stay down, asshole," Hannibal said, lifting the left side of his jacket to show the pistol in his shoulder holster. Then to Cawfee, "Stay here, man. Just watch my back. Cawfee smiled and nodded. Hannibal maintained his bored expression as his steps echoed across the concrete floor. The woman behind the bar matched his facial expression until he reached her.

"Only a couple kinds of people walk in here like they own the place," she said. "You police?"

"No."

"Then what you selling?"

"Hannibal Jones," he said, presenting his card. "I'm a private investigator."

She looked from the card to the man. "Private, eh? Well, you walk like a cop. This says you're a troubleshooter. Am I in trouble?"

"No, ma'am, but one of your customers is. Are you the manager?"

She held out a hand at the end of a full sleeve of tattoos. "Wanda. Owner and manager. So, who's in trouble and what do you expect me to do about it?"

Hannibal liked her, a woman who could get to the point. "I'm trying to track down a missing person. Tall black guy, forty or so. His name is Alexander Brown and he was…"

"Zander?" Wanda's expression shifted from disinterest to shock and concern. "Zander is missing? Oh my God."

"So, you know him."

"Who the hell doesn't?" she asked. "Damn. He was just here Friday. Good man, soft spoken for a baller." She dropped two shot glasses on the bar and filled them with something red.

"Yes. As far as we know that was the last time anybody saw him. Did he meet someone here? A date perhaps?"

"Oh yeah. His regular girl. Ximena." Wanda lifted her glass with two fingers and threw it back, then shook her head and smiled into Hannibal's lenses.

"Ximena?" he asked. That was usually enough to prompt more details, but not this time. Wanda smiled down at the other glass, then up at Hannibal. After a few seconds he took the hint and swallowed the shot. Cinnamon fire ran down his throat and his eyes flared open behind his Oakleys.

"Ximena," Wanda continued. "Pretty Spanish girl, long black hair, big ass. That was his shit."

"She works for you?"

Wanda shook her head while refilling their glasses. "More an independent contractor. She pays me to use my space. What she does while she's here is none of my business, really. But she stays clean, and I've never heard any complaints about her."

"So she might be the last person to see Mr. Brown."

Wanda leaned on the bar, winked at Hannibal, and did the second shot. Hannibal took a deep breath and emptied his own glass. He was glad he wasn't driving that afternoon.

"Nope, not the last," Wanda said. "She didn't even see Zander Brown Friday night. He asked for her, but she was busy upstairs when he came in. Now, he'll usually wait, have a couple of drinks, you know, he's a sociable guy. But then some other bitch stepped to him. Girl I ain't never seen in here before. Don't know what she whispered in his ear, but he left with her."

Hannibal glanced over his shoulder. Cawfee and the man in a kilt were facing off like boxers do while the ref reads the rules. He better make this quick.

"I'm thinking you know your regulars pretty well. She look like his type?"

"Oh, yeah," Wanda said. "Not as thick as Ximena but taller and she did look Latin. Legs for days and black hair down to her ass. She stepped in, hooked him and pulled him out the door just as Ximena was coming down the stairs."

Damn. He left with a girl with no name. "Sounds like Brown usually stayed here when he visited, so probably her idea to leave. Any chance he mentioned a destination?"

That appeared to be worth another drink. Wanda poured and drank. After another deep breath, Hannibal followed suit.

"Well, she ain't say shit to me," Wanda said. "Seemed like she was in a hurry to get Zander all to herself. When Ximena came to the bar I told her what happened, and she ran to the door. She was pulling her earrings off. I figured there'd be blood on her nails when she came back, but no. She was fuming though." Wanda put an elbow on the bar and leaned in to Hannibal. "She got there just in time to see them peel out of the parking lot." Here Wanda left a dramatic pause. "In a red Porsche 911."

Well, it was something, and Hannibal sensed that was the end of the story. He was on the edge of tipsy for it but had to admit that Wanda was a lot more open than most witnesses.

"Thank you. Thank you very much. You've been very helpful." He backed from the bar but stopped when he saw her face cloud up. She was looking from the glasses to his face and back. After a couple seconds she finally said, "The drinks?"

"Ahhh…" Not a gift, not a challenge, but the cost of talk. Hannibal pulled out his wallet and dropped two twenties on the bar. Wanda raised an eyebrow. He dropped a third twenty. That got a smile.

"Thank you, sir. Come again."

He gave her a wink and moved back to where the silent standoff continued. He tapped Cawfee's arm and pointed to the door they had entered. After two steps the big red head grabbed Hannibal's arm. Hannibal spun, pushing in until he was nearly nose to nose with the other man.

"I ain't hurt you the first time but don't get it twisted. I am the last nigga on earth you want to fuck with right now." The bigger man stepped back and watched Hannibal and Cawfee leave.

They were clear of the Statuz Club's parking lot and off of warehouse row before Cawfee said, "You don't drink much, do you? For a second there I thought you were going to fuck that boy up."

"No, not much tolerance for alcohol. Or assholes."

"You get anything out of the broad besides shots?" Cawfee asked.

"Not much. She saw Zander go but he left with some girl she didn't know. No clue as to where they might have gone."

Cawfee stopped at a light. "Maybe he took her to his apartment."

Hannibal sat forward. "His…what?"

"Zander got a little place in DC," Cawfee said. "Back in the day it's where he went to get high but now I think it's just when he wants some privacy. You know how some guys got a man cave? Well, when you got it like that you get a man apartment. He could have took her there I suppose."

"Well then, that's sounding like our next stop."

CHAPTER 5

Apartments in Washington, DC range from crumbling ghetto hovels to luxury homes. Alexander Brown's was closer to the high-end ceiling. Hannibal had his doubts when Cawfee steered them to Southeast DC, but the building at number 10 K Street, SE met his expectations.

Cawfee rang the bell before letting them in. Hannibal didn't ask why he had a key. He led them into a contemporary space with hardwood floors and floor-to-ceiling windows. Straight ahead they walked to a kitchen island that looked like quartz with the rest of the gourmet kitchen to the left. Past the island stood a dining table and a living room beyond that. It was all spotless. No glasses out and nothing in the sink.

"Doesn't look like anyone's been here since the cleaning crew." Hannibal said. He turned right to look into what he thought would be the bedroom but instead was an office/den set up with leather furniture. After confirming that the desk drawers held nothing but pens and an impressive collection of staplers, he slid through the variety of papers on the desk. There were a couple of amateur-looking business proposals. One that did not look so amateur was a full color tri-fold brochure for a company called Optilorus. They apparently manufactured advanced, high-tech, next level, 128GB, all-in-one virtual reality headsets. All the buzzwords you could eat for just 399 dollars. On a hunch, Hannibal pocketed the brochure and left the one for Lobamba high performance socks.

Cawfee trailed him into the bedroom. If this was where the magic happened, there was no evidence that it happened recently. Silk sheets on a bed made Marine Corps tight. An old-school stereo with a stack of CDs beside it. Nothing jumped out, but Hannibal knew the treasure, if there was any, would be in the walk-in closet.

"You got to do that?" Cawfee asked as Hannibal started through Brown's clothes.

"Only if we want to find him." Police training, Secret Service experience and years as a private eye had taught Hannibal that clues often hid in pockets. As he went, he piled his booty on the small dressing table. Most of it was cash. Brown seemed to seed his pants with money, so he'd never accidentally leave home without any. There were also a couple pairs of cuff links, gum, mints, and one nice pocketknife with a Damascus blade. Nothing useful.

Nothing special on the dresser, so Hannibal started on the drawers. Socks, underwear and tee shirts all neatly rolled. Sweats and workout gear. Then Hannibal pulled out a rolled-up poster of a black woman named Samantha Tucker. She wore a colorful dashiki style dress and was holding an acoustic guitar. Her hair was in dreadlocks and her face was right on the edge of what Hannibal would call pretty, but she had dark eyes and a nice smile. The poster was signed, "From your biggest fan," with a black Sharpie. Pinholes in the corners showed that the poster had been displayed at one time.

"Ever seen this before?" he asked Cawfee, who shook his head. Hannibal looked closely at the wall and found small holes, the kind that pushpins would make, above the dresser, facing the bed. Displayed for a certain visitor perhaps? He looked again at the CDs.

"Zander old school like me," Cawfee said. "Nowadays people have their music on their phones or some device, all electrons. Some of us still keep the CDs."

Among the fifteen CDs on the dresser, seven of them were by Samantha Tucker, and one of those was a Christmas album. Hannibal opened the top CD's case and found that the booklet was signed.

"Cawfee, you know this girl?"

"I know who she is," Cawfee said. "Never met her. Or seen her with Zander if that's what you're thinking."

Hannibal returned to the living room and stared out the window for a moment. The eastward view of the nicely landscaped courtyard was darkening, shadows lengthening as the afternoon slid away. Based on the description he had, Samantha Tucker was not Porsche girl, but she just might be Zander Brown's best-kept secret.

Back at what Hannibal called the Brown Mansion, Charlotte and Frankie met him in the broad foyer, their faces open with anticipation. Hannibal spoke first to avoid being cross examined.

"Mrs. Brown, would it be too intrusive for me to see the bedroom? It would help me get a clearer picture of your husband."

"Of course," she said, and led the way up the curved stairway. Frankie and Cawfee followed. Charlotte pushed the door open and stayed in the hall until Hannibal walked in. He scanned the room with some surprise. The four-poster bed and white lace appointments over light wooden furniture made the room aggressively feminine. This was a woman's space with no hint of male presence. Zander had given his wife a free hand with decoration. The dressers and vanity displayed only a woman's items. He saw women's magazines in the sitting area, on the chair closest to the fireplace.

"May I?" he asked, stepping to a closet door.

"Oh, that's my closet," Charlotte said. "I'm sure you want Zander's. Over here."

Hannibal stepped into what was more like the dressing room in a high-end store than a closet, with eight doors on each side and a marble-topped island in the middle. He opened the first to find shirts hanging in an orderly spectrum, from white to black from left to right.

"I don't want to dig into your process, but you do have some leads, right?" Charlotte asked.

"Lots of maybes," Hannibal said, moving to the second door on that side. Here he found suits, as orderly and organized as the first space. "He was out at a club Friday night, and I may have an idea of how to track his movements from there. There are also friends in The District I need to interview and from what you said I need to follow up on a business he might have put some money into. Those places like to hold your attention as long as they can. It makes people more dedicated and that often means more generous."

The first surprise was that every pocket he checked here was empty. Not a match book or cuff link, and no cash anywhere. Zander was very careful not to bring the party side of his life home.

"Do you have like DNA or fingerprints or something?" Frankie asked. "Maybe some security cameras caught him going someplace."

Hannibal smiled and shook his head as he started through the drawers of the island. "I think you've been watching too much TV. Even the cops don't really work that way. The truth is, what we do, what any investigator does, is mostly legwork. I'll talk to a lot of people and piece the info together, look for inconsistencies, and chase every little clue that's too small or too much trouble for other people to chase. It hasn't changed that much in a hundred years."

Hannibal was just as thorough in Zander's closet at home as he had been in the apartment, but he turned up nothing. He thanked Charlotte for her patience and they moved downstairs. Back in the sitting room he faced Charlotte in the same chairs they had used before but this time, Cawfee and Frankie shared the sofa. The housekeeper appeared, offered them all cocktails, then evaporated before conversation resumed.

"I just want you to know that I for one appreciate your efforts," Charlotte said, raising her glass. "I'm sure you know more than you're sharing and that's all right. You are professional, and I'll not look over your shoulder any more than I do our attorney or accountant." Then, as if it were an afterthought, she added, "Would you like to stay for dinner? I think it's the chateaubriand tonight."

Frankie shifted her weight to the front of her couch cushion and leaned forward, her pendulous breasts threatening to burst their tee shirt bonds. "You know, Hannibal…can I call you Hannibal? You know we have lots of empty rooms here. Might be easier for you to just stay here while you work the case. What do you think?"

Her smile made it more a request than an offer. Her mother's smile stayed neutral. But Cawfee's eyes shot daggers at her, then snapped to the floor. If Charlotte saw Cawfee as family, he was happy to step into that role and be as over-protective of Frankie as an uncle, or even a father might be. Hannibal spent a few seconds pretending to consider the offer, and when he responded it was to Charlotte.

"That is very generous of you, really. I need to get home and take care of some other things. But I'll be back on the job first thing in the morning, and I'll keep you posted."

He said his goodbyes and they all followed him to the door. Cawfee went out to get the car. Frankie shook his hand, winked and whispered, "another time" before jogging up the spiral staircase. As Hannibal was about to step outside Charlotte lightly gripped his arm.

"Something?" Hannibal asked, turning to her.

"The one thing I haven't told you," Charlotte said. Her eyes were down but now she raised them to lock onto his. "I love that man. Really, really love him. This isn't about the money. And if he's unfaithful, well, I don't care right now. Just please, please bring him home."

CHAPTER 6

A hot shower pushed Hannibal's workday down the drain. Off the clock now he pulled on tan slacks and a sport coat with a Hawaiian shirt Cindy had given him. Thirty minutes later, he pulled up in front of Cindy's Alexandria townhouse and trotted up the steps. She met him at the door and as he so often did, he took a moment to admire his Cuban princess and consider how lucky he was.

"I love you in red, and that dress is just…well, they'll all be jealous of me tonight."

"Why thank you, kind sir," she said. "You make a girl blush."

He held his elbow out and she took his arm. Cindy's figure was robust, her face exquisite with highlights in the deep brown hair that tumbled to her shoulders in natural waves. He had no doubt that she was the most attractive attorney in the District of Columbia, Maryland and Virginia combined. He worked all over that collective area, known to natives as the DMV.

He opened the black Volvo GLT's door for her to climb in. He dropped into the driver's seat and pulled out onto Washington Street. Day was just considering handing off to the night as he drove toward the Washington Monument.

"I'm thinking about Cane, up on H Street. You good with Caribbean tonight?"

"Like there's a time I'm not good with Caribbean? But now, tell me about this case. I mean, Zander Brown for Christ sake. What's the family like? And what about the house? I read a piece on it in The Washingtonian when they bought it. Come on, tell me everything."

Hannibal laughed. "Oh, so I'm somebody now cause I got a client you've heard of."

"Honey, you're looking for a star that they don't want the police to look for. This is really cool and I want all the details. I know you'll be hard at work tomorrow, but I've got you for tonight so spill."

They rode into The District with Cindy's hand on Hannibal's thigh the whole way. He didn't like to talk business when they were together, but this wasn't exactly that. He answered her questions as best he could, although he hadn't bothered to check how much staff the family had or the size of the swimming pool. The conversation continued until they were seated, had ordered, and were sipping their frozen margaritas.

Cane was a pretty small place, and the tables were snug. It made Hannibal feel as if he was dining in some friend's kitchen. Mouthwatering aromas wrapped him like a warm blanket of love. Too many spices and flavors filled the air for him to separate them. Run by siblings from Trinidad and Tobago, Cane's menu showed exotic influences from half the world.

"So you think Brown is fooling around?" Cindy asked, licking salt from the rim of her glass and tasting her drink.

"Yeah, maybe with a singer but I'm not ready to convict him yet. It's one possibility. Looks like he's still a party boy." Hannibal bit into one of their jerk chicken wings, savoring the pimento smoked flavor. "Damn. Babe, if you want one of these you better grab it fast."

Despite their focus on eating, their entrees arrived before the wings were gone. Cindy's oddly named "omnivore" arrived in five round metal containers. Hannibal wasn't sure if that was nan or some sort of tortilla in the largest one, but the others were a variety of curries. He knew he'd get to help her finish it all. Then his grilled oxtails landed in front of him, and he began to doubt his capacity.

"You going to eat all that?" Cindy asked between bites.

"Going to do my damnedest," he replied. Biting into the tender, spicy treat he was so occupied with the experience his mouth was having that he almost missed a familiar face at the bar. That skinny dude with the short afro had to be Lenny. He stared so long that Cindy checked over her shoulder.

"Who you looking at, lover? I don't see any fine women at the bar."

Hannibal jerked his attention back to Cindy. "Babe, they ain't made a woman so fine I'd be looking at her when I got you in front of me. I just spotted a dude I know. Goes by Lenny Mack. Might even be his name. Local music producer."

"Well wave him over," Cindy said. "Introduce me."

That was easier than I expected, Hannibal thought. He was past the knife and fork portion of his oxtails and was using his hands to enjoy the bones. The layers of spice needed to be sucked out of the flavor-packed bones. He wiped his hands on his napkin and stood up to wave toward the bar. When he caught Lenny's attention he was rewarded with a big smile. Lenny grabbed his drink, slid off the stool and began weaving his way through the full tables toward Hannibal.

"What up, my man?" Lenny said when he reached their table. "I see you wiped out them oxtails, but don't sleep on that coconut rice. I don't know how they get so much flavor into rice for God's sake."

"I know, right? Rice ain't got no business being this good. You still waiting for a table?"

"Yeah," Lenny said, "but this rum makes the wait okay. Now who's this charming lady with you?"

"Lenny Mack, this is Cindy Santiago, ace attorney and the woman who tries to save me from the darkness my business drowns me in."

"I know that's right," Lenny said, dropping into a crouch with his elbows on the table. "Hannibal bailed me out of a tough spot with some blackmail BS a while back. Hell of a guy you got here."

"So Lenny," Hannibal said, "You still booking singers in the area?"

Lenny sipped his drink. "Still in business buddy, but not so much on the hip hop stuff. That's a little old school, which is not the way to get rich around here."

Hannibal nodded and seemed to be thinking about something for a moment. "Do you know this girl singer, Samantha Tucker?"

Cindy's head popped up. "Samantha Tucker? Neo soul star like twenty years ago? I loved her stuff." Then she reached across the table to tug Hannibal's sleeve and asked in lower tones, "Is she the girl?"

"Yeah, I know Samantha," Lenny said. "Worked with her a little back in the day. Not much work these days but she's still in the game. Why?"

"You ever see her around?" Hannibal asked. "Know who she hangs with?"

Lenny looked up and to the right as if he was flipping through a stack of mental index cards. "Yeah, yeah I seen her in a couple local clubs. You trying to find her?"

"She might be able to help me with a case. Ever see her with this retired basketball player…"

"Zander Brown?" Lenny laughed. "Damn, you're good. Yeah, I seen her with Brown a couple times. But more often I see her with this other nigga. Not so tall, but real light skinned, like…"

"Like me," Hannibal said. "Any idea who this guy is?"

"Nope," Lenny said. "But a real sharp dresser, lots of gold, and flashing cash. Never met him. Samantha, she's a sweet kid but something about this dude says 'back off' you know. That kind of vibe." Lenny stopped to pull a flashing disk out of his pocket. "And speaking of vibes, this thing went off, so they got a table for me. Nice catching up. Catch you later, brother." Lenny stood but Hannibal tapped his arm.

"You said Tucker's still in the game. Where she been working?"

"Bad times for her professionally," Lenny said. "I think Huge Wilson took pity on her. I heard she's been singing hooks and backup tracks for him."

Lenny vanished toward the front of the room just as their waitress dropped dessert on the table and scooped up their empty dishes. Sesame palmier with coconut pudding for both of them. Cindy stared down into her food, eating quietly, so Hannibal followed suit. Hannibal loved the little cookie/pastry hybrids, so buttery and somehow crispy without being dry. Coconut pudding was the perfect complement filled with sesame brittles that were just short of burned. Then, Cindy's voice cut into his moment of joy.

"That wasn't chatting with a pal. That was business." She looked up and her eyes blazed at him. "You knew he'd be here, didn't you?"

"Well, yes, I knew he hung out here," he said. "It wasn't a sure thing by any means, a possible opportunity but…yes."

"Honey, I love you, but we're on a date. This is my time."

"And yet you seemed very curious about the case," he said. She responded with a huff of anger. Then she lowered her head and gave him the pout. Cindy had a pout that could break your heart.

He slid his hand across the table to grip hers. "I know. You're right. I'll make it up to you."

"Oh you will?"

"I promise," Hannibal said. "Even if it takes me all night."

That brought the smile back to her face.

CHAPTER 7

Morning found Hannibal southbound on I-95 toward Huge Wilson's studios in Virginia Beach. He drove with his window down to enjoy some fresh air before the heat later in the day forced him to switch to air conditioning. An outsized September sun cloaked the trees on the left side of the road in shadow and lit up those on the other side, trees grudgingly beginning to turn their leaves from green to brown or red or gold.

Some things, Hannibal thought, were inevitable. The crisp morning air would become too warm and humid by mid-afternoon. Summer would surrender to winter. Boring green leaves would become beautiful, crisp leaf corpses. Men with money they weren't born to would succumb to the flattery of flashy women. It was pointless to deny such things. That's why there were coats, and rakes, and private investigators.

Four hours on the road brought Hannibal to Huge's studios. It could have been any middle-class home from the outside, but from past visits Hannibal knew better. The owner greeted him at the door with a big smile.

"Hannibal, my man. What it is, bro? Long time!" Huge Wilson's business name was not based on his physical form. He was a slight man with close cut hair and two armfuls of tattoos showing below the sleeves of his vintage tee shirt. He got the name from the first musician who trusted him to produce his tracks. After hearing the results that singer said, "Man you gonna be HUGE in this business." That prediction had come to pass and when a competitor threatened him physically, Hannibal had been there to defend him. Very quickly their relationship segued from bodyguard and client to friends.

"So, you said you was looking for Samantha Tucker?" Huge asked in a natural voice that sounded like a falsetto. "Is she in trouble? Or is she trouble for somebody else?"

Hannibal followed him down a narrow hall lined with gold and platinum discs. "Neither really. She's a lead. She might be able to help me find a missing person. Dude named Zander Brown."

Huge spun so fast Hannibal bumped into him. "Zander Brown is missing? Damn, dog, what happened?"

"Don't really know, and I'd appreciate you keeping this on the DL."

"I got you, brother," Huge said. "The press would go crazy and he and his family don't need that kind of crap. You think Samantha might know where he is?"

"Maybe. And when I heard she was working with you I thought I might manage a sighting."

"And you was right on," Huge said. "She over in B right now. The woman's a true talent and I, you know, try to keep her busy enough to make sure she's buying groceries. I can introduce you."

"Let's hold off on that, Huge. This is kind of a delicate matter."

"No sweat, brother. Come on in the control room with me and just hang at the back of the room. You can see her, but you'll just be a silhouette to her."

Entering the room, they plunged into an electronic beat so thick Hannibal felt it like a heavy blanket wrapped around him. Huge went to the bewildering bank of lights, sliders, knobs and switches at the front of the room and pulled on headphones. Leaning against the back wall Hannibal's vista was the backs of Huge and another man facing a room-wide, ceiling-high glass plate and beyond that, a more brightly lighted room. At the center of that room stood a lone woman.

Her hair was tall, her head wrapped in a black scarf. It was the woman from Brown's poster except her cheeks were a little fuller. She stood, swaying with the music, her hands up just above shoulder level, eyes closed, smiling without showing her teeth. She wore a simple but colorful shift and sandals. She was a little narrow up top but broader below the waist.

A gritty voice joined the beat. It was rap, and like most rap Hannibal only caught every third word or so. It could have been any of a dozen hip hop artists Hannibal had heard on the radio. He couldn't tell them apart and really had no interest in that stuff.

But then the woman's voice joined the beat. He would have to describe it as nonsense syllables…ooooo morphing into ahhhh and back…. But he was struck by how melodic the sound was. Her voice was an instrument mixing with the others, but a magnificent instrument adding just the right smooth tone to the mix. She gave the electronic base and drumbeats life and humanity.

Had that smooth sound seduced his quarry? And if so, what now? For all he knew, she was a good woman, twenty years into a career that peaked early and now reduced to singing hooks and background sounds for someone else's potential hits. It seemed demeaning work for a former star, especially since the jobs were only offered out of pity. How would she react to a stranger asking if she had stolen another woman's rich husband? If his guess was wrong, he would have insulted her for no reason. Even if it was true that would probably earn him a slap across the face. And, even if it was true, did that make her a villain? It could be Brown who was looking for a change. Either way, he didn't get paid to judge. And, he might be able to do what he was getting paid for without confronting Tucker.

Huge spoke some direction into a microphone, clicked it off, and restarted the track. Tucker was swaying again, and Huge stepped back to Hannibal.

"So, what's next, brother?"

Tucker began a different series of soothing sounds. "Wasn't the first one good?" Hannibal asked.

"It was dope, man, but the next one might be better. Always get a few takes."

Hannibal nodded. "Makes sense. Listen, I don't need to talk to her today. But thanks a lot for letting me sit in today. It gave me a sense of who I'm dealing with. In this business you spend a lot of time trying not to hurt the wrong person, you know?"

"That's why I love you dog," Huge said, throwing an arm around Hannibal. "You try to do right by people. Not so sure every PI is with that."

Hannibal spent the next hour in his car listening to classic rock, partially to wash the rap out of his head. He was halfway into a nap when Samantha Tucker came out of the studio and slipped into a little white Mazda MX-5 Miata. He started his car and as she pulled away from the curb, so did he.

Tucker pulled onto I-64 and settled into a steady sixty-five miles per hour. Northbound traffic wasn't bad, so Hannibal didn't need to crowd her to keep her in sight. If his prevailing theory was correct then maybe Zander Brown was kicking it at her place, planning his next move. If so, Hannibal could just follow her home, make a positive sighting, and report the location to Zander's wife. It wouldn't end their problems, of course, but it would end his job.

By the time they were on I-95 a pretty strong crosswind had come up, pushing the little Mazda, forcing Tucker to slow a bit. Hannibal stayed with her, starting to wonder if she lived right in The District, a couple hundred miles north of Virginia Beach. If so, it was a long commute to work but he figured she went where the work was.

Hannibal's music mix was petty eclectic that day, and Joan Osborne was singing Pretty Little Stranger – she wondered who the next fool would be - when Tucker surprised him by holding her northbound course. They were crossing the Wilson Bridge, bypassing Washington completely. The giant Ferris wheel at the National Harbor on his right was the signpost for entering Maryland. After a few more minutes she pulled off onto Route 5 and he had to be more careful now. She navigated progressively smaller streets through a suburban neighborhood until Hannibal was very happy he had GPS because he was convinced he would never find his way home otherwise. Houses were farther and farther apart until Tucker pulled into the driveway of a surprisingly modest, older home.

Hannibal pulled to the side, under an overhanging elm, a good fifty yards away. From there he could see that the side-facing garage was open, yet Tucker parked in the wide driveway, climbed out and sprinted inside. Well, it was a long drive with no stops. She probably needed to get to the bathroom.

Hannibal gave her five minutes before he got out of his car. As he approached, he saw that it was a nice, middle-class house with two stories and a porch that spanned the front. It stood proudly behind a manicured lawn holding a couple of mature trees. A bank of colorful flowers separated the lawn from the porch. The area was wooded with solid stands of trees separating Tucker's house from her closest neighbors on either side. More house than a single person needed but it did offer plenty of privacy. That made it easier to look around. If challenged, by her or Brown, he could just be a realtor with a client who was interested in the house.

Curiosity drew Hannibal to the garage. What else did she drive? But when he reached it he found more questions instead of answers. The three-car garage was empty. Tucker had parked so that another vehicle could get around her car. Maybe she was expecting company. Tire tracks in the dirt on the garage floor told him something with a much wider wheelbase than the Miata had parked there recently. Did Brown keep a truck or jeep there?

From behind him a gruff voice asked, "The fuck you doing in here?"

Hannibal turned to find himself facing a very dark black man with yellowed teeth in a wifebeater, brown slacks and work boots. Calling him big would be like saying giraffes are kind of tall. To Hannibal's eyes the man was built like a refrigerator with a head with fists like twelve-pound hams. This was certainly not Zander Brown. Also, certainly no one Hannibal wanted to come up against in an enclosed space.

"Hank James," he said, hand extended. "This is quite a property you've got here."

The big man's face seemed locked in anger and his arms shook as if his hands were eager to hit someone.

"You just walk into somebody's place?"

"Well, it's just the garage," Hannibal said, stepping closer. "I just wanted to see…"

"The fuck out of here," the big man snapped. Hannibal sighed, shrugged, and started past him.

"Didn't mean to get you upset," Hannibal said as he walked past. The big man turned and followed. Three steps out of the garage he stiff armed Hannibal. His huge right palm thumped into Hannibal's shoulder hard enough to send him flying forward. He hit the blacktop but quickly regained his feet, brushing off the knees of his pants.

"Better not come back," the big man said. Hannibal swallowed his response. This was no time to flex. He needed to stay in character so he showed the man his palms and headed to his car.

Once behind the wheel he pulled out his phone. It didn't make sense that any woman would be with the flashy basketball star and this bum. But maybe she was a sports groupie. The monster he just encountered could be a retired football player, or even a professional wrestler. But that didn't fit the profile he had mentally built for a has-been singer either.

His thoughts were cut short when the number he called was answered. "Hey, Hannibal, what's up?"

"Hey, Quaker, you busy today? Want to make a few dollars?"

"Not much work the last week or so," Quaker said. "Love being self-employed but carpenter work kind of comes and goes. Anyway, I got time on my hands and could definitely use some dollars. What you need?"

"Need you to watch somebody. Write down this address and come meet me."

"Cool. Where you at?" Quaker asked.

Hannibal hesitated. "Not really sure. Not far. Maryland. Clinton? Suitland? Upper Marlboro maybe?"

"You kill me," Quaker said. "But the GPS will tell me once I punch in the street address. See you in a bit."

Hannibal drove back to the last intersection where he would see anyone leaving the house. He was grateful for good friends who were also good neighbors. Quaker lived upstairs from Hannibal, along with Sarge, Virgil and Ray. Hannibal had met all but Ray at a homeless shelter where he volunteered. He hired them to help him clean out a crack house in Southeast, one of the less desirable neighborhoods in The District. Ray, Cindy's father, was living with her at the time. After the team chased all the drug dealers and users out of the building the owner offered Hannibal a very attractive deal to stay there, and the others decided to take apartments in the same building.

In the half hour before Quaker's aging green Chevy Cruze parked behind his own car, Hannibal had not seen another vehicle. Quaker got out and walked up to Hannibal's door. He was tall and lanky with an angular face and hair that looked like it was assembled from what's left on a barber's floor. Hannibal sometimes wondered how a white man could be so comfortable in his neighborhood. Of course, deep down he knew the reason. Quaker was one of those lucky people who just didn't give a damn what anyone else thought.

As Hannibal lowered his window, Quaker said "Just so you know, you're in Brandywine. Now, what you need me to do?"

"You're watching for the woman who lives at the end of the cul de sac. Black woman who drives a white Mazda Miata. If she goes anywhere, please follow her. If you see her meet up with a big, tall, basketball player type, let me know right away. That's who I'm really looking for. His name is Alexander Brown. I don't have a picture but…"

"You kidding?" Quaker asked. "Who don't know what Zander Brown looks like?"

Who indeed, Hannibal wondered.

"I got you covered, buddy," Quaker said. "I take it she's seen your car."

"Probably. Don't want to take a chance of spooking her."

"No sweat, man," Quaker said. "Nobody ever notices my piece of shit beater. If she takes off I'll give you a call when she lands someplace."

"Appreciate you, brother," Hannibal said. "Going to go crash at the crib for a bit."

"Yeah, right," Quaker said with a grin. "She wore your ass out, didn't she? You need to leave that woman alone."

Forty minutes spent mostly on Suitland Parkway got Hannibal from the suburbs on the edge rural to the urban surroundings of his three-story, inner-city apartment building. Once home, he microwaved a frozen dinner and carried it across the hall to his office. He barely tasted his food which was okay since it barely had any taste. His focus was on his internet search for Optilorus. The company had an impressive Facebook page, a Twitter feed and even a couple of TikTok videos. He found them on Instagram too. It was impressive for a company whose products were all still "in development." And everything he saw seemed to point to what a great investment this company would be. Not really so weird for a young, high-tech startup. What did strike him as odd was that the company's CEO, one Ira Johnson, had no social media footprint at all. Not even a LinkedIn account, despite the fact that his smiling blonde, blue eyed face was all over the company's pages.

Hannibal had picked up the pot to pour his after-dinner coffee when his cell phone buzzed.

"Damn, Hannibal, you didn't tell me you was tracking Samantha Tucker," Quaker said. "You taking only celebrity work now? I want a raise."

Hannibal grinned, enjoying the coffee's aroma as he leaned his butt against his desk. "Everybody pays me the same, Quaker. The rich stay rich by not giving anything away."

"Yeah, sucks don't it. Anyway, she's here at the W, and I expect she'll camp out for a while."

"Outstanding," Hannibal said. "Who's she with? You got eyes on her?

"Sorry, Hannibal. She headed for the rooftop terrace, and I'm not exactly dressed for that."

"Thanks man," Hannibal said. "Just watch the door in case she decides to move on. I'll be there in a few minutes. I think it's time for a chat with her."

CHAPTER 8

The W Hotel on 15th St. NW in Washington was an artsy kind of place, working at being flashy and modern even though it lived in a hundred-year-old building barely a block from the White House. As Hannibal approached the front, he thought it could just as easily have been an office building. Lenny met him at the door with a brisk handshake.

"Good to see you again so soon,"

"Thanks for coming," Hannibal said. "I know it was kind of short notice but…"

"Are you kidding? A chance to party at the POV on your dime? I wasn't going to say no to that."

"Yeah, just hope we can get in," Hannibal said. "This place is kind of exclusive."

"Not to worry, friend," Lenny said as they headed inside. "They don't keep a list here, just cut it off when the place is full. Now, on a weekend, The Terrace would be jammed with superstar athletes and TV stars, but on a Tuesday night it shouldn't be too bad. And look at you: black suit and tie, those damn Oakley sunglasses and diamond cufflinks. You look like you must be somebody." He paused, looked around and whispered, "You're not packing heat, are you?"

Hannibal grinned. "Wow, do people actually say that? Relax, man. Half the clubs in The District have metal detectors and some still pat a brother down. My weapon's in the car. And, I see you dressed to impress too." He knew he couldn't pull off that red two-button suit with black shirt and tie, but for Lenny it worked.

At the lobby door they were carded, which made Hannibal smile. Only one couple stood in front of them.

When they were ushered in past the velvet rope Lenny leaned toward the attendant.

"We're meeting Samantha Tucker. She's already upstairs waiting for us." His bored, straight-faced delivery must have done the trick because they were immediately allowed past the velvet rope and up the elevator to the terrace.

They grabbed two seats at the bar and Lenny ordered while Hannibal took in the astonishing view through the floor-to-ceiling retractable windows. He'd have to save up some cash to bring Cindy here. Then he broke his eyes loose to scan the tables. He spotted Samantha quickly thanks to her signature head wrap. She was not alone, but the man with his back to them was neither Zander Brown nor the linebacker type he'd met at her place. But now his description was in Hannibal's mental database for later examination. A light skinned brother, dressed to the nines with gold around his neck and both wrists.

"Found our girl?" Lenny asked, sipping his cocktail.

"Yeah, but she's here with the wrong guy. Wish I knew who he is." Then Hannibal sipped his smokey drink. His brows furrowed. A second sip. "Damn. What is this you got me?"

Lenny chuckled. "It's called a Ghost In The White House. No idea what's in it besides gin, but it sure is good."

"You got that right." Hannibal sipped again. A little sweet for his tastes but still pretty good. He watched Samantha over the rim of his glass. She was animated, speaking to the man who seemed too still, like he was listening but really didn't care about anything she said. Anyway, she wasn't going to lead Hannibal to Zander Brown while her other man was there.

Lenny made some arcane gesture. The bartender, a mature gentleman with a ready smile and a sallow complexion, interpreted small movements the way an auctioneer does. In seconds he was there with two new drinks. He had the look of a major domo. He must be pretty observant to have caught that drink order.

"Excuse me," Hannibal said as the drinks landed on their assigned napkins. "What goes in this drink? Aside from gin."

"Oh, that's aperol, Pimm's number one, dolin rouge, and a little cinnamon smoke," the bartender said. Both his face and vocal delivery were deadpan. Then he moved on to another customer.

"Did that help you?" Lenny asked.

"Nope. I don't know what any of that shit is."

That drew a chuckle from Lenny. Hannibal went back to staring at Samantha although he might just as easily have been looking at the illuminated Washington Monument rising behind her through the window. As the bartender passed again, he flagged him down, as if they were old friends now.

"Isn't that Samantha Tucker over there?" Hannibal asked, his voice just above a whisper.

"Yes sir."

"Well listen," Hannibal said, "We wanted to go over and say hello but, you know, don't want to offend anybody. So, the guy with her, is he a singer too? Somebody we should recognize?"

The bartender managed to crack half a smile. "No, sir, not a celebrity. That's Nelson."

As the bartender moved on, Lenny asked, "Well, did that help?"

Hannibal nodded. "As a matter of fact, yeah. I've heard about this guy Nelson."

"Nelson. Is that his first name or last name?"

"No idea," Hannibal said, pouring half of his second drink down his throat. "That's all I've heard him called. Never met him, but I've heard plenty. A major player. A dangerous man who plays around the edges of crime."

"What the hell does that mean?"

Hannibal turned to face the bar, staring into the bottom of his glass. "Haven't heard of him killing anybody or robbing anybody or human trafficking. But if you need weapons smuggled in, or need to fence some stolen goods, or need a place for your underage hookers to stay…"

"I get it," Lenny said. "Support staff for the criminal infrastructure."

"Very eloquent," Hannibal said, and Lenny grinned, clearly pleased with his own brilliance.

"And he's getting up," Lenny said.

Hannibal glanced over to see Nelson push back from his table and toss a stack of bills on the table. Hannibal turned back to closely examine the bottles behind the bar, as if he was trying to choose his next libation. He felt some small advantage knowing what Nelson looked like without being recognized himself. He felt the man walk past behind him, then watched him get into the elevator and disappear. Even those last few steps were telling. He walked like a boss.

In Hannibal's mind, new pieces had changed the gameboard. Now he feared Zander Brown was involved in something shady. Mixed up in something he didn't want touching his family maybe? That would explain taking off for a few days. Or, if he got in too deep, maybe coerced into something he couldn't wriggle free of. Either way, Samantha Tucker still looked like his best shot at finding him.

Lenny snapped his head toward Samantha. "She's still sitting, and I'm thinking that lady needs another drink."

"You read my mind," Hannibal said. "Can a brother get an introduction?"

CHAPTER 9

Lenny walked over to Samantha with Hannibal in tow. Hannibal stood with shoulders down, eyes darting and showing a nervous smile. Samantha looked up from her drink with the smile people wear when they're being patient.

"Hi, Samantha," Lenny said. "This is my good friend Henry Jones. Henry, Samantha Tucker."

"Miss Tucker, I'm a big fan" Hannibal said, managing to affect a minor stammer. "When Lenny said he knew you I harassed him into introducing me. I hope you're not...I mean, I didn't want to bother you."

"Oh it's quite all right," Samantha said with a tinge of Jamaican accent. "Always happy to meet a music lover."

Lenny patted Hannibal on the back. "Got to bounce, buddy. You're on your own now."

As Lenny walked off Hannibal stood quiet for a few seconds, until Samantha looked at him quizzically.

"Miss Tucker, it is such an honor. I have all your CDs, even the Christmas album. I just...do you think...I mean, can I maybe buy you a drink?"

She blessed him with a glowing smile. "Sit down, Mr. Jones, and please call me Samantha."

Hannibal dropped into the booth facing her and signaled a waiter the way he'd seen Lenny do. The waiter hurried over, swept the money from the table with his eyes on Hannibal, who in turn looked at Samantha.

"Bring another of whatever the lady is having, and I'll stick with that gin drink, the...ghost in the white house is it?"

As the waiter slipped away Samantha asked, "What do you do Henry?"

"Securities," he said. "Boring stuff. But you. Oh my gosh. What have you been up to the last couple years? Will we be seeing a new CD soon?"

Drinks arrived. Samantha's had an umbrella and a slice of orange on the rim. She dropped the fruit on the table and drained the glass down to half while Hannibal sipped at his own.

"Oh, I've kept pretty busy," Samantha said over the rim of her glass. "Staying out of the limelight but doing some work down in Virginia Beach."

"Now that is exciting," Hannibal said. A close look told him she had upped her makeup game since the poster in Zander's place. She was trying to disguise her aging and a person had to look really close to see it wasn't quite working. "And to think I almost didn't come over. I saw you with that guy and thought, well, he must be your husband, or boyfriend or something."

Samantha clearly heard Hannibal's implied question and rushed to dispel the notion. "Him? Nah, Nelson's just a guy I know. There's no husband and I don't belong to any man."

"Okay," Hannibal said, sighing relief. "I sure don't want to piss nobody off. Just wanted to hear all about the latest on your career."

She nodded, emptied her glass, and looked him over with hooded eyes. Hannibal could see in her eyes she was moving fast. He guessed strangers didn't approach her often and he was making himself look harmless. He figured they had reached the go or no-go moment.

"So here's the thing," Samantha said, sliding her hand across the table to let one fingertip touch his hand. "You seem like a sweet guy, Henry. And I do want another drink. But not here. This is kind of Nelson's place, you know?"

Yes, he did know. Nelson was either scary or more likely, a cash cow she didn't want to offend with talk of her being seen out with another man. He nodded solemnly.

"I'm down for whatever, Miss Tucker."

"Samantha." That made Hannibal smile, but probably not for the reason she thought. In his mind, here sat two people, each thinking that they had set the hook and were reeling the other in. And it was to his advantage for her to think she had hooked him.

"Whatever you like, Miss, er, Samantha. Do you have another favorite place? Where can I buy you that next drink?"

Her eyes lit up as she stood and signaled him to follow her.

Tourists who want to hear great live music flock to Blues Alley. Canny local residents will often drive six miles further up Wisconsin Avenue and slide into the Bethesda Blues and Jazz Supper Club, where parking is a bit easier. Nelson had driven Samantha to the W Hotel, so Hannibal took her in his car to the supper club.

The entrance was still that of an old-time movie house, with an outside ticket booth under the huge marquee advertising a jazz band Hannibal had never heard of. The music met them at the door, soft and soothing, and followed them as a young woman showed them to a table back near the bar. Inside it was the cavernous space of an old-time movie theater, the main floor covered with tables for the diners, most of which were still occupied. Beyond that, the huge stage hosted a five piece that was rolling through a smooth but catchy improv.

Samantha asked for a Manhattan and Hannibal followed suit. Drinks came fast and Samantha again drank hers halfway down. She was smiling, fully into the music, and totally relaxed. Exactly as he had hoped.

"Man, it's good to know you're still in the game," Hannibal said. "So, who's the lucky producer down in Virginia Beach? You working on something with Timbaland?"

Samantha shook her head. "Naw, Henry, it was Huge Wilson." She raised a finger to forestall Hannibal's positive reaction. "But that's past tense. Wasn't really working out. I got to head down to his studios tomorrow morning, but after that I won't be doing any more tracks with him."

"That's too bad." Then, as if trying to change the subject, Hannibal said "Well, I like this place. It's bright and cheerful, all orange with blue accents. It just feels old school and that band is kicking it. I'm guessing that guy Nelson would never bring you here."

"No, child, been here with a different man. Nicer man." *Close,* Hannibal thought, *but not enough*. At that moment his phone began to vibrate in his pocket. Probably Cindy wondering what he was up to. He ignored it. This was not the time for an interruption that might take them out of the moment. He was trying to think of a way to point the conversation toward Zander when Samantha waved to the waitress and pointed at her glass. The girl was thin and wearing a beehive wig. When she placed two more glasses on the table Samantha slapped her arm playfully.

"I like the service in this place. Listen, this here is Henry and I'll make sure he takes good care of you."

"You're sweet," the waitress said, "But you haven't finished your first drink yet."

"Well, it's actually about my fourth or fifth tonight, and anyway…" With that, Samantha drained the half empty glass and thumped it on the table.

"You are too much, Samantha," The waitress said. "Wish you came in more often."

"Yeah, it's been a minute, ain't it? You know, different, er, escorts like different places."

"Yeah," the waitress said. "So what happened to the baller?" Then her eyes cut to Hannibal. "Oh, God. No offense, sir."

"None taken, hon," Hannibal said. And thank you for opening that door, he thought.

Samantha laughed and waved the waitress's comment off as if Hannibal wasn't even there. "Girl, it ain't like he gone be jealous or some shit. That nigga with some other bitch up in Baltimore."

"Well looks like you got a good replacement," Waitress said, winking at Hannibal. "You treat him nice, now."

Samantha gulped half her new drink and turned her eyes on Hannibal. "I know what she thinking."

"Hey, I'm not making any assumptions," Hannibal said. "But I am curious about this baller she was talking about. A real basketball player?"

"Retired," Samantha said, eyes turning to the stage. "But a sweet man. Zander Brown. He loved this place and he always drew more fans than I did."

"Are you close? I'm not trying to get between you and anybody."

Samantha leaned in, both elbows on the table with that smile some woman only find when they cross the line from high to drunk. "For a little while we was a thing. I even made some private recordings just for him. Among other things."

"Well I'm glad I'm the one here with you tonight. Where you suppose he is right now?"

Then over her shoulder Hannibal spotted a familiar face. It was Cawfee, scanning the bar as if he was looking for someone. Samantha was weaving back and forth, eye half closed, feeling the music. Hannibal wasn't sure she had even heard his question, and he couldn't really wait for an answer anyway. He knew Cawfee wandering over to their table could destroy any chance he had of getting information from his singer companion.

"Excuse me, Miss, er, Samantha. I need to find the men's room in this place."

"Go drain that snake, baby. I'll be right here when you get back. These boys got a serious groove going on."

Hannibal caught up to Cawfee halfway across the floor and waved him over toward the bar. The driver greeted him as if it was a wonderful surprise to see an old friend.

"What in the world are you doing here?" Hannibal said in a stage whisper just loud enough to get past the music.

Cawfee shrugged. "We didn't want to just sit around, doing nothing, after all that happened. I ain't no detective but I know where Zander hangs out cause I'm the one that takes him. So we figured I could go look for him in some of his old party spots. This here is one of them spots. Figured it was worth a shot, right? It ain't like I'm out on a date. And really, I know it's late but I didn't figure you for a nine to five kind of guy."

Hannibal bit back his initial response. There was no benefit in sparring with Cawfee. "As it happens, I am still on the job. I'm here with the girl."

"What? The girl he drove off with?"

"No, the girl on the poster in his little love nest," Hannibal said.

Cawfee stared across the floor, then his eyes widened and his grin increased. "I'll be damned. That does look like Samantha Tucker. She tell you anything?"

"Not yet, but I think she might if I can get back to her before she's too drunk."

Cawfee nodded. "Yeah, maybe the money's really for her."

"What money?"

"The money," Cawfee repeated. "You know. Didn't Charlotte call you?"

Hannibal pulled his phone out and saw two missed calls, both from the Brown's land line.

"I wasn't in a position to answer this evening," Hannibal said, glancing back at his table. "What happened? And what's this about money?"

"Charlotte says she got an email from Zander. I didn't see it but she says he's fine and he's asking for a pile of cash. Like a million dollars for some deal he couldn't pass up. That's a lot of cash and she said she would do what he said - it was his money after all - but she wanted to see him first. She wrote back but figured I should go looking anyway."

Hannibal closed his eyes and shook his head, shaking up the puzzle pieces to see if the new ones fit together in another pattern. They did of course, but he liked the new picture even less than the possible patterns he had looked at before.

"Let's be clear, Cawfee. Did she say 'money' or specifically 'cash' do you think?"

"Oh, specifically cash," Cawfee said. "She was mumbling about if even banks kept that much cash on hand."

Hannibal mumbled, "damn" under his breath, then held his hands straight out, clapping each on one of Cawfee's arms to make sure he had the man's attention.

"Listen, I need to follow this lead for a bit longer, but I want you to go home. I know it's late, but Mrs. Brown should get hold of Young and tell him to get ready to handle this. This is sounding less like a runaway, or a man suckered by a grifter, and more like a coerced communication."

"Wait. What?" Cawfee's brow knit in confusion.

"I think it's time to get the police involved. We might be dealing with a kidnapping."

CHAPTER 10

When Hannibal got back to his table Samantha had emptied her drink and had started on his.

"You was gone a long time," she said, offering a fake pout. "I thought you wanted to know about me and Zander."

"I was kind of curious."

"Well, I'll tell you what," she said. "I'll tell you what the deal is." This was her teasing face, Hannibal thought. She was in that place where she'd want to hold his interest, so she'd let her story out in tiny pieces. He just needed to be patient.

"I'll tell you all about that deal in the next place," she said.

"Next place?"

"Yeah, I've had enough smooth jazz," Samantha said, getting to her feet. "We need to hear something with a bit more of an edge to it, and I know just the place."

The next place turned out to be a bit down scale from the first two. It was a small club called Indigo, tucked into the middle of a strip mall in Charles County, Maryland, somewhere between Waldorf and LaPlata. A burly doorman gave Hannibal a quick pat down at the door and asked to glance into Samantha's purse. Inside, the place was dark and close, and a bit too warm, but that was because of the standing room only crowd. The clientele was completely African American, and every person in the room was wearing his or her sharpest party gear. People lined the bar, drinking with one hand and using the other for their wings and nachos.

Samantha led him to the end of the bar on their right. Music boomed from the stage at the other end of the room, where a go-go band was pounding out a deep, hard beat. Samantha flagged down drinks and wriggled her way forward until she was leaning on the bar. Hannibal squeezed in next to her. His right arm pressed hard against Samantha's left breast. She didn't seem to mind. He leaned into her, figuring that it was so loud no one could hear their conversation even if someone wanted to.

"So, what were you saying about this Zander Brown?"

Samantha threw her head back and laughed. "Henry, you a good man. I wish I could pull you into this deal. I bet you good with money."

"Well, investing is what I do. You in business with Brown?"

"Oh, yeah," Samantha said, leaning on Hannibal's arm harder. "It's business for real. Big time. It's going to make us both rich. Course he already rich but this going to make me as rich as he is. At least, if he can raise enough cash. Oh, wait. Here's my girl."

Samantha's attention was stolen by a thick woman in long dreadlocks and a shiny gold minidress who had stepped to the mic and started rapping in a fierce, aggressive style. Hannibal, no fan of the genre, had to admit this girl had a solid flow. But Samantha was still his focus. Maybe his earlier guess was wrong. Maybe this business deal she spoke of was the reason Zander Brown needed a million dollars. Still, if he needed the money in cash, it was surely a shady deal.

Samantha hooted at the girl on the stage for a couple of songs, then she lurched against him as if someone had pulled her plug from its socket. She tried to give him a kiss but narrowly missed.

"Hey, daddy, I'm about done for the night. You going to take me home? And tuck me in?"

Hannibal put an arm around her waist to steady her. "Really? Tuck you in?"

"Oh, yeah, daddy," Samantha said, hugging him. "I really need to get tucked real good tonight." Again, she threw her head back and laughed hard.

Hannibal had used his GPS to navigate his way home from Samantha's house earlier and that was a good thing because she fell asleep after giving him the first step in the directions. He figured she wouldn't remember getting home at all so there was no risk in telling her she had directed him. He parked behind her car in the wide driveway, wondering if he was going to encounter the bruiser he faced earlier in her garage. He didn't look or sound like he was on her level, but you never know. He nudged her and her eyes slid open.

"We're here. Is anyone home?"

Samantha laid a hand on his thigh. "Oh, no, handsome. This is my place and mine alone. Tonight it's just you." She tried to touch a fingertip to his nose and just missed.

He got out and helped her out of his car. Once he had her standing she could walk fine, although she was weaving quite a bit. She fished keys out of her purse, but he had to push one into the lock for her.

Pushing the door open, Hannibal stepped into a living room furnished from a catalog. The leather sofa, recliner, coffee table and end tables had come as a set. Probably the lamps with them. There was nothing personal here, just what someone thought would give the right impression.

Samantha winked at him, she kicked off her heels and headed for the stairs. Hannibal hesitated. After three steps Samantha hit her knees. With a curse under his breath, Hannibal helped her to the landing, then picked her up entirely. She was dead weight, but after a deep breath and steadying his balance, he carried her the rest of the way up.

"I might have had one too many," Samantha said in slurred tones as Hannibal carried her into the master bedroom. He lowered her to her feet but held one arm around her waist while he used his other hand to pull back the covers. She stood, docile and compliant, while he unzipped her dress and slipped it over her head. She betrayed no modesty standing before him in bra and panties, only an apologetic sadness he didn't grasp right away.

"You are so cute," Samantha said, her voice softer than he had heard all night. "I know you were hoping to get some from a bona fide star tonight but honey I don't think I can..."

"Don't be stupid," Hannibal said, sitting her on the bed. "You made no promises, and I made no assumptions. Besides, sounds like you've got enough men in your life. Now lie down and get some rest."

Samantha fell back on the triple stack of pillows. "Wow. Ain't you the gentlem..." The end of the word slid away as her eyes shut down and she fell into a gentle snore.

Hannibal scanned the room. For a tract house inside the Beltway it presented an absolutely normal, average picture. Glass end tables, a little settee and a vanity over by the windows in the sitting room area. Big screen television, bookcase, small desk with computer just before the bedroom door. Then the walk-in closet and private bath. The only thing out of place was the cardboard box, like an Amazon delivery, between the bed and the bathroom. If she got up to pee before she was sober, she'd fall over that and break her neck. So he did what came natural, he pushed the box to the side and against the wall.

Then he realized it may have looked like an Amazon delivery box, but it had not been sealed with the tape they usually use. And it was heavy. What could be inside? From its size and weight, the carton could hold a forty-pound box of cat litter, but there was no sign of any pets in the house. Not his business of course, but he was a detective, and curiosity won over propriety. With a glance over his shoulder at the sleeping woman, he lifted one flap. That raised his eyebrows.

Here was something he'd never seen before. A box full of money. Old and worn bills but neatly stacked. Only tens and twenties in evidence and he sure wasn't going to go shuffling through them. But even if they were all those denominations it would add up to quite a bit of money. Her part of the cash for this big deal?

He jumped at the jarring sound of a phone ringing. Scanning the room, he zeroed in on Samantha's purse. She had not stirred. He scooped the bag up off the floor, pulled the phone out of it and pressed the lighted button. A sharp voice burst out. He could hear both the words and the laugh in the woman's voice even with the phone an inch from his ear.

"Bitch is you crazy? I can't believe you walked in here with another man. I won't say shit, but I ain't the only one who saw you. You better watch your ass. You know Nelson will be all up in your shit if he finds out."

The speaker stopped to take a breath. In the pause Hannibal heard familiar music in the background and the chatter of a crowd. Then she continued with less energy "Sam? You there? I ain't mean to yell at you. I just don't want you to mess up that deal. Hey, you okay? Damn. Well, I'll be here until closing if you want to talk."

The caller broke the connection. Hannibal turned the phone off and returned it to the purse. Let her think Samantha answered, then passed out or something.

Hannibal looked at the sleeping woman again. Her mouth hung open and the gentle snore continued. He couldn't classify her yet–player, pawn or innocent bystander– but his instincts said she was part of whatever was keeping Zander Brown from home. Whatever was going on, it was bigger than just her.

From habit Hannibal looked around the room to make sure there was nothing there that would betray his presence. From all appearances Samantha had staggered home, crawled up the stairs and fallen into bed. For all he knew, she might remember it that way, which was fine. He pulled the door halfway closed and trotted down the stairs trying to decide on his next move.

Three steps down from the landing he froze. A small pistol's muzzle centered on his navel. The man holding it stood relaxed but alert with his back to the door. He was showing his teeth, but that wasn't really a smile.

"And just exactly who the hell are you?" Nelson asked in a soft, flat voice.

CHAPTER 11

Hannibal's mind raced. Had word of Samantha's wild night reached Nelson already? And what was the relationship? Was this a suspicious partner in crime wondering what Samantha might have spilled? Or a jealous boyfriend coming home late to find he was being two-timed? While he tried to guess the right response, Hannibal forced an embarrassed smile, his hands up and to his sides. He decided the safe play was to stay in character.

"Hey. Sorry. I didn't know she had a man. And honest to God, I didn't touch her. We just had a couple drinks and…look I'm not looking for any trouble."

Nelson stood silent for a moment, scanning Hannibal up and down, calculating, evaluating. This man was no fool. He would look for clues in a person's body language, his grooming, his voice. The knot in Hannibal's stomach tightened. Nelson's pistol was small, maybe a .38, but all guns look big when they're pointed at you. Hannibal focused on the finger pressed against a trigger. If Nelson decided to shoot, could he sidestep and reach the gun hand in time?

Nelson's left hand pointed at the recliner. "Have a seat. Get comfortable."

"I really think I should just get…"

"Sit."

Hannibal backed toward the recliner, keeping his eyes on the gun. Once he settled onto the brown leather Nelson lowered the gun a couple inches.

"Now, who are you and what's your story?"

"Henry Jones," Hannibal said. "I wasn't trying to do anything, I swear. I recognized Miss Tucker sitting alone in a bar and I just wanted to buy her a drink."

"And did you?" Nelson stepped closer, the gun now aimed at Hannibal's right knee.

"Yeah," Hannibal said, making his voice shake. "But she had already been drinking. She was in no shape to drive so I brought her home."

Nelson closed his eyes slowly and opened them again. "She's here?"

"Wait, did you think I was a burglar or something? I didn't break in, I just brought her home and..." He stopped, thinking "...and got her into bed" might not be received well. But his eyes had already gone to the stairs.

"You been upstairs?" Nelson asked, raising his aim point to Hannibal's face.

Hannibal held his hands forward and spoke slowly. "I helped her up the stairs, but I never touched her, I swear. I think she just passed out."

Nelson nodded. Hannibal could see the wheel turning in his head. He would want to verify Hannibal's' story. He wouldn't want to leave Hannibal alone. He'd take him upstairs at gunpoint. That would give him a chance to disarm Nelson and end this. Hannibal was ready.

But instead, Nelson said, "Push the chair back. All the way."

There was no lever or button, so Hannibal leaned hard. With a groan of protest the back went almost horizontal while the pad under his feet came up to straighten his legs.

"Now you sit there and relax while I check things out upstairs," Nelson said. He moved with an animal grace that made Hannibal wonder if he was a dancer in an earlier life. He slipped up the stairs and out of sight without making a sound, and Hannibal released a breath he didn't know he was holding.

Once, years ago, Hannibal had been pushed into a bathtub and told to put his feet up on the edges. He had never felt so helpless, that is, until now. There was no getting up quietly. Nelson would hear the chair creak upstairs. There was no getting up quickly either. He would never reach the door before Nelson was on the stairs with an easy shot at his back. His only option was to wait.

He heard Nelson push the bedroom door open. In his mind's eye he saw Nelson lift the comforter. A couple of seconds of silence. Then he thought he heard one piece of cardboard scrape another. Looking in the box maybe?

Less than a minute had passed before Nelson was back in front of Hannibal. The left side of his mouth moved up. Half a smile? A derisive smirk?

"So, you got her into bed." Hannibal nodded. "But you didn't strip her down."

"That would have been disrespectful," Hannibal said. Suddenly, they seemed to be two peers talking. Nelson's gun drooped to the side.

"And you didn't take anything from the room."

"Not the way I'd get a souvenir," Hannibal said. "I had a pleasant evening with a woman I admire. That's all I want to take away from here. Now I know there's a man looking out for her I won't be back. Actually, I was kind of surprised she was out there all by herself."

Hannibal stared into Nelson's light brown eyes, mentally pushing him to say something. He looked like he considered it but decided not to take the bait. Instead, he waved his pistol toward the door.

"Okay. Get out."

Hannibal stood up and forced himself to walk slowly to the door. He refused to look scared. He flipped the lock, turned the knob and pulled the door open.

"Jones, right?"

"Yeah." Hannibal looked back over his shoulder.

"Listen. Thank you. For getting her home. And look. If we ever meet again…"

"I don't know you," Hannibal said, "and this never happened. We good?"

"All good," Nelson said, slipping the pistol into his pocket.

CHAPTER 12

Back at the Volvo, Hannibal slid off his jacket and laid it on the back seat, pulled out his shoulder holster and slipped it on. He got into the car and sat for a moment with the music blaring. AC/DC was ringing Hell's Bells. He pulled his Sig Sauer P229 out of the glove compartment and slid it into the holster under his right arm. A small part of him wanted to storm back into the house and plant a forty-caliber slug in Nelson's brain. A bigger part liked the idea of disarming Nelson and planting a leather gloved fist in his face. After ten deep breaths his brain got control of those parts of him.

It was late. He was tired. And the incident with Nelson had pumped him full of adrenaline. Not a combination that helped his judgment. But he knew that confronting Nelson would get him no closer to finding Zander Brown. He might know where Brown was but even if he did, he would never give that up to Hannibal. But a good friend of Samantha's might know and might see no reason to keep it a secret. It was a slim lead, but it was easy to follow up, if he moved fast enough.

At one time Rte 301 was a main road cutting through Maryland, and it was still the best way to get some places. But most of it was one or two lanes each way, twisty in spots and poorly lit almost everywhere. A necessary evil for those areas not touched by the beltway.

He retraced his earlier path and parked in the Indigo lot. A quick glance at his watch told him it was about twenty minutes before closing time. The woman on the phone said she'd be there until closing and he was pretty sure he recognized that voice. She certainly saw him with her girlfriend that night. He hoped that was enough to gain a little trust. Reluctantly, he returned his automatic to his glove compartment.

Inside the crowd was still jumping. It must have been a strong final set. The woman who was performing earlier was still on stage, riding the beat like she had just started. He marveled at her energy, but he imagined that standing in front of a really good band was much like being plugged into a generator. He stood with the crowd on the dance floor, unnoticed by the dancers, until the song ended.

"Y'all been a good crowd," she said, "and you know your girl Kronik would stay up here and spit it all night but I gots to go. Time for y'all to get those last drinks and I'll be back tomorrow night."

The lights went down on stage and the woman turned to talk to each of the band members in turn. Most of the dancers rushed the bar. Hannibal saw a few men scanning the group, probably deciding who they were going to settle for since hunting time was running out. There were also women, a little tipsy, who had clearly given up on spotting Mr. Right that night and were now looking for Mr. Right Now.

The rapper took the long step down from the stage, momentarily offering a flash of spectacular thigh. Hannibal wasn't the only one to notice how short her dress was. A brother in a bright blue Armani suit and mirror shoes stepped to her. The man couldn't see that she was shields up and set on stun. Too bad for him, but maybe a conversation starter for Hannibal. He moved toward her, hanging a couple feet behind Armani man, who stepped right in front of her.

"Damn, Kronik, you the bomb, girl," the man said. "And you way too fine to be leaving here alone."

Kronik leaned back and gave him the side eye. "Seriously? You ain't got nothing better than that? You better step before you get your feelings hurt."

"Come on now. Don't be like that," Armani man said. "I got what you been missing, baby."

Kronik choked back a laugh. "Nigga, you ain't got nothing I want."

This was the moment for Hannibal to step between them, pushing himself into the man's face. "You should take the hint, brother. You aiming a little too high. Suggest you move on."

The man glared at Hannibal for a couple of seconds, but he didn't seem to be up for any trouble. Hannibal knew how to look like the kind of trouble nobody wants. After a brief staring contest, the man shook his head, turned to Kronik, tossed the word, "Bitch" her way and stalked off. She followed him with her eyes for a couple steps, then turned to Hannibal.

"Appreciate you, brother, but don't think that'll get you..." Her voice trailed off as her brow wrinkled. She raised a finger to point at Hannibal while she searched her memory.

"You saw me earlier with your girl Sam," Hannibal said.

Kronik nodded her recognition. Then she looked around Hannibal and her shoulders rose. She was so easy for him to read.

"She's gone. She had a couple too many, so I took her home."

"Uh huh. And turned around and came back out?" Kronik moved to a table at the side of the stage, one apparently reserved for her and the band.

"Sort of," Hannibal said, trailing along. "I was hoping to talk to you."

Kronik stopped short and spun on him, her lip curled in derision.

"Oh, no," Hannibal said, "It's not like that. I wanted to talk to you about her. She said you two were tight, and I figured you could give me the 4-1-1 on this girl."

Kronik sat and crossed her legs.

Hannibal continued to stand. "Look, this woman is special. I think you know that. But I'm not about causing any grief, you know. So I figured, before I get too deep in this thing, it would good to know what's up."

He went quiet to let her think. She sighed and swung a finger downward into the facing chair. Now Hannibal sat. A drink landed in front of her. She nodded thanks to the man who brought it, sipped and looked over the glass at Hannibal.

"What you want to know is, do she got a man," Kronik said.

"And if not, would she stick with one man, if he treated her right?" Hannibal filled in.

Kronik nodded with her lower lip out. So far, Hannibal had passed all her tests. She looked away to gather her thoughts, then refocused on him.

"Like you said, Sam's my girl. That don't mean I like everything she do. But I like you. I go by instinct, and you feel like a good one. So listen, Sam needs a good man. She with this one nigga, He think he a gangster or some shit. He got her twisted, but I think he'd cut her if she didn't do like he say."

"That's not what she needs," Hannibal said. "I can't believe somebody legitimate hasn't come for her."

"Well she was with this other man, a baller. He was fine and he treated her good."

"Really," Hannibal said. He didn't want to push too hard. Slow and easy was the way. "And she ends up with the bad guy. That's crazy. What happened to the guy you said you liked?"

Hannibal's words were cut off. A beefy fist had grabbed the back of his collar and twisted hard. A familiar voice said, "You one nosy nigga. What you selling this time?"

Kronik looked up over Hannibal's head, showing none of the surprise he was feeling. "Fridge, what the fuck you doing?"

"This boy was nosing around Samantha's house earlier. I was up there making a delivery and he shows up with this bullshit story about being a real estate man. Now he's asking questions bout her."

"What's your deal?" Kronik asked Hannibal. "You a reporter or something?"

Hannibal shook his head with both hands on Fridge's wrist.

"Smells like a cop to me," Fridge said. "Let me take him outside and school him a little."

Kronik shrugged. "No skin off my ass."

CHAPTER 13

Hannibal was getting lightheaded when Fridge pulled him up out of the chair. Fridge maintained the pressure, twisting the back of Hannibal's collar, making it almost impossible to breath. He saw the floaters swinging around his eyes like colorful planets released from their orbits. He stumbled as the bigger man dragged him down a hall. He felt a rush of cooler air and knew Fridge had shouldered a door open and they were outdoors. Rough brick scraped his face. He tried to push away from the wall. Sudden pain exploded in his back, radiating out from his right kidney. He grunted but refused to cry out. He tasted whatever that last drink was.

Then the pressure on his throat eased, he spun, and his back slammed against the same wall. His legs turned to rubber bands, but a huge hand pressed against his chest kept him from falling. A single light high on the opposite wall backlit Fridge, turning his face into a dark demon's visage broken by a wide, bright grin. Hannibal managed to raise an arm just enough to blunt the impact of a right cross, but still his jaw throbbed from the impact. His ears were ringing, the familiar sound of his brain bouncing off his skull. He clung to consciousness through pure stubbornness, but he knew it wouldn't be enough.

Then Fridge's head jerked to one side. The momentary pause gave Hannibal a chance to draw one full deep breath. He managed to slam a right into Fridge's gut. He snapped a left into Fridge's face. Another good breath, and he cocked his left leg, stamping out into Fridge's solar plexus.

His burst of energy depleted, Hannibal fell back against the wall. Fridge started forward, but another hand gripped the back of his shirt and yanked. Fridge's head bounced off the wall behind him and he dropped forward, dazed.

A strong arm looped under one of Hannibal's and helped him walk down the alley. The world began to come back into focus as he dragged more of the cool air into his lungs. They were moving across the nearly empty parking lot, toward the back where Hannibal was parked. Another car stood two spaces away from his. A black Mercedes-Maybach. He looked to his right to see Cawfee's face, smiling back at him in the moonlight.

"I can walk," Hannibal said, pulling away from Cawfee.

Still his steps were unsteady. Cawfee pulled the passenger side door of his car open and Hannibal dropped onto the seat. He took several deep breaths, wishing his corner man would squirt some water into his mouth. Wait, this wasn't then. But his fighting mind had crawled to the surface, reminding him that two punches hardly made a fight. He flexed his hands, wishing he had his gloves on.

"Okay. I'm ready for round two."

"The hell you are," Cawfee said. "But damn, you sure got in a couple good licks when you got the chance."

"I've been kick boxing since high school," Hannibal said.

"Damn. So what happened?"

"Sneak attack," Hannibal said. "Choke hold followed by a kidney punch. Don't even know why, really, but I can't leave this unfinished."

"Maybe come back and finish it later," Cawfee said. "That guy's a monster. If I hadn't smacked him upside the head with that gin bottle, he would have put a hurting on you. If he works here, he might have friends around at closing time. And you ain't in no shape for a serious throw down. Trust me."

Just standing up convinced Hannibal that Cawfee was right. There in the darkness, the parking lot between him and The Indigo was a barren landscape and just getting across it looked like a major task. He needed to let it go and catch up with this Fridge after he gathered his strength. He plopped back down in the seat. Cawfee went around and got in the driver's seat. Hannibal looked over at his own car, thinking those few steps seemed quite a ways away. Maybe he'd sit for a minute. Just for a minute.

"Hey, thanks for bailing me out back there," Hannibal said. "Not to sound ungrateful but, what were you doing here anyway?"

"Oh, well, I'm still looking around for Zander and this is one of the places I used to bring him."

Was there a beat of hesitation before that answer? Hannibal wasn't sure about his own perceptions right then. And he was mentally juggling a lot of disconnected threats.

"When you were driving Zander around did you ever meet this guy called Nelson? Light skinned, handsome, snappy dresser, wears a lot of gold? Sound like somebody Zander might have hung out with?"

"That sounds like somebody I'd remember," Cawfee said, "but I don't think so. Who is he?"

Hannibal shook his head. "Just one more guy who's pointed a gun at me. Met him with Samantha Tucker. Thought they might have all hung out."

"I'll admit I've driven her and Zander together a couple of times. And I've heard them talking about this guy Johnson, the dude that runs that company Zander dumped so much money in, Opti something."

"Optilorus," Hannibal said. "I saw the brochure at Zander's DC place. So she knows him." And the trail split again. Across the parking lot, the last light in the Indigo went out.

"What do we do now?" Cawfee asked.

"We? No, you go home. I go home. I'll grab a couple hours of sleep and jump back on this. I still don't have a clue where Zander Brown is, but I have the feeling that he's in danger and time is running out."

CHAPTER 14

The sun stabbed into Hannibal's eyes burning right through his eyelids. The bedroom of his railroad apartment was only one room removed from the street. When he moved in, he was happy about the three big wall-to-wall windows in the living room but that morning they seemed more like a punishment than a perk.

He had barely gotten his clothes off before passing out on the bed. He slept hard and deep, except for that one dream of running down a dark street without getting anywhere, as if the sidewalk was a treadmill. Some days he wished his subconscious wasn't such a smartass.

He checked his watch, the absurdly expensive Porsche titanium watch Cindy gave him for Christmas. He landed home four hours ago. Enough sleep to feel better, but not enough to feel good. Too bad. He had work to do.

After a shower, a shave, getting dressed, making coffee and toasting a bagel it was still a little early to harass anybody. So he smeared the bagel with butter, cream cheese and a little marmalade and carried it across the hall to his office. At his desk he fired up his computer for a little research.

After trying a few variant spellings, he managed to find Kronik's website. She described herself as stronger than a bag of weed, and more addictive. She also made herself sound a lot more successful than a girl who would be performing weeknights in a club twenty-five miles outside The District. There were several photos in a variety of outfits that showed nearly everything she had to offer. Her bio made it clear that she was proud of her criminal past, including a stint at Joliet for an unnamed offense that only ended a couple of years ago. Street cred mattered in the rap game and she wanted her fans to know she was a genuine gangsta. In fact, her public persona seemed the exact opposite of Samantha Tucker's. It was hard to see them as friends, but the public personas were probably both exaggerated a bit, just in opposite directions. One thing he did not find on her website was an actual name. He had no clue how to find her again unless he wanted to wait for tonight's show.

That meant Samantha Tucker was still his best lead. Sober, she might be convinced to tell him what she knew about Zander Brown's disappearance. Or, if he could find Nelson, he might know something useful. So Hannibal knew his next steps, after he made sure Zander was still missing. That meant picking up his phone. He hoped he wasn't waking anyone up.

After only two rings he heard her breathless voice. "Mr. Jones? Is there any news?"

"Sorry, Mrs. Brown, I don't have anything substantial to report. But I do have leads to follow up on. Before I headed out, I wanted to know if you had any further communication…"

"Just that email," she said. "I got your message from Darrell, but I don't know." Hannibal smiled. He'd bet only Mrs. Brown and his mother called Cawfee that.

"It's up to you of course but…"

"I'm really not ready to involve the authorities," she said. "What if someone is holding him? Don't they always say don't go to the police? I'm going to call Gene and see if it really is possible to gather a million dollars in cash. Whether it's an investment, a con game or even if he's kidnapped, it would be worth it to get my Zander back."

When the client rules out the smart move, a private detective still does what he can. In this case that would be to call for backup.

Hannibal went up to the apartment above his office and knocked on the door. After a slow ten count he knocked again. The door opened and Hannibal faced a beefy, balding black man in boxers and a tee shirt.

"Morning, Sarge. Did I wake you?"

"No big deal," Sarge said. "I had to get up to answer the door anyways. Come on in."

He went straight to the kitchen and pushed the button that got his coffee maker working. Sarge's smile came easy, one of the reasons Hannibal saw him as his best friend. His mild demeanor was not at all what Hannibal expected from a Marine Corps veteran, but he was still the man to have at your back when things got ugly.

"Sorry to say, it's not a social call," Hannibal said, dropping onto a chair at the kitchen table.

Sarge chuckled. "H, you come to my door, glasses and gloves, I know you're on a case. Who's in trouble, and how can I help?"

"Missing person," Hannibal said. "Might be a runaway husband, but he's rich so could be a kidnapping. You probably know this Alexander Brown."

Sarge froze. "Whoa! Zander Brown? THE Zander Brown. Hell, who doesn't know him?"

"Who indeed?" Hannibal said, rolling his eyes. "Well I think I know who can give me some clue as to what happened to him, but the last time I went there I was met by a guy with a gun and I didn't have mine."

"So you're thinking it might be better to go back with a little backup, eh?" Sarge grabbed the coffee pot as soon as there was enough to fill two cups.

"Yeah. When people see you, they tend to be less aggressive. Guess that's what makes you such a good bouncer."

"I suppose," Sarge said. "Well, Tuesdays are slow so the club closed early last night. I'm up for a little action, for the usual fee of course."

An hour later, Hannibal pulled his car over to the curb, within a foot or two of where he was parked on his last visit to Samantha's house. As before, he saw no one outside, no dog walkers or kids playing outdoors. In some neighborhoods people stay inside. Her garage was still open and empty, and there was no vehicle in the driveway.

"Looks like we're too late to talk to her," Sarge said. "Too bad, too. I remember Samantha Tucker and I'd have liked to meet her."

"I think she's working in Virginia Beach today," Hannibal said. "Guess she had to be there early."

"Wasted trip?"

"Not necessarily," Hannibal said. "I can't question her, but I can still examine the house. I didn't get much of a chance to look around in there before. There might be some valuable clue to Zander's disappearance inside. Mind hanging here as lookout?"

Sarge shrugged. "Just to be clear, this is breaking and entering, right?"

"Well, I don't intend to break anything."

Hannibal snugged his gloves on his hands and went to the front door. If anyone was watching him, they'd have seen him pull a key out of this pocket like he lived there. What they couldn't have seen was that it was a bump key, a modified key blank designed to defeat typical pin tumbler locks. He slid the key into the lock one notch out. Then he pulled out his pocketknife, a one-handed folder from SOG that clipped onto his pants pocket. With one sharp swing he used the end of the knife to bump the key inward. The specially designed teeth of the key jiggled all the key pins in the lock. The key pins transmitted the force to the driver pins, which separated from the key pins for a split second and were pushed back by the spring, allowing Hannibal to turn the key and open the door.

Inside, Hannibal looked around the living room, kitchen, family room and first floor bathroom for anything out of place. All looked normal if unusually clutter free. It was starting to look like Samantha used this as a place to crash when she was tired but little else. Most walls were bare. There were no personal photos on display, no recipes stuffed into a kitchen drawer, no signs of any pets. Hannibal wasn't sure what he was looking for, but whatever it was, it was more likely in the bedroom.

Upstairs revealed a lot more about the resident. The bedroom was tidy and she had made her bed before leaving. An orderly vanity showed all the tools of beauty a woman in the public eye would need. The bathroom was as expected except for a basket holding a small collection of men's gear in a corner by the second sink. The walk-in closet was quite full with a broad variety of women's clothing, well organized and well cared for. On close inspection many pieces showed the subtle signs of wear quality clothing shows as it ages. So, in the good times she bought quality, but from all appearances the good times were past.

That realization sparked a memory. The box of money he saw in his earlier visit was gone. He looked under the bed and took a second look in the closet with no luck. He was about to explore other rooms when his phone vibrated. He had a text from Sarge. "Delivery at garage."

Hannibal bounced down the stairs three at a time. A delivery man could tell him much about Samantha's normal schedule. And maybe it was a regular delivery. Why else would she arrange to have it put in the garage?

Hannibal opened the door that led to the garage. Samantha must have been expecting this delivery. That would explain why the garage door was left open. Hannibal was outside by the time the delivery man opened the back of his van, which was still running. It was the familiar blue Ford Transit with the stylized swoosh on the side and the white letters spelling "prime."

"Good morning," Hannibal called.

The uniformed driver's face showed confusion as he squinted, straining for some kind of recognition. He took five or six steps toward Hannibal, not returning his smile and stopped beside the driver's door.

"You got something for us?" Hannibal asked.

"I don't know you," the driver said, and hopped back into the driver's seat.

"Wait!" But, ignoring Hannibal, the driver backed the van out of the driveway. Once fully in the street he spun around to leave.

Sarge must have seen Hannibal outside because he got out of the car, stood in the street and waved his arms to stop the van. The van could not swerve around Sarge without hitting Hannibal's car. But it never tried to swerve. Instead of slowing down, it sped up. Hannibal's heart froze for a second, Then he saw Sarge dive to the side with no time to spare.

CHAPTER 15

The blue van zoomed down the street. Hannibal ran to Sarge, offering a hand to get him up out of the street.

"What was that about?" Sarge asked, getting to his feet and brushing himself off.

"Not sure. Clearly whatever he was delivering was for a specific person, and I'm not him. Or her."

"You don't think that was a real Amazon truck, do you?"

"Could be stolen, I suppose," Hannibal said, getting back into his car.

Seated beside him, Sarge said "I know you, man. I know you got the license plate. And it's a pretty easy kind of van to identify. I'd sure like to have a little conversation with the man who tried to run me down."

"That would be nice," Hannibal said. "But the rear plate was covered with so much mud I could only make out two letters and they weren't next to each other. And no, it's not natural for mud to stick to a plate like that. I'm sure it was put there on purpose. Beyond that, there's a billion of those Amazon vans zooming around the area and people see them on their street almost every day. They're in plain sight but kind of invisible."

He stared at the house for a moment, as if his stern expression might make it give up its secrets. Then he threw the Volvo into gear and turned her around. He wondered what someone might be delivering that was worth a whole box of money.

An incoming call broke his focus.

"Hey, lover! What's going on this morning? Wanted to hear your voice before I dug into the day."

As Cindy's honeyed tones filled the car, Sarge turned his face to his window.

"Good morning, babe," Hannibal said. "I'm driving and Sarge is here with me. Heading home after checking a lead."

"Oh. Okay." Cindy's voice became slightly more businesslike. "So how's that case going? Are you on the trail of our missing sport star yet?"

"Nothing solid yet. Looks like our boy is mixed up with some bad actors. Then the wife got a request, apparently from Zander, asking for a million dollars in cash."

"That can't be right."

"No, but she's not so sure. Anyway, despite the wife's feeling I think it's time to bring in the law. After I drop Sarge off I'll go talk to Orson and see if we can get something going informally."

"Then you going to report in to the wife?" Cindy asked. It was that voice she used when she was setting him up for something. Did she know he could spot that? Well, he knew it didn't really matter.

"Yes dear. I'll be talking to her this afternoon."

"Well…" Cindy left a short pause, "This sounds like a situation where you might want to have some legal advice. Just to be on the safe side."

Hannibal sighed, and heard a small, snorted chuckle from Sarge. "Yes dear," Hannibal said. "That does sound like a good idea. Gee, why don't I pick you up before I head down to Fairfax to chat with Orson?" It was good to have a well placed county police detective on your friends list.

"A lovely idea!" she said. "Well, I need to wrap up some things before I can leave the office, but I know I'll see you soon. Later, lover."

Hannibal was lost in thought while he drove back to The District. Phil Collins sang, "I Missed Again," and Hannibal had to agree. Music aside, the car was pretty quiet until they were within a block of Hannibal's building. Sarge still faced forward when he spoke.

"You know, Hannibal, with that amount of cash in play, you might want to consider having some extra security involved in this. I'm free for a couple days."

Behind his glasses Hannibal's eyes rolled to the ceiling. "Seriously? You too? He's a basketball player for God's sake. And you realize he won't even be there, right? You that excited to see his wife?"

"The house, man," Sarge said. "I want to see that house. You know it was written up in that magazine, *The Washingtonian*, and they did a TV piece on the news. I looked it up."

"Wait. What? When did you do that?"

"As soon as Quaker came back and started telling us about this case…"

Hannibal pulled into his usual parking space across the street from his house. Once he got the car into park, he dropped his forehead into one hand. "So, Q told everybody about the case. Great. I don't get all this. He's just a basketball player."

Sarge looked at Hannibal as if he had just blasphemed. In a lower voice he said, "Zander Brown is not just a basketball player."

"OK, look, we'll see how this plays out, okay?"

Hannibal picked Cindy up at her office downtown and forty minutes later he pulled into the Fairfax County Government Center parking lot. Cindy released a breath she might have been holding since she got in the car.

"Damn, baby. I didn't know 66 was like the Indy 500 this time of day."

"I-66 is mostly two lanes of hell during rush hour," Hannibal said. "But regardless of the time of day, people drive as fast as they can. And I don't think I've ever seen a cop on that road."

Cindy waited until Hannibal walked around and opened her door to say, "Doesn't mean you have to lead the pack."

He held out his hand for hers, to help her to her feet. She had chosen the navy blue power suit for this trip and put her hair up. "Don't worry," Hannibal said with a smile. "The ride to the Browns' house will be much slower."

Once through the metal detectors they followed the familiar path to the major crimes office. The secretary recognized them and waved them into Orson Rissik's private office in the back. There they found Hannibal's only friend in law enforcement, running through papers at his desk. As usual, Rissik's desk was obsessively neat, his outbox half full and his inbox empty. After all the years Hannibal had known him, the same three framed citations clung to the walls left and right of the desk. That same single picture hung behind Rissik's head. It was a poster of a pelican trying to eat a frog. His head already in the bird's mouth, the frog had reached out and wrapped a hand around the pelican's throat, preventing it from swallowing him. The caption under the picture said, "Never Give Up."

Rissik himself was a medium size white man who somehow seemed bigger than he was. He worked with dress shirt sleeves rolled halfway up. His suit coat hung on a rack by the door. When he finished with his papers he looked up, saw Cindy for the first time, and stood up.

"Morning, Ms Santiago. I didn't know you were coming today. Is this about a client of yours?"

"Not really," she said.

"Maybe legal support," Hannibal said.

The comment prompted Rissik to focus his dangerous blue eyes on Hannibal. "Okay, Jones, what's this about? If you were just reporting a crime you'd have called, not driven all the way out here."

Rissik was not prone to small talk. Hannibal pointed to the small table with three chairs at the side in the office. "It's a little delicate. Can we talk a minute?"

As they settled in around the table, the secretary entered with two coffees. She was tall with mousy brown hair held in a bun at the back of her head. She sat one mug in front of Rissik, the other in front of Hannibal. Then she smiled at Cindy.

"I wasn't sure about you dear,"

Rissik said, "Gert here keeps the place running. She's been my admin assistant since back when we called them secretaries. Gert, this is Cindy Santiago, Hannibal's lawyer friend and…"

"Yes," Gert said with a wink. "Coffee dear?"

"Please," Cindy said.

As Gert stepped out Hannibal said, "Orson, I'm on a missing person's case. I'm here because I've got reason to believe the missing man is actually kidnapped. If I'm right about the people involved, he could be in danger."

Rissik nodded. "Okay, so it is a crime report. And you think it's a kidnapping because…?"

"His wife got an email, apparently from him, requesting a million dollars in cash."

Gert eased into the room, delivered one more cup and vanished like a spirit, not even disturbing the air carrying their conversation. That gave Rissik a few seconds to digest the situation.

"Got you. The client is actually…?

"His wife," Hannibal said, sipping his coffee. It was hot and fresh and strong. In other words, perfect. "The man missing is retired basketball player Zander Brown. Your face tells me you've heard of him."

"Hell, everybody knows Zander Brown," Rissik said. "Got to respect the talent. Still, there's something bad wrong with a world where a man gets paid slave wages for saving lives every day and another guy get millions of dollars a year just because he can consistently drop a ball into a hoop from the three-point line. No surprise somebody wants to take a little of that money from him. But you came here in person because…?"

"Because my client doesn't want the police involved. She thinks that would make it public knowledge and she doesn't want the publicity."

"So, what, you expecting me to do some investigating on the down low. That's your job, Jones. That's why private eyes exist, isn't it?"

"I'm not asking you to take over my case," Hannibal said. "But I think there's a connection to this club in Charles County, Maryland, The Indigo. Asking questions there got me this bruise on my jaw."

"Maryland? That's way outside my jurisdiction."

"Yeah, I know," Hannibal said. "But my client lives in McLean, which is in your county. So if you open an investigation into this…"

"Missing person," Rissik said.

"Kidnapping," Hannibal corrected. "At least that's the way it looks to me. With an open investigation you can go wherever it takes you, or at least get the local boys to do some checking for you."

Rissik took a few seconds of silence. Hannibal felt the air conditioner brushing his face while he held his breath.

"What happens when your client finds out you brought me into this?"

"I'm probably fired," Hannibal said. "But maybe we save a man's life."

Rissik leaned back in his chair. That was apparently the right answer. "Okay. You got a suspect?"

"Well, sort of." Hannibal sipped his coffee while collecting his thoughts. One thing Rissik's admin assistant could do was brew a damned fine cup of coffee, strong without being bitter. "I talked to a woman Zander Brown is connected with, and through her encountered a man called Nelson. That's all the name I've got but he pulled a gun on me, so I guess that puts him on the bad guy list in my book. I can give you a good description though." Hannibal stopped when he saw Rissik's eyebrows go up. "You know this man?"

"I read the bulletins," Rissik said, "for the whole DMV. If you're talking about the guy I've read about, he's a person of interest in a number of shady deals. And you've actually made two connections. That club, The Indigo? He owns it."

"You're kidding. Can't be a coincidence."

"Yeah, the PG County boys been watching that place for a long time," Rissik said. "He bought it from some singer a couple years ago. She bought it from a gambler a couple years before that."

"Happen to remember the singer's name?" Hannibal asked.

"No, but I can check into it. Why?"

"Just one of those hunches," Hannibal said. "So, can you hook up with the PG County police and maybe question Nelson when he shows up at the club?"

"You are a pain in my…" Rissik glanced at Cindy. "behind, Jones. But yeah I'll see if I can drum up some reason to ask my Maryland brothers to detain this Nelson guy for questioning. On one condition."

"We got conditions now?" Hannibal said, standing.

Rissik got to his feet as well but addressed Cindy. "Keep your man away from this Nelson guy, would you? Don't let him go after this guy. They haven't been able to pin anything on this clown but people who cross him have a bad habit of disappcaring."

CHAPTER 16

When Hannibal pulled up in front of the Brown house Cindy lit up, but it wasn't the jaw drop he expected. No, what he saw on her face was more a wide-eyed look of glee. It was the look he saw when he took her on that shopping trip to Bloomingdales which, he suddenly realized, was quite nearby.

"Good to see you, Hannibal," Cawfee called, trotting down the front steps. "They waiting for you in the sitting room. And I see you brought some class to the party. Who's this lovely lady?"

"Cawfee, this is Cintia Santiago, my personal legal advisor. Cindy, Cawfee here handles security for the estate."

"Among other things," Cawfee said. "Pleased to meet you, ma'am." Cawfee then held his hand out, palm up, toward Hannibal. When Hannibal looked from Cawfee's hand to his face, Cawfee said, "I park the car."

Hannibal surrendered his key fob and Cindy took his arm as they walked to the door. As he reached for the knob the door swung open, as if by magic. The woman who had met him at the door before stood beside it, smiling.

"Welcome back, sir," she said. "The ladies await you in the sitting room."

"Thanks. I know the way."

On their way down the hall Cindy leaned toward Hannibal and whispered, "That's how you know you're rich," she said. "When you got a weepy-eyed white girl answering your door."

Hannibal knew he didn't have time to explain everything he thought was wrong with that remark before they were in the sitting room. Charlotte and Frankie rose from the two easy chairs like synchronized swimmers on land.

"Welcome back, Hannibal," Charlotte said. "And this is your legal expert?"

Cindy stepped forward before Hannibal could speak, extending her hand. "Cindy Santiago, ma'am, and let me say it's a pleasure to meet you both. I understand this is a trying time and I can assure you I will proceed with the utmost discretion. I'm only here as an advisor."

Handshakes were exchanged, then Frankie broke the ice. "Hannibal, do you have a line on daddy's whereabouts?"

"Nothing solid," he admitted. "I think you have the best lead."

"Yes," Charlotte said, handing him a sheet of paper. "The email. I printed it out."

Mother and daughter lowered to their seat as smoothly as they had stood. Hannibal wondered if they practiced. He waved Cindy down on the love seat and he sat beside her. She read the email over his shoulder.

Hi, Babydoll,

I've stumbled on a business deal that's just too good to pass up. But to get in on it I have to move fast. I need you to gather one million dollars for this. It has to be cash, but if you get 20s and 50s it should all fit in a couple of duffl es okay.

I'll get back to you tomorrow about where to have the money sent. Love you.

Zander

Hannibal stared at the paper for a moment, as if he might glean more by osmosis. Charlotte looked as if she was eager to speak, so Hannibal just watched her and waited.

"I replied to the email but there's been no response yet," she said. "Still, I can't be sure, but I do think it might be real."

"Seriously?" Cindy said. Hannibal rested a hand on her knee hoping to quiet her.

"Well, yes," Charlotte said. "He always likes to call me Babydoll. That's his private nickname for me. So it's got to be, right?"

"Really?" Cindy said again, staring right through Hannibal's pleading expression. "Really? Your husband of all these years would be gone for four days, no contact at all, and when he does message you, no 'how you doing?' No 'sorry I've been out of touch.'"

Charlotte pressed her lips together and raised an eyebrow at Cindy. Then her expression softened, and she turned to the man she knew to be a detective. "What do you think, Hannibal? It's possible, isn't it?"

Hannibal wished they still cut letters out of the newspaper and glued them to a sheet of paper. Emails didn't have fingerprints or any physical clues. To Charlotte he said, "Well, there are a couple of things. If he was free to move it would make more sense for him to come here and pick up the money than to tell you where to ship it, right? And what business prefers cash to an electronic transfer of some kind? But most important: If he wanted anything at all done with money, you'd think he would contact Young, the man who handles all the finances, not expect his wife to handle this."

He could see on Charlotte's face that every sentence hit her harder than the last, melting her hopes that this email was indeed from her man, making it difficult to stay positive.

Hannibal's phone buzzed. He had a text. With any luck it was Rissik with some news, but he couldn't just pull his phone out. This would be an awkward time to answer, but he'd hate to wait. He looked at Cindy. With subtle head movements he managed to tap into that near-psychic communication some couples develop over time. Her brows went down in confusion, then up in understanding, and she turned to Charlotte.

"Mrs. Brown, I'm really sorry if I was a bit off-putting at first. I know you're worried and I do respect that. Can we start over? You have a lovely house, and I'll bet there are some special places here. Any chance…?"

Charlotte seemed all too happy to let go of grim thoughts and accept both the apology and the flattery. Also, perhaps, to move to more mundane actions. "Thank you, Miss Santiago. Would you like a tour?"

"Oh, that would be wonderful," Cindy said, bouncing to her feet. "And it's Cindy, please."

The two women left the room, but Frankie didn't move. Clearly, she was not ready to take her mind off her adoptive father's fate. So Hannibal rose as well. "If you'll excuse me," he said, trailing the others. Outside the room, and Frankie's line of vision, Hannibal spotted the two women and wandered in the opposite direction. He pulled his phone out when he found himself in the kitchen although, to him, kitchen was rather an understatement.

With hardwood floors, off-white cabinetry and marble topped everything, he would have been afraid to cook here for fear he'd spill something. The split-level island had three chairs at the rounded raised end, but he didn't imagine that anyone ever ate there except the staff. He parked on one of the chairs and opened his text. It was from Rissik as expected, terse but all he needed:

Police watching Indigo for Nelson. Bought Indigo 2 yrs ago from Samantha Tucker.

So, their connection was more than romantic. Or, maybe less than romantic. Either way, another layer that took it past coincidence.

Cawfee wandered into the kitchen and pulled open the door to what Hannibal had thought was a cupboard but was in fact a refrigerator. Cawfee pulled out a bottle of Coke then looked up as if just noticing that Hannibal was there.

"Hey, Hannibal. Want a soda?" When Hannibal shook his head, Cawfee came closer, twisted the cap off his drink, and leaned on the island. "What's next? She showed you the email, right? So, what you thinking?"

"I'm thinking Zander Brown is in real trouble."

"Don't have to be," Cawfee said after a long drink from the bottle.

"You've known Zander a lot of years," Hannibal said. "You really think this could be him?"

Cawfee finished the soda and pointed the neck at Hannibal. "Look, Zander, he a good man and all, but after all the money and all the years he still a hustler. The gangster runs deep. I can see him getting into something a little shady with a quick profit. Like, I don't know, drugs or something."

"How dare you?" Frankie's voice cut across the kitchen like the blade of an ax, to slice deep into Cawfee's heart. She marched into the room with eyes blazing and teeth bared for battle.

"Hey, I didn't mean nothing," Cawfee said, backing toward the arch at the other end of the kitchen.

"How you gone badmouth Daddy like that?" she screamed. "You supposed to be his friend. After all the shit he done for you. And you gone put him on blast like that?"

Frankie stopped halfway across the room because Cawfee had backed out and now was probably out of ear shot. She stood with fists clenched and took three slow, deep breaths. Hannibal just watched her until she regained control and turned back to him.

"My daddy is not involved in anything illegal," she said in the softer voice he had heard from her before. "He didn't ask for that money. It's just like you said, somebody wants money from us and then they'll send him home."

Hannibal thought about putting his arm around her, but decided she might react negatively. Instead, he allowed her a few seconds to calm down a bit.

"You don't think Zander would take a chance like Cawfee says? Well, I don't either. But I'm surprised you're so sure."

Frankie's mouth slid to one side, forming a sarcastic expression. "Look, Mister, I might look like a spoiled little bitch. Maybe I am. But my daddy's been good to me and Mama, and I won't listen to that shiftless fool talk him down."

Hannibal nodded. "I bet he gave you anything you asked for. Stepdads do that a lot. I can guess how losing him at this stage might hurt you."

That gentle probe earned Hannibal the dagger eyes Cawfee got before. Frankie came within striking distance. Anger, sorrow and fear were pulling her face in different directions, distorting her features into a horror mask.

"You listen to me," She started low, but it was building. "Daddy loved me like his own, and I loved him. You think this is about money or lifestyle? He loved me enough to set up an endowment for me. There's more money in that trust than I could ever spend. But yeah, losing him now would hurt like hell. I probably look like a spoiled, lazy bitch to you but I'm at that point, you know? I got to figure out what I'm going to do with my life, but there's so much to think about. Mama don't always listen, but Daddy, he was going to help me figure it all out. I need him. I…"

That was where it ran out. Her head dropped and tears slapped the hardwood floor. Hannibal had little to offer, but he gave her what he had.

"I'll find him. And I'll bring him home to you."

Over Frankie's shoulder Hannibal saw Charlotte and Cindy. They looked equally surprised and concerned to see Frankie breaking down but neither wanted to cross the threshold. Charlotte got Hannibal's attention by hooking a thumb toward the front of the house.

"Gene Young is here with all that money."

CHAPTER 17

Charlotte and Cindy left, and Hannibal moved to follow, but stopped when he realized Frankie wasn't moving.

"Hey, you okay?" he asked. "We're on our way to ending this and getting Zander back."

Frankie pulled a cloth from a drawer to wipe her eyes. "Yeah. Thanks. Need to get myself together before Gene sees me."

"Young? You like him?"

Frankie nodded and produced a genuine smile. "Yeah. We're dating kind of. He's a good man and Mama thinks he'd be a fine choice for a husband."

"Really? What do you think?"

"I'm not really ready for that kind of decision," Frankie said.

"Well, come on," Hannibal said. "Let's get this business done so you can get some guidance from your father."

Frankie led him to a larger lounge room dominated by a flat screen. He didn't know they made them that big. The L-shaped sofa facing it had a chaise lounge at each end and the section beside each of them was a recliner. Charlotte occupied the center cushion. Two cushions to her right, Young sat with his feet straddling a large black duffle bag. Cawfee had the seat to his right. On the other side, Cindy sat leaning forward on the chaise. In fact, no one was sitting back.

Frankie settled in the space held for her between Charlotte and Young. Hannibal guessed he belonged beside his woman. As soon as he was down the housekeeper ghosted in with a tray of drinks. The room held its silence until everyone took a drink and the woman returned to what Hannibal imagined as a human docking station, waiting to be needed again.

"I take it that bag contains Zander's investment," Hannibal said. "Or, if I'm right, his ransom."

"Yes, sir, and this was no easy task," Young said. He looked tired, as if he had hand cranked the machine that printed every bill in the bag. "First, banks don't keep this kind of cash on hand, and they are naturally suspicious of this kind of behavior. I had to liquidate some good bonds and tell some interesting stories at five different branches. But it got done."

"Okay, so what's next?" Frankie asked. All eyes turned to Hannibal.

"Well, that depends." He said. "Have you heard from Zander again?"

Charlotte shook her head.

"So you don't know where this money is supposed to go."

"I'd bet money it's all going to Ira Johnson at Optilorus." Young said. "That guy's a scam artist, I'm telling you, and he's convinced Zander to sink another pile of money into that bogus company of his."

While he spoke Young's left hand was wrapped around the duffle bag's handles as if he were afraid the money would get away from him. His other hand rested casually on Frankie's knee.

"Not arguing with you," Hannibal said, "Although one might wonder why he wouldn't just take a wire transfer. Right now, we don't know what the money's for, if Zander Brown is really involved with the request for it, or where it's supposed to go. So, we wait for instructions."

The quiet rolled in again, thicker than before, and Charlotte checked all the faces before speaking again. "Am I the only one here who's uncomfortable with all this money sitting here?"

"It is a lot of cash," Hannibal said. "It makes me nervous too. And if the request didn't really come from Zander, then somebody knows Young gathered it and brought it here. One possibility is that you aren't supposed to take it anywhere. This could be a setup to robbing the house."

Charlotte and Young exchanged worried glances before she said, "So what do we do?"

First things first," Hannibal said. "You got a safe that will hold that bag?"

"There's a safe room," Young said. "I can stash it there. But what else?"

Now it was Cindy and Hannibal looking at each other. Her expectant expression was followed by his sigh of surrender. "Good options are few. It's a huge house with a lot of entry points and that wrought iron gate would be easy to climb over. And this level of privacy isn't really a safety feature. I recommend added security personnel."

"That would make me feel better," Charlotte said. "No offense, Darrell."

"None taken," Cawfee said.

"Hannibal, can you arrange for more security people to be here?" Charlotte asked. "I'd sure sleep better."

"Yes, I know a few men I'd trust to do this. I'm sure they are available and would be happy to be here."

Hannibal, Cindy and Cawfee stood at the front door a couple of hours later when the black limousine pulled up. Hannibal knew he should not have been surprised at the scale of response to his request. All four of the other men who rented apartments upstairs from his own were eager to see Zander Brown's home and hoped to meet Zander himself when he returned to it. Cindy's father Ray owned a limo company so naturally he used one of his cars to bring the team out.

Cindy trotted down the steps to greet her father when he stepped out of the driver's seat. No one would think this man would do security work. Ray was a short, bulky, balding Cuban who was starting to thicken around the middle. Today he wore khakis, a dress shirt, his tweed sport coat and highly shined shoes. Who was he trying to impress, Hannibal wondered.

Then the other men climbed out of the back and Hannibal realized they had agreed to present an image. They had decided on Khakis, sport coats and dress shoes as their uniform. Hannibal went down to introduce everyone to Cawfee.

"Guys, Cawfee here is the driver for the Brown family and personal protection for Zander most of the time."

Virgil said, "Good to know you," in his deep, low voice, and shook Cawfee's hand. Virgil was a big man with mahogany skin, yellowed eyes and puffy hands. Cawfee seemed hesitant. Maybe he was intimidated by so much help. Or maybe he recognized the subtle signs of a man who was once a heroin addict. Hannibal introduced him to the others.

"So, this here's your posse," Cawfee said as he shook Sarge's hand, then Quaker's. After shaking with Ray he left his hand out.

"Need the key, bro. I need to park the limo."

"Oh, just tell me where it…"

"No. My job," Cawfee said.

As Ray surrendered the key fob the housekeeper appeared at the door. "Ladies and gentlemen, we are set up for a late lunch in the outdoor dining area. Please follow me."

They trailed the woman to a different flagstone covered area Hannibal had not seen. A long wooden table stood under a cover extending from the house supported by white columns at each end. Ten wicker chairs surrounded the table. Charlotte sat at one end in an off-white sweater dress very similar to the one Hannibal met her in. Frankie, at the other end, wore a more casual yellow button-front dress. Sleeveless with a V-neck, it showed her assets to best advantage. Young sat beside her. Hannibal's friends lined up on the far side of the table, so Hannibal held the chair beside Charlotte's on the near side for Cindy. Hannibal introduced his friends once more, then sat beside Cindy.

Fans overhead provided a breeze that gently tossed Cindy's hair. There was a moment of awkward silence. No easy icebreaker presented itself, so Hannibal chose to dive right in.

"If I may ask, where is the money?"

Charlotte stared at Young until the pressure forced him to speak. "I locked it in the panic room. Outside of me, only the residents can get in there."

Safe from everybody except all our suspects, Hannibal thought.

Cawfee walked up just ahead of the housekeeper who was pushing a wheeled cart loaded with covered dishes. He scanned the table and squeezed into the seat between Cindy and Young.

The housekeeper distributed meals. Hannibal was a fan of lettuce wedges covered with crumbled bacon and blue cheese dressing, and everyone he knew loved a good crab cake. Conversation chilled until the food was gone, except at the end of the table where Young chatted with Frankie between bites.

Everyone stood and stretched a bit while the housekeeper refilled lemonade glasses and cleared the table. Charlotte followed her, giving instructions about accommodations for their overnight guests. Young and Frankie headed into the house. Cawfee followed them with his eyes. Hannibal moved close to him to discuss plans, but it seemed Cawfee had other things on his mind.

"You know he going for that broad, right?"

"You jealous?" Hannibal asked.

"What? No, man, she's like a little sister to me."

"I see," Hannibal said. "Protective. Well, think he's got a chance?"

Cawfee checked that Charlotte was out of hearing distance before answering. "Sure. He look like a big shot, but he in Zander's posse too, just like me." When Hannibal raised an eyebrow, Cawfee continued. "Look, in this world you either got a posse, or you in a posse. If you in somebody's posse you do what they want you to do, go where they want you to go, say what they want you to say. And while you doing that you learn how to work them, to get what you want. And what that nigga wants is right there."

Frankie stalked out of the house, her face set in a determined scowl. At that moment she did not look like anybody's little sister, but Hannibal understood the dynamic Cawfee was talking about. He had watched his old friend's daughter grow up so she would be off limits to him. Frankie stopped in front of them, staring into Hannibal's face the way a woman does when she's going to ask you for something and you're going to say yes. Hannibal broke eye contact to address Cawfee.

"Listen, Sarge retired from the Marines and still thinks like a gunnery sergeant. He's kind of the unofficial leader when we do security work. Why don't you get with him, give the boys a tour of the grounds, figure out the weak points for entry? Then y'all can figure out who should post up where."

"Yeah I'll get on that now," Cawfee said, and went to join Hannibal's friends on the other side of the table. Hannibal turned his attention to the young woman standing so close to him she had to look up to see into his eyes.

"Listen, you heard what Gene said about Ira Johnson," Frankie said. "He thinks the man's a hustler."

"Right. And he's got a point. The whole Optilorus operation could be some sort of con."

"Well, I've been thinking. At first, I thought Daddy had got hooked by this guy and was being hustled. Wouldn't be the first time."

"At first," Hannibal repeated. "But now?"

"Now I'm thinking, what if Daddy is in on it?" She looked back over her shoulder, breathing a sigh of relief when she spotted her rmother and Cindy on their way into the house. "Daddy's a pretty smart guy. What if he's part of the whole Optilorus thing? What if this million dollars is part of some scheme to get out of paying taxes or something? Or maybe he's investing in something that's not entirely on the level."

"All possibilities," Hannibal said. "But until we get instructions about what to do with all that cash all we really have is possibilities."

"But what if Daddy's with Johnson," she asked, flipping her hands forward as if she had just revealed a magician's secret. "They might be sitting in that plant laughing at us all right now. And if he is kidnapped, that might be who's got him, in which case, he'd be in the same place."

Hannibal held up his palms. "Slow down, Frankie. What is this plant you're talking about?"

"The Optilorus plant slash office building. The whole operation is there. It's out in Ashburn, maybe half an hour from here. I think it was all built with Daddy's money."

"Might be worth checking out at least," Hannibal said. "Exactly where is this place?"

"Oh, you'd never find it," Frankie said with a mischievous grin. "But Daddy took me a couple times to meet this guy. I can get you there."

CHAPTER 18

"This is an absurd idea," Charlotte said, standing in the wide foyer.

"Come on Mom," Frankie said. "It's a good lead. Hannibal thinks it makes sense, and even Gene agrees there might be something crooked going on out there."

When Frankie turned her laser eyes on him, he nodded, although he and Hannibal both kept their distance from the women. Cindy, standing to Charlotte's left, was looking around as if she was seeking a good hiding place.

"That may be, but there's no reason for you to be involved," Charlotte said. "I can see how this may be a good lead, but if bad actors are at this plant or whatever, then it's no place for you, Frankie."

"He knows me," Frankie said, raising her voice a bit. "And I'll know if he tries to lie to us."

"It's just too dangerous," Charlotte said.

Frankie surged forward, backing her mother up against the spiral staircase. "You're not listening. I've got to go. If Daddy's there, I've just got to see him. I have to know he's okay."

Cindy pushed her open hand between the women like a referee pausing the fight. To Frankie she said, "You need to calm down, young lady." Then she turned to Charlotte. "I have to say, she has a point. He might be there of his own volition. If he's hiding, he may not reveal himself to Hannibal but he's not likely to hide from his daughter, not after he sees and hears how worried she is. Besides…" Cindy cut her eyes to the two men and dropped her voice to a whisper. "…they don't need to see you and your daughter do this."

Charlotte blinked twice, searched the other faces in the room, took a deep breath and refocused on Frankie.

"All right. Do what you need to do but Hannibal is responsible for you. Promise me you'll do what he says. And if you find - anything - you call me right away."

Rather than answer her mother Frankie turned to Hannibal. "Got to find Uncle Cawfee and get him to bring your car to the front." Then she was out the door.

"Let me know," Charlotte said, and headed up the stairs.

Young lightly held Hannibal's sleeve. "Please, please take good care of her. I know Frankie can be a ball of fire sometimes but just keep her safe."

"Your concern is noted," Hannibal said. "Now let me get going."

Cindy followed Hannibal out the front door. Side by side, he gathered her hand in his. The afternoon sky was robin's egg blue, but clouds on the edge of the horizon warned that you can't always trust the promises the present makes. Storms feel no obligation to warn you of their approach.

"Nicely handled in there," Hannibal said. "You have a gift for knowing what to say to calm a situation down."

"No magic there," she said. "A woman who wears a twenty-five-hundred-dollar Bottega Veneta to lunch in her own house because she has company is more concerned about how she looks to her guests than she is about her real relationship with her daughter."

"A twenty-five hundred dollar what?"

"The dress, dear," Cindy said with a grin.

"You'd look sweet in that dress." Hannibal said.

"I'll add it to my Christmas list."

Hannibal's car rolled up in front of them with Frankie riding shotgun. Hannibal gave Cindy a quick kiss and traded places with Cawfee. Frankie tilted the seat back just far enough that Hannibal couldn't see her face in his peripheral vision.

"You do know I could find this place on my own, right?" Hannibal said. "It's a business with an address, and that's why God created GPS. So let's be clear: That line was for your mother's benefit. You just wanted to make this trip with me."

"Wasn't trying to insult you," she said. "Now, can you find Route 7 from here? Optilorus is down near the end of the Tech Corridor."

The Dulles Technology Corridor is a business cluster comprised of defense and tech companies gathered near Washington Dulles International Airport. Sometimes called the Silicon Valley of the East, it's home to more satellite and telecom companies than anywhere else in the world. The electronic pathways there carry half of all the traffic on the internet. And people live there too, in communities strung along The Dulles Toll Road and Route 7.

Hannibal drove them westward through those areas, from Tysons Corner, past Reston, then Herndon, and finally near the end of the toll road into Ashburn. To Hannibal it was much as he imagined it would be driving through Disneyland's Tomorrowland. Glistening towers of steel and glass rose up on one side of them, then the other, monuments to how much money and power can be generated without anyone doing actual physical work.

Hannibal kept the music at a moderate volume, and Warren Zevon was just asking his dad to send lawyers, guns and money when Frankie said, "What's your story, Hannibal? I don't figure you for sports, and you're not like any of the hustlers I've met. Or white collar like Gene. Daddy, he grew up on the streets of Baltimore. Basketball was his way up out the hood. How about you?"

"Grew up in Berlin," Hannibal said. "so I didn't have a hood to get up out of. My father was a soldier, married a German lady. And actually, college was your father's way up and out. He went to Howard, right? Basketball was just his way to wealth and fame."

"You right," she said, easing her seat forward far enough to see his face. "I know he worked his ass off to make the pros. So, how does a brother become a private detective?"

She was looking for equivalents, making comparisons. Hannibal guessed that Zander Brown was her only point of reference for manhood.

"A brother becomes a New York cop," he says. "If he's good he becomes a detective. Then if he's real good he moves to DC and joins the Secret Service. Then if he pisses the wrong people off, he gets asked to leave that job. So then he gets a private investigator's license. Three actually if he wants to work here, cause cases rarely stay in The District or Maryland or Virginia. Oh, and this brother lives in Ward 8, in Anacostia, so I guess he went backwards and ended up in the hood."

She stared straight ahead for a while, as if hypnotized by the lowering sun. The toll road seemed to stretch forward to infinity. He wondered how he stacked up against her father. From the dashboard Jackson Brown told them he was running on empty, running into the sun but he was running behind.

"Hannibal, how do you tell the bad guys?"

"Tell them what?"

She chuckled. "Not like that. I mean the world has good guys and bad guys, right? How do you tell them apart?"

"I don't know what your father told you, but I think you're starting with a false premise."

"Well, take my dad," she said. "He's been good to me. But what if we get out here and find out he's going to invest a million dollars into some crooked scheme? Or illegal drugs or something? Does that make him a bad guy?"

"I don't believe in bad guys," he said. "There's just guys. Guys who do mostly good things, and a few guys who do bad things. Not good guys and bad guys. More like hunters and prey. Givers and takers. Wolves and sheep. But a lot more sheep than wolves."

"Over here," she said, sitting up. "Down Gloucester Parkway. We're close now."

Residences gave way to shopping centers which surrendered to an industrial park. Hannibal eased down a long winding private road into the parking lot of a structure that looked like the illegitimate child of an old school factory and a modern office building. The grounds were well kept, and the image was one of wealth and efficiency. Only four other cars shared the lot. A Bronco, an F150 and a little Chevy Hannibal wasn't sure about sat at one end. He parked up front, two spaces from a BMW convertible. The sign mounted on the front wall said "Optilorus – your view of the future." Before they got out of the car Frankie regarded Hannibal with appraising eyes.

"And which are you? Wolf? Or sheep?"

He got out of the car, walked around to the other side and opened the door for his passenger. When she stood up, he said, "That's not for me to say. Cindy would tell you I'm neither. She says I'm the sheepdog."

When they were within ten yards of the door a man burst from the door. Hannibal recognized him from his web site. Blond hair, blue eyes, fit, well dressed and aggressively handsome. He froze when he saw them. He seemed to recognize one of them.

"That's him," Frankie said. "That's Ira Johnson."

CHAPTER 19

Johnson's face held a tan that Hannibal knew came from a booth, not beach time. Like his teeth, his tan was too perfect to be natural. His bright blue eyes scanned his two visitors and Hannibal imagined this man vacuuming in information about them, the way a carnival mentalist does to tell marks their futures.

"Miss Brown, how lovely to see you again." Johnson's smile dripped honey as he moved to meet them. "You've never visited without Zander, so I'm thinking this is an official visit of some kind?" He ended the statement as a question.

"We drove out looking for Daddy," Frankie said. It seemed the only path she knew was the direct one.

Johnson turned his questioning gaze on Hannibal, who thought he should answer the unasked questions to move things along.

"Not a cop. Just a family friend. Hannibal Jones." Hannibal held his gloved hand forward and received a solid, firm handshake. A politician's handshake. A 'trust me' handshake. "I came with Frankie because Charlotte, Mrs. Brown, thought her husband might be out here today."

Johnson did stunned surprise like a pro. "Why would Zander be here? I haven't seen him in weeks. Is he okay?"

'Left for the weekend and never came back," Frankie said, stepping into Johnson's personal space. "Did he come to give you more money?"

"What? Of course not. Like I said, I haven't seen him. I'd certainly tell you if I had." Righteous indignation. Hannibal had him marked as a world class confidence man. That meant that every word out of his mouth was suspect.

"Look, we don't want to cause you any trouble," Hannibal said, matching Johnson's smile. "But I do want to put poor Charlotte's mind at ease. Besides, this looks like a pretty cool place. Want to give us the tour? Just so I can say we looked around for him, you know?"

"Well, ordinarily I'd be happy to, but I was just on my way home. It's been a long day."

Hannibal raised a palm to Frankie to stop her predictable attack. "I understand. I'm sure a member of your staff can show us around."

"Well, no," Johnson said. "There's no one else here right now, except of course a couple of security people."

Hannibal checked his watch. "Really? It's barely three."

"I let everyone off early."

In the middle of the week? Hannbal thought. *What a nice boss.* Aloud he said, "Then at least we won't be distracting anyone from their work. Just want to have a quick look around is all. You've got nothing to hide, right? There's no telling what Charlotte will do if we can't reassure her. She was talking about going to the police and the press, but I told her she didn't want those people questioning all of Zander's friends and so forth."

Johnson's smile never wavered but his eyes slid off Hannibal and zoomed in on the determined set of Frankie's jaw.

"Well, I can't refuse you, Miss Brown, and I guess we don't want your mom to be upset. Sure, let me give you the ten-cent tour."

Johnson unlocked the big glass double doors and escorted Hannibal and Frankie into a wide, modern lobby. Marble, steel and glass made it the high-class lobby of the future. Fresh flowers adorned the reception desk, the ceiling lighting was chandeliers, and the walls were dark hardwood. No expense had been spared to give the feel of success.

"Our offices are upstairs," Johnson said, punching an elevator button.

They rode up and in seconds stepped out into what looked like a typical office cube farm with spaces for sixteen workers. Johnson flipped on the lights to reveal a vista of empty desks. To the right stood a single enclosed office. Johnson pulled the door open and stepped inside. Frankie followed. Hannibal stayed just outside but he could see the rich appointments filling it.

"This is where I get it all done," Johnson said. "There's a conference room at the other end if you want to look under the table or something."

Hannibal nodded and looked into the conference room, but he knew he would find nothing of interest. He walked down two rows He found it minimalist, nearly devoid of any human touches. Indeed, almost Spartan. He doubled back to the entrance where Johnson and Frankie waited for him.

"Are you satisfied…friend?" Johnson asked, running a hand back through the blond thatch on his head. "I think I've been indulgent, but I really do have to get home."

"Yeah, we're good," Hannibal said. "And thank you for indulging us."

The three rode down to the lobby, their steps echoing off the walls on their way to the door. Johnson again locked up and waved goodbye as he headed for his car. Hannibal and Frankie got back into his vehicle and watched the BMW pull away. The second it was out of sight Frankie gave Hannibal's shoulder a light punch.

"Jesus, did that guy set off your bullshit alarm or what? What do you think?"

"I think you've got some good instincts," Hannibal said, "But I'll bet he's much better when he's not caught by surprise. His pitch to potential investors must be pretty strong to keep them from noticing the rest."

"What rest? This place sure looks good."

"Yeah, out here," Hannibal said. "And the lobby's pretty convincing. I'm sure the girl he puts there is top notch. But upstairs, not so much. Computers in every cubicle, but no personal items at all. No plants, no abandoned notes, no family pictures. Who works like that? And the cubicles at the back and on the far side had a little dust on them."

"So, you don't think anybody works here?"

"Not office personnel anyway," Hannibal said. "I'm thinking when he's got potential investors, he hires a few girls to sit up there and look busy while he pitches the investors in the conference room."

"So you figure this is all a front for some big con game, right?" Excitement raised Frankie's voice. "So why we sitting here? Let's go back and tell Mom."

"Yes, he's a con man running a game," Hannibal said. "And we're sitting here because we haven't seen half the operation and that could be where your father is. The loading docks are in the back, and I'd guess that's also where the supposed manufacturing area is, where they build these virtual reality thingies. If I had a partner, he might have been in the office areas, but if I was holding somebody against their will they'd be in there someplace. So now that it's clear Johnson's not coming back, I figured I'd go around back and see if I can get a look."

He popped his door and as he stepped out Frankie said, "I'm coming too." Hannibal knew it was pointless to debate it. In the entire history of film and television dramas "stay in the car" was a command that was never once obeyed. Real life was much the same.

The unshaven fellow standing on the loading dock wore a navy-blue uniform and boots Hannibal assumed were steel-toed. His sidearm sat in a holster with no restraining strap. His reddened skin was probably due to standing outdoors all day. His eyes tracked Hannibal as he walked up the steps to the dock. He took a step to block Hannibal's progress and his hand settled on his weapon.

"Whoa," Hannibal said with a smile. "Ira Johnson just sent us back here. We're just going to look around the warehouse area. He said…"

"No, he didn't," the guard said. "And no you ain't. Get moving."

"Now look, your boss said…"

"The boss ain't never sent nobody back here." The guard growled. "Nobody sees in the warehouse, nobody nohow."

While Hannibal choked back a Wizard of Oz reference a second security guard emerged. Aside from his mocha skin and crooked teeth he was a clone of his white co-worker.

"Problem here, Bennie?"

"Nah," the first guard said. "These two were just leaving."

"This is bullshit!" Frankie snapped, rushing toward the guard. Hannibal grabbed her arm and yanked hard before she got within arm's length of her target.

"Now now, dear. Let's not provoke the animals. I'm sure Mr. Johnson can straighten this all out later."

Hannibal gently but firmly pulled Frankie back and pointed her toward the parking area. He had shoved her into her seat and gotten strapped into the driver's seat before she managed to get past fuming to speak.

"What the hell, Hannibal? You could have taken that guy."

"Probably," he said, pulling out of the parking lot. "And maybe the second guy. But I couldn't see the third guy. He might have been inside with his gun drawn already."

"Third guy?"

"Count the cars in the parking lot," Hannibal said, easing back onto Gloucester Parkway. "Nobody there today but security, and none of them was at the front of the building. But don't worry. I'm planning to go back to see them when I'm better prepared."

He was less than a block away from Optilorus headquarters when a blue Amazon delivery van passed him going the other way. Nothing odd about that, he told himself. Those things are everywhere. Just a coincidence, he told himself.

But he was having a hard time believing himself.

CHAPTER 20

Driving was at once one of Hannibal's great joys and one of his greatest frustrations. Getting back on the toll road was a little tricky, and Hannibal half thought Frankie was playing with him to take out her own frustrations. She directed him onto Ashburn Farm Parkway which dragged him past churches, schools and doctor's offices.

After a bit of very nice residential space the scenery reverted to business again. It was still commercial space, but not industrial. Stopped at a light Hannibal could see the kinds of businesses that only the deeply overpaid would welcome. Nothing called a Kiddie Academy would appear in the inner city, and he wondered at a sign for a Russian School of Mathematics.

Madonna snarled "What are you looking at?" from his speakers when the light changed, and he could move forward. He turned left following the signs for the Greenway, which was yet another name for the Toll Road. A car turning onto Ashburn Farm caught his attention. A red Porsche 911 convertible with the top down. The driver was a tall woman, maybe Latin, with long black hair flying in the wind.

"Damn," he said. "One coincidence too many." Frankie gasped as he executed a U-turn in the intersection. Tires squealed, and snapping the Volvo straight on the road threw Frankie into him for a second. His car had plenty of power and he quickly closed the distance between himself and the Porsche. He saw the other driver's head tip slightly as she looked into her rearview mirror, and she slowed to exactly the speed limit. The normal caution of the sports car driver?

Maybe. Or, was this a woman who was always worried about being followed?

The road wound through the residential area again with Hannibal keeping a reasonable distance between himself and his quarry. He finally noticed his passenger was talking.

"Will you just tell me what you're doing?" Frankie screeched. "Are you following that Porsche or what? What the hell's the matter with you?"

"A car like that one turned up in my investigation."

"What, like it's the only one?" Frankie said. "We're in Loudoun County, brother. That Cabriolet's probably the cheapest car on her block. You need to get a grip."

The Porsche turned back onto Gloucester Parkway. Hannibal maintained a safe follow distance. Hopefully he was just one black sedan among the crowd of BMWs, Benz's, Lexus's, Hondas and other Volvos in her wake, all of which looked pretty much the same at a distance. If she was going to Optilorus he might have a concrete connection between Zander's disappearance and Ira Johnson's scam.

The Porsche slowed and turned into the industrial park. Yes! She slowed to a crawl so Hannibal did too as he turned to follow.

Then, like a spurred stallion, the red sports car leaped forward.

"Damn," Hannibal said. "Now she's sure she's being followed." He mashed the accelerator to the floor as the Porsche skipped through the narrow paths and back out onto the main highway. He followed hard, tuning out the ongoing narrative on his right.

"Who is this woman and why do you want her so bad? Is she connected with Daddy's disappearance? Why are you - whoa!"

Frankie's hands hit the dashboard. They were racing down the Parkway, away from the toll road, weaving around slower moving vehicles. Hannibal gripped his steering wheel hard, leaning forward as if that would make them go faster. Under the ongoing chatter he could hear his tires humming against the road. His eyes flicked down to the speedometer. He was pushing 100 miles per hour and the Porsche was pulling away. His Volvo had an easy twenty miles an hour more under her hood, but he was chasing a two-hundred- mile-an-hour car and a driver who clearly knew what she was doing.

Hannibal slammed on the brake pedal as a Jeep SUV changing lanes slid over in front of him. He searched for a way around but the cars in the next lane made it impossible. He didn't notice how hard his heart was pumping until the Porsche disappeared ahead. He turned on the next side road and pulled to the curb.

"Okay, that was crazy," Frankie said. Her eyebrows were trying to reach her hairline. "You trying to get us killed. Are you fucking crazy?"

He turned to her with complete calm, his voice soft, both hands still locked on the wheel. "I think you have me confused with someone else. You can talk to your mother like that, or the servants running around your house, but I'm not your family and I don't get paid to take your shit."

After a moment of stunned silence, Frankie came back with, "Just who do you think you are?"

"I think I'm the man driving the car you're sitting in," he said. "Also, the man who will have no problem putting your ass on the street right here. So you can get the hell out, or you can sit back and shut the hell up. Choose now, cause I got places to go and things to do."

Hannibal knew how to execute a genuine hard look. Frankie must have read it correctly because after four deep breaths she faced forward and leaned her seat back. Hannibal pulled back into traffic and turned around to head back to the Browns' house. Once on the toll road he set the cruise control on sixty and tapped Frankie's leg.

"Look, in the moment I had to focus on what I was doing. I'm about to get on the phone and I need you to be quiet. If you pay attention to the call, you'll probably hear the answer to all your questions. If you don't I promise to answer them all afterward. Okay?"

"I suppose."

Hannibal pushed buttons on his steering wheel and in less than a minute he was connected to Orson Rissik again.

"Could use some help with that issue we discussed earlier." Hannibal said.

"You making this official?" Rissik asked.

"Not yet but give me an hour. Driving now but when I'm face-to-face with the client, I'll make her bring you in."

"All right. You know, whether it's a missing person or an abduction time is of the essence."

"Agreed, Chief," Hannibal said with a quick look at Frankie. "And after that it will be your investigation and we'll all do what you say."

"Good. Now, what have you got?"

"In an earlier interview I was told that Zander Brown was last seen getting into a red, Porsche 911." He glanced at Frankie who was staring at him with wide eyes. "I'm told it's a Cabriolet."

"So?"

"Same witness described the driver. A tall female, probably Latin, with very long black hair."

"Reliable witness?"

"I think so," Hannibal said. "Thing is, I spotted a car and driver that fit that description in the vicinity of a business that's known for getting money from Zander. Might be nothing, might be a crucial link. Thought you might hunt this woman down."

"Are you serious?" The voice coming in from the dashboard dripped with sarcasm. "You expect me to dig through Motor Vehicle records for all the 911's registered in the DMV?"

"Actually, I think it will be a lot easier than that," Hannibal said. Afternoon traffic backed a line of cars up at the next toll booth. Even with his EZ pass this volume of traffic caused annoying delays. "Let's think this through. Do you think a woman who owned a Porsche would be doing this? Would she take this kind of risk for a measly million dollars?"

"I see your point," Rissik said.

"Good. I think the car was chosen to let an out-of-towner blend in. I'm thinking it's most likely a rental."

Even over the phone, he could hear Rissik nodding. "Can't be too many places that rent this kind of high-end vehicle."

"And I can help you narrow it down a bit," Hannibal said. "I didn't capture the whole plate, but I got the first three letters."

"A partial plate's a whole lot better than nothing. Hit me." While Hannibal gave Rissik that information. He was aware of Frankie's wrinkled brow, her eyes in constant motion. The two men said their goodbyes. Madonna, from the car stereo, decided to be annoying.

A man can tell a thousand lies
I've learned my lesson well
Hope I live to tell
The secret I have learned, 'til then...

Frankie stayed quiet and stared out the side window until they were on Route 7, close to home. When she broke her silence, she still didn't look at him.

"Somebody saw Daddy in that car?"

Hannibal nodded.

"With that woman?"

A deeper nod.

"And you don't know who she is.'

Hannibal shook his head.

She turned to face him. "Don't tell Mama. It will break her heart."

"Didn't want to tell you," he said. *For the same reason,* he didn't say aloud. To him, Charlotte's love for her husband was not obvious but Frankie's devotion to him shone very clearly.

The ring of his phone took him by surprise. Could Rissik have found something that quickly? He hit the button, hopeful for fast answers.

"Hannibal? It's Cindy. Are you on your way back?"

"Not far out, babe," he said. "What's going on?"

"Get here as fast as you can, honey. Things have changed and Charlotte's a mess. We have a ransom note."

CHAPTER 21

Hannibal tossed his key fob to Cawfee and ran up the stairs to the front door behind Frankie. Charlotte, Young and Cindy, gathered in the sitting room, all sprang to their feet when Hannibal and Frankie ran in. Frankie dove into her mother's arms. Charlotte held a plain white envelope clutched in her left hand. Hannibal guessed what it was. He gave Cindy a quick fly-by kiss and grabbed Charlotte's arm, yanking her out of her daughter's embrace.

"You. Me. Kitchen. Now."

Charlotte stumbled after him as he dragged her out of the room. Behind him he saw that Frankie had moved from comforting to being comforted in Young's arms. In the kitchen, Hannibal pushed Charlotte into a chair at the island. Dried tears crusted her cheeks, the remains of the shock of reality. And he knew he was about to make it worse.

"I need you to listen to me," Hannibal said. "Now that we know what we're dealing with, things are going to have to change. You understand?"

"Just tell me what to do. I just want Zander back."

"Is that the note?" Hannibal asked.

Charlotte nodded and handed him the envelope. Nothing on the outside but her name, Charlotte Brown, printed in black ink, in Times New Roman font, twelve point. The single sheet of paper inside was standard cheap copy paper, folded in thirds. Near the top in the same font were two sentences in all capital letters.

LEAVE THE MONEY IN FRONT OF THE FIRST GAS
PUMP AT MANASSAS COSTCO AT MIDNIGHT TONIGHT.
IF YOU DON'T ZANDER BROWN DIES AT 1AM.

Hannibal folded the paper and returned it to its envelope.
Frankie came into the kitchen, headed for her mother.

"Not yet," Hannibal said. "Out." He needed Charlotte's
full attention.

Frankie froze. Young, behind her, placed his hands on her
shoulders, whispered something to her and eased her back
out of the room.

"Charlotte, you understand that this is now a criminal
situation," Hannibal said. "There can be no doubt. Your
husband is in serious danger."

"Yes. Yes, but we can pay."

"Of course," Hannibal said. "But that's no guarantee
we'll get Zander back. In a situation like this, you have to
involve law enforcement."

"No," Charlotte shook her head hard. "No cops. This is a
private matter."

"Think this through. If things go poorly, you'll lose the
option of secrecy and in a case like this the wife is the first
suspect. I'm afraid you have to involve the police. Now you
do have options there. I should alert the FBI. Kidnapping is,
after all, a federal crime. But time is short, and I think we
can work with local county police. I have a contact, a friend,
who I know will be discreet. But you'll have to cooperate
with him. All right?"

Charlotte looked around the room as if searching for
another option. Finding none she faced Hannibal and
nodded.

"Good. He'll be here in a few minutes. I called him right
after I heard there was a ransom demand. I figured you'd be
mad, but I knew you'd get over it and time is the enemy now,
even more than I knew at the time. Now, you good?"

Charlotte's face closed. Her mouth, her eyes, even her hair seemed to be clenched tight. After ten long seconds she opened her eyes and clutched both of Hannibal's hands.

"I put this in your hands from the beginning," she said. "Whatever it takes. You just bring my Zander home."

They were headed back to the sitting room when Hannibal's phone rang.

"Hey Sarge."

"Yo, Hannibal. There's a car here at the gate. It's your boy Rissik. Hold him?"

"No, man, send him on through," Hannibal said. "He's the reinforcements."

The housekeeper escorted Rissik into the sitting room. Hannibal and Cindy greeted him with handshakes, and Hannibal introduced him to Charlotte, Frankie and Young. Rissik stood while everyone else sat. He was polite and precise and pointedly unimpressed by his surroundings. Hannibal figured that working major cases in Fairfax County had exposed him to the most extravagant homes and big-name victims.

"Mrs. Brown, I'm really sorry you are faced with this awful situation," Rissik said. "High profile kidnapping is not all that common in the U.S. anymore, mostly because of the difficulty level. There are extreme logistical challenges involved in successfully exchanging the money for the return of the victim without getting caught. So you have reason to be optimistic. I understand that you didn't want law enforcement involved with your problems. I'll have to notify the FBI with what I know tomorrow. With any luck, this will all be over by then. Now, if I can see that note…"

He accepted the ransom note and stared at it for a minute, then closed it up and slipped it into a plastic bag he carried in his jacket pocket.

"I'll get this checked for prints later," Rissik said. "I don't expect to find anything except all the people in here who probably handled it, but you never know. How'd you get the note? In the mailbox?"

Charlotte shook her head. "Victor found it."

"Who?"

"Our cook," Charlotte said. "He was headed out to pick up some fresh ingredients and found this envelope taped to the gate. Thank God he was going out, or we might not have seen it until hours later."

"What about right now?" Frankie asked. "Do we pay?"

"I think so," Rissik said, with a sarcastic smile. "Not much choice. I take it you have the money together."

"Yes," Charlotte said. "That much is ready to go."

Cawfee hustled into the room and circled the perimeter to stand behind the sofa. Feeling like a student in some odd criminology class, Hannibal raised his hand.

"Orson, what do you think of these kidnappers?"

"What, you want a profile?" Rissik asked. "I think they're rank amateurs with big egos and small ambitions. Pros would ask for lots more money from a mark like this, and they'd want bearer bonds or precious stones. And only one-way communications, with no proof of life offered, and no way for you to ask for it. And obviously it's an inside job."

Aside from Hannibal and Cindy, every other jaw in the room dropped. Young was first to recover his voice.

"Obvious? Why obvious?"

"Well, no proof of life means they know for sure you'll pay without questioning," Rissik said.

"Demanding the money tonight means they know you were able to get the funds together," Hannibal added, "and that you actually did it this fast."

That set everyone to looking at each other.

"Just who do you suspect?" Charlotte asked.

"Everybody," Rissik said.

"I see." Charlotte's tone said she was offended.

Rissik's expression said he didn't care. "I suppose you'll want to interrogate us all," she added.

"I'd like to start with the staff. How many do you have here?"

"Just two," Charlotte said. "There's Victor of course, and Betsy, who runs the house. She showed you in."

Hannibal was happy to learn that they both had names. No one had bothered with an introduction. And in the past, he had known overlooked servants to be resentful enough to do bad things.

"Two people?" Rissik asked. "To run this house? I'm thinking, what, fifteen thousand square feet? Sitting on four acres? That's a lot of house for one housekeeper."

"Zander, he didn't like having, well, servants." That last word was hard for Charlotte to push out. "Betsy runs things, manages the house as it were. She has people come in every week to clean and hires the crew that takes care of the grounds."

"So just those two," Rissik said, "and the fellow over there who parked my car."

Hannibal turned to look at Cawfee standing behind him. Charlotte turned her offended tone up a notch.

"Darrell has known Zander longer than I have. He is my husband's oldest and best friend."

Rissik redirected his gaze, his dangerous blue eyes zooming in on Cawfee. "Is that what it says on your tax returns, Darrell? Professional friend?"

"I'm Zander's chauffeur," Cawfee said, "and I ain't ashamed of it. Unofficially, I'm also his muscle, his bodyguard."

"Under the circumstances, you might not want to boast about that part," Rissik said, straight faced. To Hannibal he added, "Speaking of driving, I did do a check on that red vehicle you asked me about. Found one with plates that fit the partial you gave me. Rented to a woman who the attendant says matched the description you gave me. Of course, the address she gave was bogus, but it might have been her real name."

"That sounds like you've got a suspect who doesn't live here," Charlotte said.

"Tell you about it later," Hannibal said. "Orson, you said there wasn't time to reach out to the FBI. I take it that means we go ahead with the drop."

"I think that's the plan," Rissik said. "I'll get a map and lay it all out."

Cawfee put both hands on the back of the sofa and leaned forward. "I'll drop that money off at the Costco pumps."

Young snapped to his feet. "That's okay man, I can take the money to the drop spot."

"It's my job, man," Cawfee said, stepping around the sofa toward Young. "It's my job to look out for Zander."

Young turned to face Cawfee, but left one hand on Frankie's shoulder. "And it's my job to look out for his money. I got this."

Hannibal stood also, stepping into the space between them. The two men faced each other over Hannibal's shoulder until Rissik interrupted.

"Fellas, fellas, it's too hot for that nonsense," he said, walking over to stare one, then the other, down. It seemed to be enough to make them both back off. "Besides, you'll both be here in the house while we make the drop and, I expect, the takedown. I need a disinterested party to make that drop. That means you." Rissik pointed at Hannibal, then turned back to Charlotte. "Right now I need to talk to Hannibal for a minute, then I'll want to question the three staff members."

"In that case, you can talk to Betsy first," Charlotte said. "I'll have Victor put together something quick, maybe some sandwiches, for everyone and lay them out in the formal dining room."

Rissik snapped his head toward the archway. Hannibal got the message and followed him out of the room. When Rissik muttered, "this place is a maze," Hannibal guided him to the kitchen which had become his makeshift headquarters.

He opened the disguised refrigerator and pulled out a pitcher of lemonade.

"They keep milk in there?" Rissik asked. Hannibal pulled it out and opened a few cabinet doors until he came upon glasses. He poured milk for Rissik and lemonade for himself. The two men sat side by side, drinking.

"You get why I want those two yahoos in the house, right?'

"Of course," Hannibal said. "They're suspects."

"There won't be any cash to guard so can you get your boys to watch them? Keep them pinned down?"

"They're getting paid," Hannibal said, "They'll be glad to do it." It was really good lemonade, just sweet enough, and Hannibal wondered if rich people got special lemons or if Victor squeezed fruit and made it from scratch. "Hey, that bit you said in the other room, about not having time to alert the FBI. I mean I threw that out before you got here as an excuse to call you, but between us, you know you could have half a dozen agents down here before the drop."

"Yeah, but why muddy the waters? I don't trust the Bureau boys to think about the victim first. Besides, they tend to follow policy, so no way they'd go along with actually paying the ransom. But this is the best chance of bringing Mr. Brown back in one piece."

Hannibal nodded. "You think you'll catch these people?"

"Oh yeah. We've got an unusual advantage this time" Rissik emptied his glass. "We know the car they'll likely use. These morons will figure they can outrun any police vehicle. Thing is, that sports car is best on the open road, so we pretty much know how they plan to escape. It's easy enough for us to close off the major roads in that area and draw the net tight."

"So you got plans to make," Hannibal took their glasses to the sink. "Map out strategy and talk to your officers and so forth. Me, I'm just the bag man. So I guess I'll get some rest. They gave us one of the guest rooms."

Rissik stood to leave but turned to Hannibal. "Who you think it is? The inside man. Or woman."

"I don't want to accuse anybody without some kind of evidence. Besides, in hours you'll have whoever they send to pick up the money and they'll tell us."

"Yeah, well, between us, I'm not feeling the wife's worry," Rissik said. "I've been around a lot of women whose husbands had disappeared. None of them cared about public appearances much, let alone entertaining company."

"I hear you, brother, but sometimes people who were born poor and get money become obsessed with living the role. It's like they have to keep proving they ain't poor."

"They get dressed for company?" Rissik asked. "They do their makeup?"

"Maybe you didn't notice how bloodshot her eyes are. I don't think she's had any sleep in the last 3 days."

"You might be right," Rissik said, "but I'm keeping my eye on her. When a man goes missing, it's the wife more often than not."

The two-man meeting broke up, Rissik headed for his office. Instead of going upstairs Hannibal headed for the dining room. There he found his friends munching on sandwiches and what looked like potato salad. Everybody looked too relaxed for his tastes, although he had to admit there was nothing urgent for them to focus on. Hannibal picked up what looked like a half a grilled cheese sandwich on whole wheat and took a bite. Well it was grilled cheese, but Havarti cheese. And artichoke. And what, pesto? It was gooey and so smooth that the flavor took him away from the case for a moment. He knew Rissik would question everyone. He also knew that whoever made this sandwich could not possibly be guilty of a crime.

"Is that the best thing you've ever tasted?" Cindy asked, walking up beside him. "Pretty sure that's a spinach basil pesto in there. I've got to get that recipe."

At the table, Virgil said, "Man I feel guilty getting paid to eat like this. Thanks for the invite."

Hannibal moved over to sit beside Virgil. "Glad you guys are having a good time. I need you to do me a favor tonight. Still paid time."

"No problem," Virgil replied. His voice and manner always reminded Hannibal of Eeyore in the Winnie the Pooh cartoons. "What can I do?"

"I've got a hunch that the kidnappers might be connected to this club down near LaPlata Maryland. It's called the Indigo."

"Yeah, I know it," Virgil said, and took another bite of his own sandwich.

"Can I get you to go there tonight and just watch the parking lot for a red Porsche 911 drop top? Might have to be there all night but it could pay off."

Virgil nodded. "On my way. But I'm taking this sandwich with me."

"Thanks, brother."

"No problem," Virgil said, although Hannibal heard "thanks for noticing" in the back of his mind. As he chewed the last bite of his sandwich, Cindy cupped his jaw, turned his face to hers and examined his eyes.

"How long you been up, baby?" she asked.

He pursed his lips. He didn't remember what time he had gotten up. "All day."

"And last night was a late one," Cindy said. "I figure you'll leave here around eleven to make this drop. I think you need to grab some sleep as soon as you finish with food. This might be a long night and I don't want you falling asleep on the road."

"Yes, ma'am. But you don't need to be worrying. This is Orson's show tonight. I want to stay on the scene, but I'll just sit back and enjoy the show."

Cindy gave a closed-mouth sigh. "You can tell yourself that lie if you want, honey, but don't tell it to me."

CHAPTER 22

Three pairs of gas pumps stood under a broad, white cover in front of the Costco automotive area. The Costco structure itself was huge, surrounded by a vast ocean of parking space. Even at night the building was brightly lit, and overhead lamps made the gas pump area an island of daylight. Hannibal wondered why the kidnappers had chosen it for the drop when there was no shortage of dark, obscure corners in Northern Virginia.

His Volvo rolled up to the center fueling island just as he would if he were buying gas. He got out, feeling the humidity wrap him like a damp blanket. He didn't really need to wear his black suit and gloves for this, but he was one of those men who dressed the same way whenever he was on the job. And this was the job. Buy Zander Brown back from his kidnappers.

In the silence of that moonless night, he imagined the cops, watching him from fifty yards away, could hear his back door open and the duffle bag sliding across his back seat. A trash can stood between the two pumps. Hannibal leaned the bag of money against the garbage can and got back in his car.

"Drop made," Hannibal said. He imagined Rissik smirking at the other end of that phone call.

"I knew you could handle it," Rissik said. "Now we got this. I know you won't sleep so I'll call you back when we got her in custody."

They said goodbyes and Hannibal drove out of the surveillance zone. He actually went two miles before doubling back. Did Rissik really think he would miss the takedown or was this a plausible deniability thing?

Hannibal had studied the map with Rissik when he was planning the stakeouts. The Costco hung onto the southern edge of the Manassas Crossroads Mall with Sudley Manor Drive on one side and lots of retail and car dealerships on the other. Sudley Manor went northerly to connect with Sudley Road at Sudley Manor Square. He didn't know who Sudley was but figured he must have been pretty important around there.

Both the road and the drive were divided highways offering nice flat, straight, one-way blacktops that would be very sports car friendly in the wee hours. To the south was Ashton Avenue, another divided highway that might appeal to an escaping felon. But barely a mile north on Sudley Road a driver would hit I-66, an even better major road. North of there the north and south lanes of Sudley Road merged, and you'd run into the Manassas Battlefield. The end of sports car territory.

Hannibal thought he understood amateur criminals pretty well. She'd want I-66 for sure. Direction was a fifty-fifty gamble. He mentally flipped a coin and pulled over on the shoulder on Sudley Road in sight of the ramp to I-66 East. If he guessed right he could fall in with the pursuing vehicle. Of course Rissik had people positioned to block her on all of the roads in the zone. Unless the bad guys had a helicopter, there was no way out.

He rolled down his window, tilted his seat back a bit, and turned down Led Zeppelin who were telling him about the houses of the holy. He wanted to be able to clearly hear his police scanner. Rissik was regularly checking in with at least seven other cops, sitting in different cars around the area.

In his time as a New York policeman, detective and finally the protective side of the Secret Service, Hannibal found that even the word stakeout made him yawn. Few things bored him more, but this time at least he could expect a rewarding finish.

The kidnappers were not punctual. An hour rolled past without incident. Leaning out his window Hannibal could not overlook the difference between night at home in The District and there in Manassas, Virginia. In Manassas the stars were bright and clearly visible. The air was fresh and clean, with a flowery scent instead of the industrial urban smell he was used to.

While listening to the occasional chatter on his police scanner Hannibal enjoyed some new, old music. He had decided to try to broaden his tastes from the classic rock he listened to as a child on AFN radio in Germany. He had mixed in some blues – Muddy Waters, Albert King, Buddy Guy - and was getting a feel for where all that rock and roll came from.

Two o'clock came and went while he sipped the last of the excellent coffee Victor had brewed at the Browns' house. Thank goodness Rissik had cleared him for now. There was no evidence that he or Betsy were involved and Cawfee seemed too cooperative for a co-conspirator. But as the occasional car whizzed past him Hannibal considered how easy it is to appear innocent until someone really suspects you.

Then he sat forward when an unfamiliar voice said, "She's here."

Rissik said, "Stay sharp. She's doing a high-speed circle in the parking lot. Call out when you know her trajectory."

An unknown officer said, "Damn. She snatched the bag up into the car. She hardly slowed down. Looks like she's headed west. Yep, she's up on Sudley Manor, headed north. Damn! That thing is flying."

Rissik said, "Smith. Johnson. You got her?"

Someone responded, "She cut left at the Taco Bell. On Sudley Road now. Repeat, north on Sudley Road."

Hannibal smiled and started his engine. She was headed toward him. Sweet!

"Miller. Williams. She's headed toward one of you. Johnson, you let me know if she cuts left or right on 66. Then we can draw the net closed."

Hannibal felt the adrenaline dump. Go left, he screamed in his mind. *Don't make me have to spin around. By the time I get to the roadblock it will all be over.*

He had not expected to hear the roar of the 640 horsepower engine push toward him. He slipped his car into drive and wrapped both hands tightly on the steering wheel.

"No!" the scanner said.

"What?" from Rissik.

"She didn't turn. She didn't turn. She's headed straight up Sudley."

Rissik said, "Miller. Williams. Fall in behind Johnson. Do not lose her."

In less time than it took Hannibal to wonder how Rissik kept them all straight, the red Porsche flew past him. He crushed the pedal to the floor. The G forces slammed him against the back of his seat. His tires squealed as the Volvo leapt onto the road and its speedometer climbed. He was now the lead dog in the pack chasing the Porsche, the others well behind him. In a minute the north and south roads would merge. She would have to slow down.

The Porsche shot under a signal light and vanished from sight. Hannibal hit his brakes, squealing to a near stop just past the intersection in front of a small, narrow road to his left. He could just see brake lights down there. He cranked the wheel hard left and followed. Now he was driving the wrong way down a narrow, one-way road cutting through the woods and into the Battlefield.

"What the hell?" the scanner said. "It's gone, boss. The car's just gone."

Hannibal shook his head. There was no way the pursuing police cars could have seen the Porsche make that turn, and they'd likely miss the little road completely. Of course, the sports car couldn't move nearly as fast now, but she didn't have to. He had to reevaluate the criminals. If not for him, this would have worked. Too bad he didn't have a police radio to alert his frustrated friend. But on this single lane blacktop with trees pushing in on both sides, driving as fast as he dared, he could not work the buttons to call Rissik on the phone.

The next surprise came when the trees cleared on his right and the Porsche turned into the clearing. Hannibal followed, both vehicles moving much more slowly over the grassy turf. Surely she saw his lights and knew he was following. What was her next play? Double back to the road? If she played around too long out here some rock or stump would end up tearing the bottom out of the Porsche's low carriage. They were slow enough now to try keying the phone on. He had her.

A sharp brightness split the night, stabbing into his eyes. No, it wasn't everywhere. The light was in his rearview mirror. Another vehicle coming up behind him, moving much faster than he was. It was higher than his car, and now the throaty roar of its engine reached him. An instant of confusion froze him. Just an instant. The other vehicle, a truck maybe, pulled up next to him on his left and swerved toward him. Reflexes yanked him to the right like a batter getting a brush back pitch. His car rocked a stand of trees with a resounding crunch sound and what felt like an angry giant's hand mashed him back against his seat.

He floated up out of the blackness. His face didn't usually hurt this much until the third or fourth round. His ribs ached too. Muscle memory of too many kickboxing matches. He checked his nose. Still not broken. He blinked and shook his head. That hurt too, and why was there dust falling in front of his face?

He pushed his internal replay button. *Oh yes.* Shoved aside by an unknown vehicle, he had slammed into some trees hard enough to pop his air bag. The powder, the aches, were remnants of the safety device that had probably spared him a concussion.

His door worked thank goodness, so he got out on wobbly legs. He looked around in the darkness. Like standing on a football field at night with only the stars for light. Two steps and he stumbled on tread ruts. Too wide for his car or the Porsche's tires. The thing that brushed him aside must have been a truck or a four-by-four.

The bad thing about being in shock is, you know it and so what? You can't do anything about it. Drive his car? Probably a bad idea. Follow the tracks, see where the attack vehicle went? Okay. Call Rissik? Yeah, that's a great idea.

But what to tell him? Hannibal didn't know where he was. In the darkness he felt his way forward, following the slight impressions of the tire tracks. The silence was oppressive. Where were the insects that usually fill the night with noise? Did they all go to sleep before four in the morning?

Ahead he detected the silhouette of a small, low building like a multi-car garage. That might give him a location to report. It was a gap in the tree line. To the right, maybe a parking lot for that building. To the left…was that a car? Yes, a vehicle in front of the trees.

Of course. It must be the Porsche. Top down, so the driver could snatch up the money bag without stopping. He adjusted his walk to the left, moving to the car as he pulled out his phone. He had really underestimated the kidnappers. They could ditch the flashy sports car here. A vehicle made for cross-country driving must have been waiting here to pick up the driver and the money and drive off through the woods. But maybe the car would yield some clues.

When Hannibal reached the Porsche, he held his phone forward to light it up. Another shock. The money was gone but the driver was there. Tall woman, Hispanic features, long hair, in what had been a bright yellow dress. Now the front of it was glistening red. That color had flowed down from the opening in her throat.

CHAPTER 23

Hannibal's phone rang before he could make the call himself.

"Hey, buddy, it's Orson. Hope I didn't wake you up, but I figured you'd want to hear right away. I'm afraid I've got some bad news."

"No, I've got the bad news," Hannibal said. "And I wasn't sleeping. In fact, I'm probably not far from you right now."

After a pause, Rissik came back with, "You in Manassas?"

"Yep."

"Well then, what's your bad news?"

"I caught the red Porsche. The driver's dead. The money's gone. And I need a ride."

Hannibal waited through a longer pause while, he assumed, Rissik tried to put it all together in a way that made sense. Finally, he just asked, "Where are you?"

"Pretty sure I'm in the Manassas Battlefield."

"That's a big target," Rissik said. "If you want a ride, you'll have to be a little more specific."

"Take it easy on me, Chief," Hannibal said. "I got my bell rung pretty good in the accident. Look, if you're going north on Sudley Road you'll go under sixty-six."

"Heading that way now."

"Okay," Hannibal said, "You'll go under two signal lights. Right after that second light there's a road on your left. It's small, easy to miss, and you'll be going the wrong way on a one-way street. When you see a clearing on your right, that's where I am."

"You were off roading?"

"In pursuit of the Porsche," Hannibal said.

"Well, if that thing could handle the terrain there, I guess my Honda can too. Get comfortable and I'll be there in a few minutes."

Hannibal appreciated a lot about Rissik, not the least being his waiting to ask more questions when they were face-to-face. But since he had a few minutes, he'd see what he could learn.

He thought of all the people who had smirked when they saw him dressed for work, always wearing sunglasses and thin black gloves. Both had saved him any number of times. In this case, he was glad to already have gloves on.

He pushed branches out of his way to reach the far side of the Porsche. The glove compartment yielded nothing useful. No registration and no personal items. He had hoped for rental paperwork but even that was missing.

The driver's purse was his next target. This time he found a pair of twenty-dollar bills and various makeup tools but no phone and no credit cards. Walking back around, he took a picture of the corpse in the driver's seat. Her left hand was still locked on the steering wheel. Her mouth hung open, perhaps in surprise.

"You weren't expecting to die today, were you?" Hannibal said aloud. Then he noticed her left hand. It bore a rubber stamp, the kind that lets you leave a bar and return without paying. On impulse, he took a close-up photo of that too,

The world was getting brighter and the sound of tentative tires approaching on dirt made him turn. Rissik must hate doing this to his Accord, Hannibal thought. His relationship with that car had outlasted most marriages. He stopped about ten yards from Hannibal and hopped out with the Accord running. He moved toward Hannibal's car, stopped and turned back toward Hannibal. Backlit by his headlights he looked like an avenging angel stalking forward, but as he closed the distance his demeanor changed.

"Are you all right?" Rissik asked. Hannibal had expected a 'What are you doing here?' or 'Why are you standing in my crime scene?'

"Thanks for asking, but I'm good," Hannibal said. "Why did you ask?"

"Black suit covered with white powder equals air bag. And your car's over there holding up a tree."

"I was barely moving when I hit that tree," Hannibal said.

"Had to be over fifteen miles an hour for the bag to deploy," Rissik said.

"Why do you know that?"

Rissik walked past Hannibal to slowly circle the car before stopping to visually examine the corpse. "I see you got pushed over by a bigger vehicle. Big enough to tear up the turf over there next to your tire tracks. Looks like they stopped just in front of the sports car here. You touch anything?"

"Of course not, chief," Hannibal said. "Besides. Gloves." Of course, Rissik knew better. He knew Hannibal. But at least now the official response was on the record in case anybody asked him.

Two more cars rolled into the clearing and Hannibal imagined the grounds keepers would have a hell of a job facing them in the morning. If they were allowed to do it. Rissik would cordon off his crime scene and have forensic guys crawling all over the Porsche as soon as the sun was up.

"Okay, you got this," Hannibal said. "I'll just get my ass out of your way."

"You don't look to me like you should be driving," Rissik said. "I'll give you a ride home…"

"Staying at the Browns' house. Will need to tell them what happened."

"I'll take you there, then," Rissik said. "I'll have one of the boys bring your car out later. Right now, go sit in my car for a few minutes while I make sure the boys know what to do with the scene."

He wanted to argue, but Hannibal suddenly realized how tired he was. He nodded and dragged himself to Rissik's car. He saw Rissik on the phone, probably to the crime scene team. Uniforms surrounded him, awaiting his direction about the crime scene, the cars and the corpse. Then his eyes wandered over to his car, the crippled Black Beauty. He wondered who the dead girl was, why she was dead, and how his odds of finding Zander Brown had changed.

When Rissik opened his car door Hannibal realized he had lost a few minutes. In silence Rissik eased the Accord back to the access road and rolled back to the highway. Hannibal wondering how anybody could drive with no music on.

Once on the road, Rissik asked, "So how do you figure it?"

"Only one way it makes sense," Hannibal said. "I'm thinking they had a pretty good plan. Kidnapper number one scoops the money, drives like hell and goes exactly where nobody would expect her to go in a hot sports car: small dead-end trail, then off road. Kidnapper number two was waiting out there in the little parking area around that maintenance garage in something made for off-road. They park the Porsche, switch vehicles and take off through the woods."

"That tracks," Rissik said. "But it didn't play out that way, did it? Looks like a double cross."

"Yeah. If it was a two-person crew, now there's no split," Hannibal said. "And if kidnapper number two was ready to slit his own partner's throat…"

Rissik gave a grim nod. "Where does that leave Zander Brown?"

Demons wrestled in Hannibal's head while he slept. He had crashed hard as soon as he reached the bed, snuggled up beside Cindy. Sleep was deep, but guilt, worry and the specter of failure chased each other around inside his mind for five hours. When his eyes snapped open, cool satin sheets did not offer any comfort. The cold sweat had nothing to do with the temperature.

He was alone. He guessed Cindy, and everyone else, had gone down to some fabulous breakfast. Charlotte really liked to entertain. He was sure there would be scraps leftover for him. Sitting up reminded him that he had been in an accident. He was achy all over, a familiar feeling for him. He took a hot shower (did all the guest rooms have private baths too?) and when he came out Cindy was sitting on the bed, dressed as she would be for the office, her expression flat.

"Are you all right, honey?"

"Physically fine," he said.

"And otherwise?"

"Not even close."

Cindy went to him and embraced his naked form, holding him close, sharing her strength. "I love you, honey."

"Never a doubt," Hannibal said.

"And I went to your place last night after dinner." She released him to pull a suitcase out of the closet. "At the time I thought you'd want a fresh change to celebrate catching the extortionists today."

"You amaze me," Hannibal said, opening the case. He found everything he needed to start his day there, his toiletries and fresh clothes, all precisely packed. He couldn't help but grin as he started to get dressed. "I'm guessing you ate with the family. How are they doing?"

"Worried, of course. I told them what little you shared before you passed out. Your car's out front and that told me a little more. I tried to assure them this morning that the kidnappers had their money, so Zander was probably okay."

"Not at all sure that's true," Hannibal said, pulling on a crisp white shirt. "But at least I might have a clue to get on their trail."

"They'll want to hear that. Let's get you to the dining room. They held some waffles and sausages for you. And the fellows will want to know what the next step is."

When Hannibal and Cindy got to the table Betsy was there, smiling and asking if he would like his brunch served now.

"Yes please, ma'am," Hannibal said, "And I should talk to the family. Where might they be?"

"I'm sorry sir," she said, "but Mrs. Brown slept poorly and has gone back in for a nap. Miss Francine was up late and has also returned to her bedroom, but I believe she is awake."

"Thanks," Hannibal said. "Please ask her to join me here so I can bring her up to date. And could you also ask my friends to join me in here?"

She disappeared and returned in what seemed like seconds with his plate and a large mug of coffee. He was barely halfway through the light, fluffy waffles before the men he relied on began filing in. All sat on the opposite side of the table.

Sarge started the conversation. "So they got away with the money. This morning Charlotte came to breakfast, all makeup and hair straight and everything, but she's in rough shape, brother. So, where do we go from here?"

From the entry arch they heard, "What the hell?" and Frankie burst into the room, a loose multi-colored caftan swirling around her. She went to the table directly opposite Hannibal and leaned forward, slamming her palms down on the table in front of his plate.

"You let them get away," she yelled. "You let them get away? What the hell?"

Hannibal diverted his gaze from the generous view the loose garment offered, its front hanging from Frankie's frame.

"Yes, they eluded the police," Hannibal said. "And while I regret that, they, and I, will continue the search to find your father. I need to know if you or your mother has heard anything further from the kidnappers."

"Not a word," Frankie said. "Nothing. So, what do we do now?"

It amused Hannibal how clients always talked as if "we" were going to do something. He pushed his plate aside.

"Well first, I wanted you to know that I'm going to ask these men to hang here one more day. I'm concerned that you and your mother may still be at risk."

Frankie pulled back. "What? Why? There's sure no big bag of money here to steal."

"One member of the kidnap crew apparently killed the driver last night. There's no telling what they might do when they figure out I'm still pursuing this case. And I am still on this case. I will find your father."

Frankie calmed, her chin shuddering a bit. "Do you…do you think he's still alive?"

"We met their demands," Hannibal said. "And they probably feel like they can make a clean getaway. The only member of the crew we actually identified is dead."

"So maybe they just take the money and run," Frankie said. "Okay. What about you? What do you do next?"

"Some research," Hannibal said, pulling out his phone. "If I can find anybody who knew the dead driver, I might be able to get closer to the rest of the gang, and your father. And I might be able to find a place she used to hang out. She had a stamp on her hand."

"Wait. You saw the body?"

Hannibal nodded. "Throat cut, almost certainly by someone she trusted. No worse way to go. But anyway, I'll spend the day digging for where they use this stamp." Hannibal held up his phone, displaying the picture, which looked like a crudely drawn Margarita glass. "I'm thinking it's a Mexican restaurant or bar and there are only so many in Northern Virginia."

"Oh yeah," Frankie said. "That's the Brazos Cantina over in Sterling."

"You know this place?"

All eyes were on Frankie and for a moment she looked like she was sorry she had spoken. "Um, yeah. That place is a dive. Totally ghetto. I checked it out this one time because I heard they had a dope DJ. But all they played was Spanish shit. The food sucked and the waitress lost my credit card after I gave it to her, but I think it was on purpose. Had to complain to the manager to get it back."

"Sounds like just the place for low lifes to hang out," Hannibal said. "And that's where I'll be as soon as they open."

Cindy raised an eyebrow. "This case sure seems to be putting you in a lot of bars and clubs."

Frankie snorted. "Ain't nobody there gone talk to you. Not dressed like that. Didn't I say this place is ghetto? And damn near everybody's Spanish."

"I might get someone to speak to me," Cindy said. "My Spanish is still fluent."

"Excuse me saying it," Francine said, "but you just too high class for that place."

"People will talk to me," Ray said, crossing his arms and leaning back. Hannibal had to agree. Pushing sixty and a Cuban immigrant, Ray was both authentic and non-threatening. And given the right script, he could tease information out of any bartender or waitress.

"Maybe so, Papa," Cindy said, "But you'd still need a change of clothes."

"Expenses," Frankie said. "That was part of the deal, right? I'll just tell Gene the clothes were a necessary expense for finding Daddy. He won't challenge me. And tell Cawfee I said to give you one of the cars. Yours is kind of crunched up."

The Brazos Cantina sat in the middle of an L-shaped strip mall - Hannibal noted that they called them plazas in Virginia – tucked in between a pizza joint and the UPS store. He saw it as a basic nightclub with its name in huge neon letters on the wall over the door, and the standard neon lights in the front-facing windows. Unlikely to find any surprises inside.

They arrived in separate vehicles. Hannibal drove the Mercedes-Maybach sedan, while Ray drove his limousine. Parking was easy, even for Ray's limo. Seven o'clock was a transition time. Most of the stores had closed and the bar had just opened.

As agreed, Hannibal pushed through the double glass doors first, dressed in jeans, sneakers and a loose faux-Hawaiian shirt that covered the side draw holster tucked into his waistband. His casual outfit matched the unfussy décor. Neon tubes lined the top of the walls, or maybe they were LED lights. Similar lighted tubes wrapped the trunks of fake palm trees at the ends of the bar. A gigantic screen stood behind the bar at the far end. Hannibal pictured screaming crowds watching a soccer game there. Turned the other way the crowd would face the stage.

A scan of the room told him that the waitress didn't want to be bothered but the woman behind the bar was bored and looking for something to do. He wandered to the bar, which had no seats facing it, and ordered a margarita. The young girl in glasses and a flowered blouse, threw the drink together in two minutes and shoved it in front of him. Not frozen, and not in a margarita glass, making the hand stamp a form of false advertising. He selected one of the round tables and settled in.

Five minutes later, Ray entered, their second customer of the day. He went straight to a table just within Hannibal's hearing range, sat down, and stared at the waitress until she got up and headed toward him. No glasses but otherwise cut from the same pattern as the barmaid except for a wider carriage accented by black tights. When she reached Ray he ordered a Corona and squinted at the girl as Hannibal had coached him.

"You new here?"

"Been here two months," the girl said in a strong accent, staring past him. She might have been just old enough to legally work in a bar.

"Huh. Didn't recognize you." Ray said, making clear he was not new here. She wandered to the bar and returned with the beer. No glass but it did have the lime wedge in the neck. Ray handed her two twenties.

"Time you get back I'll be ready for the next one," he said. She accepted the bills, showing a bit more interest. In the next five minutes he looked around the room and drank most of the beer. When he had about a swallow left the waitress returned with a second beer. She dropped it and his change on the table. Ray left it there and added another twenty to it.

"While it ain't busy can I talk to you for a minute?" he asked. When she took a half step away, he added, "Relax, chica, I'm old enough to be your papa. I'm looking for somebody who comes in here."

"Yeah, well I don't get customers' names or anything."

Two men walked in, waved at the waitress as if they knew her, and went to the bar. Ray peeled another twenty off his roll, which recovered her attention.

"I know it's a long shot," Ray said. "But this girl was so beautiful. Pretty, like you, but taller with really long legs and black hair down to her culo." That elicited a half-smile, so he added one more twenty.

"You seen her in here?" she asked.

"Last week," Ray said. "Then Friday up in Baltimore."

Almost to herself, the waitress said, "Katie said she was in Baltimore Friday."

"Katie," Ray said. "That's it. You know her? Tu amiga?"

Three more men entered the bar. Hannibal cursed under his breath. Two of the newcomers wore the gray shirts and navy-blue pants of the Fairfax County police. The third, in his standard blue suit, was Orson Rissik. They made solid eye contact before Hannibal turned away.

The two real customers eased toward the door. The waitress broke from Ray and walked toward the policemen like a child sent to bring her mother a switch. She and Rissik spoke in low tones. Then Rissik waved the barmaid over and exchanged words with her. Hannibal turned his back to that scene and finished his drink. He knew he wouldn't be waiting long. When Rissik did reach him, he walked around the table so Hannibal could see him.

"You. With me. Now." Then he walked back to stand in front of the doors. Hannibal sighed, stood and followed. One of the cops was talking with the barmaid, the other with the waitress, both with their notebooks out. Rissik stood with hands on hips staring at the floor. Hannibal stood close enough that their conversation could remain between them.

"What the hell are you doing here?" Rissik asked. As Hannibal opened his mouth to speak, Rissik pinned him with an icy stare. "Never mind. I know exactly what you're doing here. Are you trying to pollute my investigation? Or you just think I'm stupid. Didn't you think I'd see that hand stamp?"

"Honestly, I hoped it would take you a little longer to track it down." Hannibal said.

"I'm full speed ahead on this case," Rissik said. "Got dressed down good for not pulling in the FBI right away, although honestly the chief got that it was a time sensitive situation. But it's in my lap now and I need to show some real progress before the feds show up"

Four young people opened the door, brushing past Hannibal and Rissik who stepped to the side. This place would fill up pretty soon.

"Look, no offense, Orson, but your hardass approach won't get you dick in here. Ray looks like he belongs in here and he don't smell like a cop. Your boys over there will fill their notebooks with a lot of nothing."

"Really? Have you done any better?"

"Well, we got a first name," Hannibal said. "Might have gotten a good deal more if you hadn't come busting in here with the storm troopers."

"Yeah, well if you wanted her name you could have just asked me. Got that much just by running her fingerprints through AFIS. But there's still a lot I don't know that I want to know, so why don't you and your friend move on and let me do my job."

"Okay, Chief," Hannibal said. "Will you at least keep me posted?"

"I will if you will."

"Fair enough," Hannibal said. He waved to Ray and when he was sure he'd been seen he slipped out through an incoming group of party people.

He reached the car just as the sun's light surrendered to the artificial illumination from storefronts and the parking lot lamp posts. Another day had passed. Zander Brown was six days gone. The bad guys had him and the money. No phone calls, and no more notes or emails. And he was clutching at short, broken straws. He started the car. His mind was reaching for something, anything for him to follow up on. Right then it seemed there was nothing else for him to do.

The parking lot was filling up, at least the area near the club. A small knot of bodies at the door would soon become a line of people waiting to get in. A blue Amazon van pulled up in front of the Brazos Cantina. Before this case it would have been invisible to Hannibal but right then it seemed he was seeing them everywhere.

The driver got out and went around to the back. But then he noticed the two police cars parked near the entrance and jumped back in his vehicle. Hannibal put the Mercedes into gear.

He recognized the driver. It was the muscle man he knew only as Fridge.

CHAPTER 24

The Amazon van pulled out onto the highway but only for a brief moment before pulling off onto a smaller local road. Hannibal kept a lot of distance between himself and the van and he was sure Fridge had no idea he was followed. This time they both probably believed the darkness was their friend.

The borrowed car rode like a comfortable, luxury race car if that made any sense, but Hannibal wished he was in his own. He had bonded with his Volvo. He knew its quirks, and more important, knew exactly how hard to push the accelerator or brake pedal to get the response he wanted. This drive was more like dancing with a stranger.

Suburban streets soon gave way to smaller streets, backstreets, and then a fire road that crossed a highway. Wherever Fridge was heading, it was off the beaten path. Hannibal made sure to keep the van's brake lights in sight on the winding country roads.

Hannibal wanted to call Rissik to let him know what was going on. He owed him that much. But his phone wasn't paired with this car, and he was not about to figure it out while he was driving an unfamiliar car on unfamiliar roads in the dark. He would just have to call him when they landed someplace.

Virginia's long history of segregation did not apply to its trees. Hannibal drove down long lanes lined with poplars, pines, gum trees and maples whose leaves were just beginning to hint at future redness. In fact, trees on either side of the road often shook hands overhead, hiding even the meager light of the stars. The taller van occasionally brushed those leaves as it crept past the homes of people who valued their privacy and rejoiced in splendid isolation.

After twenty minutes of these winding roads Hannibal saw the headlights on his right. The van had turned and was crunching down a long gravel driveway, moving even more slowly than before. Hannibal drove past the driveway entrance and pulled over twenty yards up the road. The Mercedes filled the shoulder, so Hannibal put the hazard lights on. With luck no one would run into his loaner before he returned. He had no idea where he was, and this was no time to try to learn how to work an unfamiliar car's GPS. This was exactly the kind of remote place one might take a man who was being held against his will.

Stepping out of the car he backtracked on foot. About halfway back to the driveway entrance Hannibal climbed over the rustic wooden fence that separated the property from the road. He trudged through long-unmown grass, each step raising a fetid, swampy odor. It seemed poor drainage kept the ground from totally drying. He moved toward what looked like a traditional farmhouse. The nearest neighbors were well outside of shouting range. The cricket chorus drowned out any sound his steps made.

Light shone through only one window, so that became his target. It was toward the back of the house, probably the kitchen. The house was probably white with rattan furniture on the porch but everything looked gray in the dark. He crept up on the side, leaning against the wall with his head beside the lighted window and drew his pistol. He wanted to listen a while to see just how many people were inside before confronting Fridge. Until he heard something incriminating, he was still chasing coincidences and technically, trespassing. He didn't even know what to accuse Fridge of, besides sucker punching private eyes.

Inside, Fridge said, "This is bad. I didn't make the drop at the Brazos and I really should be at the Indigo by now. He's going to be pissed."

An unfamiliar female voice said, "No, you did the right thing. If there were cops at that joint, they might know something, and if you get jammed up the whole thing could fall."

Hannibal caught the sound of liquid pouring into a glass. He pictured the two of them, sitting at a table drinking, whining about the boss like any two fellow employees.

"Maybe," Fridge said, "But you know how he gets about timetables and shit. He wants his deliveries made when he wants them made."

Hannibal wondered what they were delivering, and what it might have to do with a kidnapping. Was he on the wrong trail? But his mouth dropped open when connections were made.

"You right about that," the woman said. "Nelson got no patience at all for things not happening to his timetable. He's already mad as hell about Katie not showing up when he told her to."

"Yeah, and it's been like a whole day now," Fridge said. "Where the hell your stupid ass sister run off to?"

"Hell if I know," the woman said. "She ain't at her place. No call, no text, nada. For all I know she just took off and left me to take the heat. Again. And by the way, you didn't seem to think she was such a stupid ass when you were putting the moves on her." She was laughing. He was not.

"Yeah, well that was before I found out she plays for the other team," Fridge said. "But hey, she ain't the pretty sister anyway."

"Thanks, I guess." Glasses clinked.

"Seriously, Leigh, Maybe I was just afraid to aim high," Fridge said. "You the girl I'd really want to…"

"Don't even try," the woman said. "Ever hear the saying, don't piss where you eat? I don't date coworkers."

"Come on. Who's going to know? Or don't you like men either?"

A chair slid back, and a glass hit the table. "Listen close, Fridge. I like getting laid as much as the next girl. But not here, not now, and not by you. I think it's time for you to hit the road while it's still friendly in here."

Hannibal had heard more than enough. He raced across the open field toward his car. He managed to get inside in time to see the Amazon van in his rearview mirror. The van eased out onto the road but turned left, away from Hannibal, who quickly turned around to follow. The van moved slowly enough that he was able to drive with his headlights out, navigating based on the movements of the van's tail lights. He had to know where Fridge was going. Zander Brown, or at least the kidnappers, could be waiting there.

CHAPTER 25

Fridge pushed his van down more narrow roads that were punishing Hannibal's back and the Mercedes' suspension. Eventually he came onto a smooth two-lane blacktop and picked up the pace. Now there were streetlamps as they wove through another suburban area, and Hannibal continued to run dark. As long as Fridge didn't suspect he was being followed he would drive at the speed limit and stay easy to follow. When they came to traffic lights Hannibal would pull over until the van was on the move again.

A sliver of the moon had arisen, offering a bit of light. Hannibal tried to stay aware of his surroundings, but nothing looked familiar to him. Or, seen another way, everything looked familiar. Small town streets and country roads seemed generic, all built in the same set shop with little in the way of landmarks or significant terrain features. Hannibal simply focused on the Amazon delivery van's taillights and hoped they didn't go too far.

Suburbia returned outside Hannibal's windows and he rolled under a couple more traffic lights before a familiar sight came into view: The entrance to an industrial park. Now he knew where the van was going. He could not follow down that long winding private road undetected, so he parked on the street.

Getting out of the car he complimented himself on following his instincts. Fridge had approached the plant on a completely different path than Hannibal had taken so surprise would be reasonable, but he had known in his gut where this chase would take him.

He padded down the narrow private road and across the parking lot in a crouch, creeping close enough to be able to read the sign mounted on the front wall, illuminated by a fixed spotlight. "Optilorus – your view of the future."

The front of the building was brightly lit and there was no sign of the van. Hannibal moved around to the back. The van was parked by the loading dock. He saw no security guards but in the distant dark he thought he saw a couple of other vehicles. Maybe they were all inside discussing their next plans. If Zander was inside this could be the moment they were deciding whether to cut him loose or cut his throat. Fighting to keep his breathing slow and quiet, he slipped up the loading dock stairs. No sound, no movement he could detect. Of course the dock itself was shut. He moved to the door at the side. With agonizing slowness he turned the knob until he could push the door open just enough to slip inside.

There's dark and then there's dark. This was the kind where you couldn't be sure if your eyes were open or closed. If he was in his suit jacket he'd pull out his Mag light but he didn't have one on him this night. Use his phone? No, if anyone else was around that would just make him a bright, shining target.

He waited long enough to know his eyes were not going to adjust. There was not a drop of light to gather. He put a hand on the wall and followed it to the corner. He continued to follow the wall, knowing that at some point he'd come to a door. Instead, his foot bumped what turned out to be an exposed staircase. At the top a slim glimmer showed. The warehouse would show him nothing, so he started up the stairs. Light leaked out from under the door at the top. He pressed an ear against the door and took silence as an invitation. It was unlocked, so he went through.

Light from the other end of a long hall revealed the vast, empty second floor. Just a gathering of empty, unfurnished offices. Part of the Optilorus façade, he guessed. The door at the other end called to him. When he reached it, he again heard nothing and again, he walked in.

Now he was in the well-lit suite he had visited before. It looked empty. Where was everybody? He took five steps into the room before movement stopped him. Ira Johnson stepped out of his private office. He turned toward Hannibal, his face reflecting the surprise on Hannibal's. Then Johnson's face softened into a small smile of recognition.

"Ahhh, Frankie Brown's family friend, right?"

"Yes," Hannibal said, moving closer. "And you're the confidence man who decided to try to rip them off. Well, let's see if I can get some answers out of you before your muscle-bound friend shows up."

"Muscle bound? Oh, you must mean one of my drivers. And you may see me as some sort of criminal, but in fact I am just a respectable businessman confronting an intruder in his workplace." Johnson stood his ground, his smile actually growing.

Hannibal rushed forward.

"Sure, if businessman is another way of saying hustler, and driver is another word for thug."

"And family friend is a euphemism for private investigator," Johnson said, "We seem to be in an era of renaming things. For example," As Hannibal came within a dozen feet of him, Johnson pulled a knife from his pocket and flipped it open with his thumb. The loud click and four-inch blade said this was a serious weapon. "I guess this is just an overly ambitious letter opener."

Johnson took one step forward, his expression changing to a menacing grimace. Now Hannibal smiled and pulled his Sig Sauer P229 from under his shirt.

"Then this must be my cordless hole puncher. I'll be happy to show you how it works if you don't tell me what the hell you did with Zander Brown. Right now."

Hannibal heard the movement behind him a fraction of a second too late. He spun in time to see the office chair rolling toward him. It thumped into his legs and he went down hard but didn't lose his weapon. He aimed at Fridge who was charging toward him.

"Hold it, big man," Hannibal said. "Is he worth dying for?" He got to his feet, his left fist holding his pistol aimed at Fridge. The door to the warehouse steps was behind him. Johnson was in the other direction and behind him, the door to the elevator Hannibal had used in his first visit to this building. Now that door opened.

"Grab this asshole," Johnson said. "He knows if he shoots one of you, that will give the rest time to jump him."

The rest? After the first two men came in Hannibal backed down the aisle between cubicles. At the other side of the suite, he moved toward the warehouse door, moving his gun to try to cover all the possible ways someone might be approaching him. When he reached the point where his back was to the door Fridge was to his immediate left, grinning like an alligator with a juicy rabbit in its sights. Foot falls came from straight ahead. Hannibal had no way of knowing if the others were armed or even how many there were. Things could get real messy real quick if he started a fire fight. So, as much as he would have loved to wipe the smile off Fridge's face, he spun, yanked the door open, and dove into the darkness.

Hannibal ran down the cement stairs, no longer caring about noise level. He thought that in the darkness he could find the door and once outside he could easily escape. He only needed a moment of peace to call in some help.

He hit the bottom of the stairs sooner than expected and almost fell forward. Moving away from the wall, arms outstretched, he hit what felt like a tower of cardboard boxes. Well it was a warehouse. It made sense that stuff was stored there. He would feel his way around the obstacles and as long as he was headed in the right direction, he'd be okay.

And then the world exploded into eye-scorching brightness. Rows of lights in the ceiling flooded every corner of the huge space with light. The ceiling had to be thirty feet above. Boxes of various sizes were stacked in no particular order that Hannibal could see.

He was navigating a maze of sorts, a cardboard labyrinth of unknown design, laid out on a cement floor. In most places he couldn't see over the boxes. The challenge was that his pursuers knew he needed to get to the only door out. The good news was, if he couldn't see them, they couldn't see him.

"To your left, Charlie!" Johnson's voice boomed out. "Maybe two hundred feet."

Hannibal looked up to see Ira Johnson standing at the top of the stairs that were against the back wall. From there he could probably see all of the players.

A big white guy in a blue shirt and ball cap popped up in front of him. He raised a baseball bat and charged. Hannibal jerked his arm back and fired. The deafening blast reverberated in the warehouse and the man dropped his bat, clutched his leg and fell.

Hannibal spun and ran, jogging around every box stack, now left, now right, working at being unpredictable. He heard his footfalls and maybe six other pairs of feet hitting the cement floor. He needed to find a corner where he could be still for a minute.

On his next turn he almost ran into another blue shirt. This time a bat came down hard on his left forearm. Hannibal snapped out a right cross that put the other man on his back, but Hannibal's left hand was numbed and he dropped his gun. He reached for it but a gunshot backed him up. The huge hole in the box on his left told him where the shot came from, and that it had only missed by a few inches.

"Mario," Johnson called. "He's right in front of you."

Damn. Hannibal sprinted to his left. He stayed low and found a column of stove size boxes stacked three high. He should be invisible to Johnson for a minute. Only one man had fired at him. Maybe there was only one shooter. If he could find that man, he might turn things around again.

Around the next corner of tall boxes he was suddenly a foot away from a man holding what looked like a machete. The blade rose over the man's head but before it could come down Hannibal whipped a side kick into his ribs. The man bent forward, and Hannibal slammed a combination into his face. Left-left-right, and the man went down. And now Hannibal had a blade.

Hannibal crept into another long path between tall stacks of boxes that could hold refrigerators. What the hell did they keep in here? How big could the parts be for the virtual reality toys Johnson makes? Or maybe Johnson rented the space to other vendors. It didn't figure that heavy appliances would be part of his scheme, but even con men might need a side hustle these days.

The pursuers seemed to be searching in the wrong corner of the warehouse right then. Hannibal stood with his back against a bank of huge boxes, taking a moment to gather his scattered wits. His heart was slamming against his chest. He saw limited options and faced serious opposition. He counted six or maybe seven men after him. They were big and nasty but slow. He had taken two of them out of the chase, and he had gotten oriented during his exploration of the warehouse. His best shot was to make a hard break for the door.

But just as he braced for a run the boxes facing him shifted. The tower of refrigerator boxes, stacked three high, silently tilted toward him. Spurred by terror he sprinted down the narrow row but the entire wall of boxes was tipping over. He dove to the floor, snugging up against the bottom of the other side hoping for a safe gap when the avalanche crashed down on him. Eyes closed, teeth clenched, he waited for the impact.

For a long thirty seconds he lay still, arms stretched forward. Luck had been with him. Nothing felt broken. He saw light at the far end of the narrow tunnel he was jammed into. Maybe he could crawl to the end. It wasn't over.

He heard boxes moving again, in front and behind him. Then the box directly on top of him lifted and flipped away. Only then did he realize he had been running through a forest of empty cardboard cartons. He looked up to see Fridge looking down on him, still grinning. Beside him, one of the security men Hannibal met on his first visit to this place held a pistol forward. Behind him more boxes moved until he was completely exposed. He was still between two rows of boxes, but now they were only one box high. And clearing the extras revealed another uniformed guard holding a gun on Hannibal, maybe five yards away. The two men with him looked like a pro wrestling tag team, despite being dressed in the blue Amazon delivery uniforms and ball caps.

So now it was over. Hannibal got to his feet and, almost as an afterthought, dropped the machete. Again he faced Fridge, who stepped to just outside arm's length. At least, Hannibal's arms.

"Okay, so what now?" Hannibal asked.

Johnson's voice echoed across the warehouse from Hannibal's left. "Now? Now you and I have a conversation about what you know and who else knows it."

Hannibal turned to face the man at the other end of the warehouse at the top of the staircase that led to the offices above. He opened his mouth to speak, but his caustic retort was lost in the impact on his jaw. Sparkling floaters confused his vision before the fist smashing into his gut pushed all the air out of him. His legs turned to rubber and against his will he dropped to his knees. He only managed one deep breath before a kick to his stomach forced it all out of him again. Then something like a twelve-pound sledgehammer collided with the back of his head and the cement floor rushed up to caress his cheek.

CHAPTER 26

He hurt everywhere. But that was good. It meant he was alive. His head was thumping in that familiar rhythmic way. His mouth was filled with the copper taste of blood but his tongue check verified that all his teeth were still in place. He tried to check his nose. It had never been broken and he wanted to keep that streak going, but he couldn't be sure because he couldn't move his arms. Shoulders ached so he had to conclude that his hands were tied behind him. He was on his left side, but this was not the cold cement floor but rather a carpet.

"Are you going to sleep the night away?" Johnson asked. Hannibal forced his eyes open to find himself staring at Johnson's swinging feet. Hannibal had to crane his neck to see Johnson's face, backlit by florescent tubes, since he was sitting on his desk. Hannibal was on the floor in Johnson's office. He tried to right himself, but his legs were bound as well. Johnson sat silent, giving Hannibal time to brace on his elbow, straighten his legs and sit up. Using his heels, he pushed himself backward far enough to lean back against the door jamb.

"Comfortable now?"

"Oh yeah," Hannibal said. "You're the perfect host. You're also going to spend a lot of time in a much less comfortable place."

"You get points for arrogance," Johnson said. "But to establish the situation more concretely…you do know that I could have one of my men kill you now, right? I mean, you did break into my warehouse. With a gun, which I have given to your old friend the Fridge for his loyalty. But if I decided to dispose of you, I'd have him surrender it to the police as evidence. You shot one of my security personnel with it."

"Well he shouldn't have tried to cave my head in with a bat," Hannibal said. "And you're too smart to have me killed. Think nobody knows where I am? I imagine you're pretty slippery, but you'd play hell trying to dodge a murder charge if I disappear after coming here. Even if I don't, they'll be here with the sun. Your smart play is to cut me loose now."

Without warning Johnson's relaxed demeanor shifted to wary awareness. It was the way some dogs react when their master walks into the room. Not so much happy, but cautious, equally anticipating a treat or a kick. His eyes shifted up from Hannibal to the doorway. He dropped to the floor and looked like he was about to greet his new visitor but was cut off.

"I was just talking to the boys downstairs," the newcomer said. "I understand this boy came by before."

"You know him?" Johnson asked.

Nelson walked to the desk and turned to face Hannibal. "Yeah, we've met." They locked eyes for a moment, each taking the other's measure anew. Without breaking eye contact, Nelson said to Johnson, "You know who this is?"

"Not really," Johnson said. "When he came with Frankie Brown she just introduced him as a family friend. At the time I thought he was a lawyer or something, but now I'm thinking private cop or something."

Nelson turned his laser eyes on Johnson. "He was here before? Why didn't you tell me?

Unlike Hannibal, Johnson averted his eyes. "I didn't know it mattered. He was just a guy snooping around with a mark's daughter."

"Yeah," Nelson said. "Just a snoop who's going to cost me for medical bills and disability benefits for one of my drivers. You've got a mess here, Ira. Samantha is not going to be pleased. I think the prudent move at this point is to shut this operation down."

"What? It's not that bad. We'd be leaving a lot of money on the table."

"Too risky," Nelson said. "It's time to tie it all off. Go tell the boys to complete their current deliveries. Then they can leave the trucks in different places in South Carolina or West Virginia, but none of them in Virginia, Maryland or The District. Got it?" When Johnson nodded, Nelson added, "And tell the Fridge to come up here, but stay outside the door."

When Johnson was gone Nelson stood in front of Hannibal with hands on hips, shaking his head. With a sigh he said, "put your feet on the floor." Hannibal shrugged and complied.

"Now, don't be an asshole, all right?" Nelson said. Then he gripped the front of Hannibal's shirt with both hands and hoisted him upward until he was standing. He spun him around and dropped him into the visitor's chair beside the desk.

"That's better, ain't it?" Hannibal nodded.

Nelson sat in the chair behind the desk, leaned back and put his feet up on the desk. "What's your story? You're not Henry Jones, realtor."

"Hannibal. Hannibal Jones."

"Right," Nelson said. "You're a private eye."

"And your name's Nelson," Hannibal said. "Small time hustler."

"Now that's kind of derisive," Nelson played with his gold bracelet. "Let's just say a hustler who knows how to keep his head low enough to fly below law enforcement radar. I'm the bug on the elephant's hide that's not quite irritating enough for the elephant to make the effort to squash."

"Well, I think you got a little too irritating this time," Hannibal said. "You know, the cops are headed here right now. They're already at the Brazos Cantina and up at the Indigo. You own them both, don't you?"

Again, Nelson stared into Hannibal's hazel eyes. Hannibal wasn't sure what he was looking for, but he held his gaze until Nelson gave one short laugh and leaned back again.

"You're good," Nelson said. "I can't tell if you're lying, and that's rare. If all that's true it's bad news for some of my people but they'll play hell tying anything to me. Unless you decide to be a fool. Are you a fool Mr. Jones?"

"How do I prove that one way or the other?"

"You're a P.I., right?" Nelson asked. "In my experience, P.I.s don't tend to have very good relationships with law enforcement. So here's my offer. I'm shutting down this operation, but I'll cut you in for half of the profits on this last leg. A cool fifty grand for you, just for having a bad memory about tonight."

"One of us is confused," Hannibal said, squirming to sit up straighter. "If you're offering me half the take you left off a zero." When Nelson didn't react, Hannibal said, "You picked the wrong time to get tired of being small time. Seriously, isn't kidnapping a little high profile for you? Not to mention murder."

Nelson moved his feet to the floor and leaned forward. "Just exactly what are you accusing me of?"

"Was that you that slit the girl's throat?" Hannibal asked. "Were you driving that Jeep or Land Rover or whatever it was that ran me into a tree? Or was it one of your boys?"

Nelson adopted that facial expression that Hannibal had seen so many times in the mirror. The mouth raised at one end, the staring up, brows lowered. The face of putting things together, of pushing the pieces of the puzzle around until they fit. Only then did it occur to Hannibal that he had put it together wrong.

Finally, Nelson seemed to see the lightbulb overhead. His mouth dropped open, then curled into a smile. He stood and went to the office door and leaned out.

"Listen, Fridge, I need you to take this asshole somewhere safe and sit on him. Don't break him, I might need him later. Oh, and can you tell me where the hell Kronik is right now?"

CHAPTER 27

It was a long, quiet ride in the back of the now familiar Mercedes. With his hands bound behind him there was nothing he could do to shorten it, but he considered that the situation wasn't all bad. Fridge had cut the zip tie holding Hannibal's feet together so he could walk to the car. He had also taken Hannibal's phone and boasted that he had Hannibal's gun and was taking what he assumed was Hannibal's car. So at least Hannibal knew where all the important stuff was and could recover it all if he just managed to survive the night.

He hated that he couldn't see his watch. He had no idea what time it was, and he wasn't about to ask the ape behind the wheel who was driving the Maybach as if it was an old beater. He just knew it would be another late night. He wished he could nap in the car, but he was too keyed up for that. He wished he had called Rissik before he went into the Optilorus stronghold. But mostly, he wished he had punched Ira Johnson in the face when he had the chance.

Through the tinted windows he could see just enough to see that again they were on backroads and narrow streets. No landmarks stood out, so no way to even know where he was until they rolled onto a long gravel driveway and Hannibal recognized the farmhouse.

Fridge parked beside yet another Amazon delivery truck around back and hauled Hannibal out of the back seat. He thought for a moment he'd meet the mystery woman, but she was absent. Fridge shoved him through the back door, through the kitchen and into a small bedroom. The final push was hard enough to bounce him off the far wall. Fridge laughed when Hannibal dropped to the floor.

"Sit there and be quiet and you won't get hurt no worse," Fridge said. "Piss me off and I'll bust you up."

He slammed the door and Hannibal heard the click of a solid lock sliding into place. Fridge walked off and soon Hannibal heard a refrigerator open and close. Fridge's bulk landed on a wooden chair. Liquid poured into a glass. A tinny television speaker broadcast what sounded like an old kung fu movie, poorly dubbed. Figuring his captor would be settled for a while, Hannibal examined his environment. Bars on the single window made him wonder if the owner was worried about someone breaking in or guests breaking out. A bed and a dresser were all the furniture, and there wasn't even a rug on the wide plank floor. Aside from the comforter on the bed the room held no sign that it was ever used. No one lived here. It was a safe house, a drop off point or a temporary stop for travelers who didn't want to be traced. Or temporary housing for involuntary guests like himself. Nelson maintained a lot of hustles, so there were lots of possibilities.

None of that mattered to him. He had to get back to civilization and rally the troops. That meant getting out of his bonds, getting out of that house, and getting Nelson.

Hannibal began rocking side to side on the wooden floor, pulling his wrists forward under himself. With some effort he managed to get his hands past his behind. The zip tie bit into his wrists and now his legs. On his back he pulled his knees up as far as he could, thankful for his slender frame. Ears tuned to the slapstick sounds of a film fight in the kitchen, Hannibal managed to get his heels hooked on the plastic tie. He gritted his teeth and pushed as hard as he could. All that did was cause the plastic to cut into his wrists. He didn't think zip ties were usually this thick. This approach was getting him nowhere, so he exhaled to deflate his body and slipped his feet back and through. Now his wrists were in front of him. It was a start.

He moved to brace his back against the bed, which smelled like the last five or six people who used it hadn't bothered to change the bedding. He untied his sneakers. He pulled one of the laces of his right sneaker through the zip tie, then tied it to one of the laces on his left. He leaned back and started pushing his feet forward alternately. He breathed through his mouth so his effort would be quieter. It only took about ten seconds of this action for the laces to saw through the plastic tie. He relaxed and moved his arms around, trying to work the soreness out of his shoulders. Now for step two.

Hannibal shoved the broken wrist restraint into his pocket. He untied his sneaker laces and retied them the right way. He stood and swung his arms like windmills a few times to loosen his shoulders and restore proper circulation. Then he went to the door and turned the knob. Well, he heard Fridge lock it, but he had to at least try. He had nothing on him with which to pick the lock. Oddly, he wasn't disappointed that he would have to do this the hard way. He backed away from the door a couple steps and shouted.

"Hey ugly! Hey out there!"

The television sound stopped. He must have been watching a video of a bad kung fu flick. A chair's legs scraped against the kitchen floor. Heavy footsteps approached. Hannibal backed against the bed and grabbed his own wrist behind his back. The door's lock clicked. Fridge pushed the door in and stomped into the room.

"The hell you want?"

Hannibal looked down. "I, er, I need to use the bathroom."

"So?"

"You serious?" Hannibal asked. "I got to piss."

"Well, see, it's like this. I ain't letting your hands loose cause I ain't got no more zip ties out here. And I sure as hell ain't holding your dick. So I guess you either gone hold it till

I hear from the boss, or you gone piss your pants. And I don't care which."

Fridge stepped back into the hall with a hand on the knob. That would not do.

Hannibal snapped, "I knew you were ugly as fuck, but I didn't realize you were such a little bitch."

That drew Fridge back into the room. "What you say?"

"I should have known. All you know how to do is hit a guy when he's not looking. I bet they call you Sucker Punch Fridge. You ain't got the balls to face a guy, even if he's half your size."

"You better shut your mouth before I put your teeth down your throat."

"Right," Hannibal said. "You'll beat up on the man whose hands are tied behind his back. You really are a whiney little bitch."

"Call me that again, and…"

"What?" Hannibal said, taking one step to his left. "A little bitch? It's all you are. I bet everybody knows it."

Fridge almost roared as he lunged forward. Three steps brought him in range and his huge right fist swept toward Hannibal's face. Hannibal leaned back and his left hand swept up, slapping the outside of Fridge's arm, pushing it past to Hannibal's right, leaving Fridge extended and off balance. Hannibal rammed his right fist into Fridge's stomach, followed by a left cross and a straight right into Fridge's nose.

The big man staggered back, stunned. But his left hand swung out as he did, catching the door. He fell back into it, slamming it shut, but didn't quite fall. His surprised expression quickly reverted to a hard grimace of rage. He wiped the back of his hand across his face, noting the blood that had come from his nose. Then he straightened his shoulders and raised his fists.

"You done fucked up now," he said. "The boss wanted you in one piece, but too bad. I am going to fuck you up."

Hannibal also assumed a ready stance, smiling as he circled to his right. "My buddy Nathan down in King and Queen County got a saying. Talk shit. Spit blood."

Fridge moved in fast, trying to corner Hannibal but he had a limited repertoire of attacks. Hannibal dodged another sweeping right and thumped left-right-left into Fridge's ribs before bouncing out of reach. Then Fridge tried a left. Hannibal blocked it and drove an uppercut into the bigger man's jaw. Fridge counter-punched and caught Hannibal a glancing blow to the jaw. Hannibal quickly moved out of reach, circling in the room as he once did in the ring.

Fridge no longer blocked the door. Hannibal no longer cared. He owed this man too much.

Fridge charged again, but Hannibal backed him off with a stamp kick to the midsection. "You think that karate shit's going to stop me?" Fridge asked. "No way."

He swung another hard right that smacked Hannibal's upraised forearms. Hannibal backed off, then lunged forward with two quick jabs and a right hook that split Fridge's lip.

Both men were panting hard when Hannibal back pedaled and his back hit a wall. Fridge grinned and threw a left that rocked Hannibal's head back. But Hannibal dodged the follow-up right. Fridge grunted when his fist smashed into the wall. *That'll cost him a knuckle,* Hannibal thought. He hopped to the side, raised his leg and stamped out and down.

At the right angle, fourteen pounds of pressure is enough to dislocate a knee. Fridge's leg quivered and he went down. Hannibal drove into his kneeling enemy, peppering his face with punches until his arms were tired. When Fridge finally raised his arms to protect his face Hannibal planted a snap kick in his solar plexus.

Fridge doubled over. Out of his opponent's reach, Hannibal waited for him to look up. He wanted eye contact. When Fridge looked up Hannibal saw what he wanted. The big man knew he was beaten.

"Goodnight, bitch," Hannibal said.

One arcing crescent kick against Fridge's head ended the fight. He keeled over, went down and stayed there. Now there was only the sound of Hannibal's labored breathing. As was so often the case he had tuned out the exhaustion until the fight was over. As fatigue replaced the adrenaline rush, he knelt to quickly frisk his unconscious enemy. He recovered the key fob for the Mercedes, ignored the loose change and pulled out the wallet. He carried a couple hundred dollars in cash, but Hannibal took nothing from the wallet except the man's driver's license. With this, Rissik would have no trouble identifying him when Hannibal pressed charges.

The next stop was the kitchen, where Hannibal found what he wanted on display in the middle of the table. He pocketed his phone and shoved his pistol into its paddle holster in his waistband. He looked back over his shoulder, considering if he should bind Fridge before he left. But now, he didn't feel like searching for something to tie him up with. Besides, he was just too tired to deal with moving that monster's body, and if he came to, Hannibal sure didn't want to deal with wrestling with him.

The cool night air hit him like a splash of water in the face. Seconds later the Mercedes engine roared to life. Hannibal drove down the long driveway thinking that he had done a lot in the last twenty-four hours but wondering if anything had been gained.

CHAPTER 28

When Hannibal pulled up to the gate that barred access to the Browns' driveway, he checked his watch. How had it gotten past three o'clock? Yes, he had pulled to the side about halfway there for a quick cat nap. Maybe it hadn't been as quick as he thought.

He rolled slowly to the gate across the long driveway to the house. Surely no one was up, and he'd hate to wake somebody to get in. Could he open the fence manually? Maybe he didn't need to. There was a box on the visor with several buttons. He pushed one, waited ten seconds and pushed another. When he pushed button number three the gates swung inward.

He left the car parked in front of the door which, to his surprise, was not locked. He padded to the room he was staying in, eased the door open and slipped inside. He stripped in the bathroom and checked for damage. Not much showed. He gently washed his face, already hating the thought of shaving his tender jaw in the morning. He was equally careful washing his hands. Gloves sure made the rough stuff easier on his knuckles, and he didn't have to worry about carrying another man's blood to bed.

When he felt clean enough for the sheets, he pulled out his phone to set his alarm. He wanted to meet with his team before the family breakfast to bring them up to speed. Zander Brown's wife and daughter didn't need to hear all that had happened. Anyway, all of that could wait four hours. Right then, his goal was to get under the covers and snuggle in without waking Cindy out of a sound sleep.

As his arm settled around her, Cindy murmured, "You okay honey?"

"All good, babe," he whispered. Her arm pulled his closer and she slipped back into a deep sleep. He quickly followed.

At seven thirty they all had coffee and were gathered around the long island in the cook's kitchen. Cindy, Ray and Virgil took the chairs at one end, with Sarge and Quaker leaning against the marble surface. Hannibal, more comfortable to be in his black suit and Oakleys again, was pacing as he talked. He ran through the events of the previous twelve hours, starting with following Fridge's van. Everyone else was quiet until nearly the end of his report, when Sarge commented.

"Dude! Would you settle somewhere? I'm getting dizzy following you back and forth."

"Sorry," Hannibal said. "I guess coffee on top of lack of sleep has made me a little, I don't know…"

"Hyper?" Quaker said. "Yeah, we get that. We were up late too. Not like you but still…"

Hannibal nodded and gulped more coffee. "Yeah, my head's in overdrive. I woke up with a wild theory and had to get into my phone to do some research. But anyway, what was going on here last night? Did these guys go anywhere? Get any visitors? Another note or email from the kidnappers?"

"No new communication," Cindy said. "I stayed pretty close to Charlotte, but she took pills and turned in early. I think that's her primary stress coping mechanism."

"Nobody came in," Sarge said, "and I stayed pretty close to Cawfee. Likes to swim at night and I think he's happy to have somebody to talk to with Zander gone."

"Me and Virgil, we kind of switched off keeping an eye on Young, but he's pretty boring. Spent some time on the phone but I could hear it was business stuff. We all watched a movie in the big room. He crashed around eleven."

"Everybody just seemed to be waiting for some news," Cindy said. "Frankie was the only person who got restless, I guess. She left at some point and didn't come home until around midnight. I crashed soon after she went to bed."

All the men turned to her. She raised her empty cup and Hannibal poured her a refill. "You didn't see her leave?" he asked.

"I didn't even notice she was gone," Ray said. "But it's a big house, brother."

Hannibal raised a palm to him. "Not attacking my girl, Ray. Just pinning down the facts." Then to Cindy he said, "You sure she was gone, babe? It is a big house."

"Well, we were all starting to watch that movie with all the shooting and blowing stuff up, and I noticed I hadn't seen her for a while, so I went looking for her. Her bedroom was empty, so then I thought maybe she was with her mother. But Charlotte was passed out and no Frankie. Then I checked around the house. Lots of exercise but no Frankie. Then I admit I had a bad thought." She slowly turned away, looking a little embarrassed.

"Well don't stop there," Hannibal said, refilling his own cup. "Seems like the detective bug bit you. What were you thinking that could be so bad?"

"Well, Cawfee is around all the time, and she wasn't in there with her boyfriend, and I thought maybe..."

"Oh no," Ray said. "He's old enough to be her father."

"That don't stop everybody," Hannibal said.

"Well, I hadn't looked everywhere, had I?" Cindy said. "So, I went over to the guest house where Cawfee stays. I knocked but there was no answer. And, well the door was open."

"You didn't," Ray said.

Cindy nodded, eyes closed. "I did."

"My girl!" Hannibal said. "So, how's he living? Anything unusual in there? Signs of too much money, or signs he's getting ready to leave?"

"Nothing like that," Cindy said. "Although I will say it seemed like a very neat apartment for a bachelor. And not much clothes. And a whole bunch of DVDs and CDs. The movies were all old blaxploitation films like Truck Turner and Superfly and Shaft. CDs were all gogo and rappers with weird names like Fat Trel, Tabi Bonney and, oh, Biz Markey."

"Good stuff, and all local talent," Quaker said. When all eyes went to him, he said, "What? White boys can't dig rap?"

That brought a round of laughter that broke any tension there was. As it was dying down, Hannibal's phone rang. His first thought was that everyone who ever called him was in the room. Then he realized only one person would call him that early.

"Good morning, Orson. Are you in your office already?"

"Been here a while," Rissik said. "I had to listen to your three long messages. Were you drunk or something?"

"No, man, just tired. And my face was a little swollen so might have slurred my speech a little."

"Yeah, well, thanks for bringing me up to date on your shenanigans. I assume you'll press charges on all these people you had to deal with, so I'm putting warrants out."

"Appreciate you," Hannibal said, thinking do people really use that word? Shenanigans. "I don't have names for any of the boys who attacked me except Fridge"

"You sure that's how you spell that? Aquiles?"

"Read it right off his license. His mother must have had spelling issues. But at least you'll know you got the right guy. And I'd sure love it if you can grab Nelson, and that grifter, Ira Johnson too."

"Did either of them hurt you?"

"Not directly," Hannibal said, "but they gave the orders for the beating and my abduction. You can pull them in for some kind of conspiracy, right?"

"Yeah," Rissik said. "Petty misdemeanors but it's an excuse to hold them while we dig for evidence of more serious stuff at the Optilorus site and the two bars."

"You da man," Hannibal said, "but I don't think you called me just to tell me that."

"You think?" Rissik asked. "You must be a detective or something. I got some research done and since you were kind enough to share what you know with me, I figured I'd return the favor."

"You're the best, Chief. Okay if I put you on speaker?"

"Sure. Is Miss Santiago there too?"

"I'm here," Cindy called.

"Good. You can stop me if I start stepping on somebody's rights."

Hannibal laid his phone in the center of the kitchen island and everyone in the room leaned in close. They heard papers rustling on the other end.

"Okay," Rissik began, "We got nothing useful off the rented Porsche 911, so for now the killer is still a mystery. The victim, not so much. We got a hit as soon as we put her prints into the system. Looks like the driver was one Katerina Rogers, small time out of Wilmette, Illinois. Parents deceased."

"Katerina?" Cindy said. "Unusual name."

"Apparently a family thing," Rissik said. "One sister, Quinnleigh Rogers, location unknown. One brother Uriah Rogers, killed in gang-related violence three years ago."

"Oh yeah," Ray said. "The waitress in the Brazos said her friend was Katie. Must be the same girl."

"Yeah, and I heard Fridge say Katie was missing."

"Anyhow, this woman has a long record, goes back to juvie. Moved from shoplifting to a little B & E to boosting cars. Looks like she was working with a partner, a Veronica Jean Walker."

"Thelma and Louise," Virgil said, in the voice of Eeyore.

"Yeah," Rissik said. "Can't be sure, but the way the records read, there might have been a…" he paused for a second. "a romantic connection between them. Got to admit the team thing was pretty smart. Two women can talk most guys into letting them in the car. Then a taser or a gun in his face gets him out of it. Last time they pulled her in was about seven years ago. Looks like they caught her alone after a high-speed chase, but she lightened her sentence by giving up the other girl. We can assume Walker never knew that, since they hung together in Joliet."

"Aww, she just didn't want to do time without her boo," Sarge said.

"Walker is the obvious lead," Hannibal said. "Since they clearly stick together. Got a line on her?"

Rissik sighed over the phone. "I know you sometimes forget, but this investigative thing is what I do for a living. Walker is on parole so tracing her won't be hard. Kind of looks like she was trying to go legit, or at least move to a more legal hustle. She's a performer now. She's put out five extended play CDs under her stage name Kronik."

Hannibal pushed himself back from the island. "What? Kronik?"

"Yes," Rissik said. "Not like an illness, but like the high-quality marijuana Snoop Dogg used to rap about."

Names and faces were swirling in Hannibal's brain as he watched pieces of his mental puzzle start to drop into place. Energized, he turned back to the phone.

"Orson, you never cease to amaze me."

"What? The white man can't have knowledge of hip-hop recordings?"

"Not that, moron," Hannibal laughed. "I know her. She's friends with Samantha Tucker, who's definitely involved with Nelson. Wasn't sure if Kronik was mixed up in this but you just tied her to it pretty tight. When I saw her, she was performing every night at the Indigo."

"One of Nelson's places," Rissik said. "She might be a person of interest in your case."

"No doubt," Hannibal said. Then his eyes widened, and he turned to Virgil. "Hey, was she on stage night before last?"

"Afraid not," Virgil said in his dour voice. "But I think she was supposed to be. Heard some people say they were pissed she wasn't there."

Hannibal made more connections. "Listen, Orson, if you spot her you might want to observe for a bit before you pick her up. If things come together the way I think they will, I'm pretty sure Nelson will be looking for her. If he moves on her you could grab both. And I think one or the other might be able to lead us to Zander Brown."

"Makes sense," Rissik said. "Let me get to work. Maybe we can wrap this whole gang up."

Hannibal rang off, his mind still pushing facts around into different patterns. There were still holes but he thought he might be able to fill some of them in. His friends watched him, waiting he guessed for the next step. All except Cindy who stared at the ceiling, wearing that expression that usually means a person is trying to remember something. Then her eyes popped open, and a smile replaced her puzzled look.

"What is it, babe?" Hannibal asked.

"Oh, nothing really," Cindy said, waving the thought away with her left hand. "I thought I recognized that name. Kronik. Spelled with a K, right? Then I remembered. It was on CDs in Cawfee's room."

Hannibal's mouth dropped open. Another unexpected connection. But did it really mean anything?

"Not a surprise, right?" Sarge said. "The man's a hip-hop fan."

"No, hold on," Quaker said. "This ain't right. This chick's from Chicagoland, right? Every other name Cindy told us about is out of DC. You remember any more, Cindy?"

She closed her eyes, searching her memory. "Let's see. Head Roc. Q Da Fool. Deetranada. Did I say Wale before?"

"See," Quaker said. "Every one of them is local DMV talent. Kronik kind of sticks out."

"And he had one or two of each, but five of hers," Cindy said. "Didn't Orson say she only had five?"

"Yeah," Hannibal said. "So Cawfee's at least a major fan, and maybe a lot more."

"Sucks, don't it," Quaker said. "Kind of sounds like Zander's best friend is the inside man."

Conversation stopped when Betsy, the housekeeper, appeared at the arch entrance to the kitchen. "Gentlemen and Miss Santiago, Breakfast is served in the main dining room. The others are already seated."

She left and everyone moved to follow. Hannibal tugged Cindy back.

"Listen babe, give my apologies, okay?" he said. "Tell them I already ate or something."

"Going somewhere?" she asked.

"Yeah. Right now we have one thin clue that points to Cawfee but I want to see if his room turns up any other evidence."

CHAPTER 29

Gloves and glasses on, Hannibal made sure no one saw him approach Cawfee's guest house. The sun was making a statement that morning, making sure he knew it was there, and birds he never heard near his home in Southeast DC celebrated loudly.

Hannibal figured Cawfee usually left the door unlocked. After all, the grounds were secure, and the cleaning crew probably took care of his place when they visited the main house. But when Hannibal tried the doorknob, it wouldn't turn. No matter. It wasn't much of a lock and it only slowed him down by a minute or so.

It was a nice little apartment, bright and airy. Windows stood open with sheer curtains wiggling as if they were tickled by the gentle breeze. And Cindy was right, it was neat for a bachelor pad. Cawfee left no shoes scattered around, he made his bed in the morning, and he didn't leave stuff lying out in the bathroom. Yes, Cindy was very observant, but she hadn't read the entire story the room told.

The closet revealed a minimal collection. Dresser drawers showed the usual socks, underwear and shirts but only enough for two or three days. Under the bed Hannibal found two medium sized suitcases. Both were packed, neatly but full. Somebody was planning a trip.

The living area held a big screen television, a Blu-ray disc player and an old school stereo setup. The sound system was a set of separate components like no one uses anymore, and two big Bose speakers. Two orderly racks held his media. One held DVDs, all action movies. The other rack displayed a collection of CDs, almost all rap as Cindy said, and stored in alphabetical order. That made it easy to see that five were missing, right where Kronik would go. Hannibal doubted the man's tastes had changed overnight.

Hannibal returned to the suitcases just to be sure. No CDs there. The house held only two trash cans, one in the kitchen, the other in the bathroom. Both were empty. So where did they take their trash? There were probably seven or eight garbage cans in the main house. It all had to go someplace to be disposed of maybe once a week. Hannibal mentally replayed his quick tour of the grounds. He recalled larger garbage bins near the outdoor kitchen and over by the shed next to the driving range.

Hannibal speed-walked to the driving range, knowing that breakfast would be over soon, and people would miss him. He wanted to be sure before throwing accusations around. The trash bins were just where he remembered, two of the four labeled for recycling. The bottles and cans filled the first one he opened. The second held cardboard and paper. The third can was filled with smaller garbage bags tied closed. He opened one that smelled of kitchen garbage. But he hit the jackpot with the second one. He pulled out five CD jewel cases.

It must have been hard to toss these. Three of the cases were autographed. One said, "You're the one" in a feminine script. Kronik had even drawn a tiny heart over the "I" in her name on that one.

From behind Hannibal, Cawfee's voice said, "What you doing digging around in the garbage?"

Hannibal turned, with a gentle smile. "Wonder what made you decide to throw these particular CDs away."

"Don't see how that's any of your business," Cawfee said. "Ain't going in my trash an invasion of privacy or something?"

Hannibal closed the trash bin and leaned back against it. "Here's what I didn't get from day one. Zander was your boy. Plus, it was your job to keep him safe. But when he didn't come home for a couple days, you didn't immediately go look for him at his private pad. You acted like you wanted to be all cooperative, but you didn't look in the most obvious place yourself."

"I ain't no detective, am I?" Cawfee said, moving in to almost within reach of Hannibal.

"At first, I thought maybe Zander had decided to sneak off for a while, and you were the only person who knew where he went. And when it became clear it was a kidnapping, well, that was still the only reason I could think of for you to not have looked in his DC apartment right away. You knew where he was."

"Don't go there," Cawfee said.

"So the only reason for you to take me to that little apartment was as a diversion. You needed to look helpful. You had no idea I'd find a clue there that would eventually lead me around to Kronik."

Cawfee leaned in, fists clenched. "If I was you, I'd shut my mouth."

"Threatening me?" Hannibal asked, shifting into a fighting stance. "The sign of an amateur. Well, another sign. These were the giveaway." Hannibal waved the CDs in Cawfee's face.

"That ain't nothing," Cawfee said. "Lots of people got them CDs."

"See? That's my whole point," Hannibal said, shaking his head. "If I found these in your place, well, they do kind of indicate a connection between you and Kronik. And you used to be a DJ, so maybe you worked with all them rappers in your collection. But the fact that you felt the need to get rid of these particular CDs, that tells me you were worried about people learning about your connection to this girl. Tell me, is she your main squeeze?"

"Don't push this too far, brother," Cawfee's voice lowered, and was more menacing for it. Hannibal took a deep breath but stayed calm.

"Did you know she was a real gangsta when you hooked up with her?" he asked. "I bet she was blown away when she saw how you were living, and how your boy Zander was living. And he was so good to you."

"Shit," Cawfee spat. "He's up here living like Trump or Steve fucking Jobs. It started out like we was partners, but after he retired, things changed. All of a sudden, I was his goddam servant. Driving his ass around." Cawfee looked down, his gaze moving back and forth across the ground, perhaps searching for his dignity.

"I think I get it," Hannibal said. "You might have loved the man when this all started, when he offered you a job to keep you close. But in time you came to resent it. Resent him. He had it all, didn't he? Not just the money, but the fame, the respect, the family you wished you had."

"Why him?" Cawfee said. "Why him and not me?" Hannibal didn't think the question was really addressed to him. He had seen it before. Men who felt that life had defeated them clutched at the laziest lifeline, but their hearts could still be corroded by failure and envy and eventually, hate. Then they were ripe to be prodded in the wrong direction.

"I'm betting this was all Kronik's idea," Hannibal said. "She did time in a hard place. She and her home girl must've been looking for that one big score. She convinced you they could take Zander if you set it up for them, right? They'd get a big pot of money, bring him home safe, and then you'd take off with them. A nice little family of three, maybe in another country, with enough money to do whatever you want."

"That's a hell of a story," Cawfee said, "But it still don't prove nothing. Anybody could have snatched Zander out of that club."

Now Hannibal chuckled a bit. "Come on, man. It just doesn't work as a crime of opportunity. The girl who lured him out had to know when he was going to be there. Once you get past that it all comes back to the only person who knew where Zander was going that night. He didn't tell anyone else, not his wife, his daughter, nobody. I figure you set it up with Kronik for her girl Katie to pick Zander up and take him somewhere."

When Hannibal dropped Katie's name Cawfee's demeanor changed. All pretense of innocence left his face. Maybe he realized this was more than just conjecture. If Hannibal pushed hard enough, maybe he could get the answer he needed.

"Did you know Katie went inside the Statuz Club to lure him out?" Hannibal asked. "That's right. The manager saw her. All we've got to do is show her Katie's picture. Her positive ID will draw the line from Zander's kidnapping to Kronik. And these CDs draw the line from Kronik to their inside man. You."

Cawfee seemed to be rocking, emotionally, between fear, anger and guilt. Hannibal didn't know which square he'd land on.

"All these years out of the game, but Zander was still a baller," Cawfee told Hannibal's shoes. "In his heart he was still a player, but he didn't toss that stuff around the house. Here he was a family man, loving husband and father and the deal was, when he stepped out for a night or two, Charlotte didn't ask no questions. He gave her this life, and that was the price, and she didn't mind paying it. He was good to her, and never disrespected her. Kept his outside action on the downlow."

"Sure," Hannibal said. "That's why nobody knew where he went to party. Nobody but you."

Cawfee's face fell in on itself. After a few seconds of silence he said, "You know, you don't have to tell nobody all that," in a surprisingly soft voice. "You could give me a couple hours' head start at least. Remember, I saved your ass at the Indigo."

"True, and I thank you for that," Hannibal said. "But that doesn't change the fact that you lied to me. You said you were looking for Zander but the truth is, you were there to see your girl Kronik, weren't you?"

"Yeah, and I never got to get with her that night. I wanted to check on Zander." Cawfee began to walk, slowly, aimlessly, around the golf shack. He seemed to be teetering on the edge of confusion.

A bank of clouds slid under the sun, dimming the world. Hannibal noticed how quiet it was, as if even the birds were holding their breath. He saw his opening and stepped into it, walking beside Cawfee.

"So…is Zander all right? He's alive?"

"Of course," Cawfee said. "We never planned to hurt him. Just wanted to get paid so we could live like we deserve to live."

Hannibal put a comforting hand on Cawfee's shoulder. "Look, you know I can't just let you run off, but that doesn't mean your life is over. You're a victim here too. You were taken advantage of, confused. You didn't get the money, and you didn't hurt anybody. Just tell me where Zander is and with the right lawyer, I'm betting you can plead out of this."

Cawfee stopped and looked up into the clouds as if searching his options. A head nod. A decision made. He turned to Hannibal.

"I could do that," Cawfee said. Then he gripped the back of Hannibal's suit coat, pulled a folding fighting knife out of his pocket and flipped it open with one hand. "Or, I could just shut you up for good."

CHAPTER 30

Hannibal saw the five inches of stainless-steel arcing toward his stomach and managed to swing his right arm down fast enough to stop Cawfee's arm, wrist against wrist. He gripped Cawfee's knife hand with both of his own and twisted hard. It didn't break Cawfee's grip on the weapon, but he did release Hannibal's jacket, waving his free arm to keep his balance.

Hannibal let go and jumped back away from Cawfee. Wrestling with a knife in the hand of a bigger man was a losing proposition. He back pedaled, trying to get more distance from that knife, but Cawfee kept charging at him.

"I seen your gun," Cawfee said, "but I saw how you acted around the women and I figured you wouldn't go around strapped here at the house. Not so stupid now, huh?"

At that moment, Hannibal felt stupid, thinking Cawfee might make the rational choice. Now he faced a man who looked like he knew what he was doing with a blade, making short feinting slashes at Hannibal. He would have to wait until Cawfee committed before he tried to disarm him.

Cawfee's eyes lit up and he leaped forward faster than Hannibal thought he could. The blade swished past in front of him, but he lost his footing and fell. His back thudded into the turf and Cawfee dropped on top of him, switching his grip to stab down. Hannibal crossed his forearms, stopping Cawfee's arm between his fists. Cawfee applied all his weight, forcing the knife down to within an inch of Hannibal's throat. Both men panted hard with the opposing effort, Hannibal gearing up to push hard to one side.

Then there was a short whoosh and a loud crack sound. The impact sounded to him just like a man driving a ball down the fairway. He pushed hard and Cawfee fell to his left way more easily than expected. And Hannibal found himself staring up at Gene Young, who was slowly lowering a driver.

Hannibal got to his feet. Cawfee lay on his back, arms outstretched. Young seemed to be grinning in satisfaction but quickly switched to an open-mouthed look of concern.

"Thanks," Hannibal said, working to catch his breath. "I appreciate the help, but how did you end up here?" Then he knelt beside Cawfee, checking the impact area.

"Well, after breakfast we were all wondering where you were," Young said. "All the guys went in different directions looking for you. I happened to spot Cawfee talking to you and headed over to see what was up. Just about when I got to the golf shack, I saw Cawfee pull a knife. I was afraid he was going to kill you, so…"

"So instead of yelling to him you decided to grab a club, ran over here and teed off on his head."

"Yeah. You're welcome," Young said. His tone was dry and Hannibal thought he may have been offended. He didn't mean to sound ungrateful, but Young had smacked Cawfee pretty hard with a golfer's accuracy, right in the temple. Cawfee was breathing, but it could have easily been a fatal blow. As it was, Cawfee was unresponsive. His pulse was strong and his breathing steady, but a solid shake and even a quick slap didn't wake him.

"Is he going to be all right?" Young asked.

"Too soon to know." Hannibal pulled out his phone. He had two calls to make in a hurry. First to 9-1-1. Then to Orson Rissik.

Everyone staying at the house had come out to watch Cawfee being loaded into the ambulance. Rissik spoke in low tones to the EMTs before they climbed back into their vehicle. Virgil offered to follow them out so he could secure the gate behind them. Two members of the crime scene unit had already collected th

06e knife and golf club and were taking what Hannibal thought was an absurd number of pictures. A plainclothes detective was taking Young's statement. Another was getting a statement from Charlotte and Frankie.

Rissik pulled Hannibal aside to hear his side of the events that had left Cawfee unconscious, maybe even in what appeared to be a coma. In terse fragments, Hannibal explained his theory on Cawfee's involvement with the kidnapping. Rissik listened without moving or speaking. Hannibal thought this must be what the confessional feels like or asking for wisdom from a Buddha. When he finished, Rissik took one long, deep breath and let it out slowly.

"So, you think this Cawfee is in love with the rapper, Kronik?" Rissik asked.

"To get him to betray his long-time friend like this? Yeah, he was sprung."

"Then it's possible she had serious feelings for him," Rissik said. "Or at least was staying in close contact. I better reach out to the medical staff and remind them about their confidentiality agreements. If she decides to look for him I don't want anybody leaking his location."

Hannibal shook his head. "They've had the money, what, seven hours? And nothing from them? You get anything from the ransom note?"

"Nada."

Hannibal moved a little closer to Rissik. "Listen, I did a quick search of Cawfee's place but, you know, just eyes not forensics."

"No surprise there. But as soon as you called I requested a search warrant for his place. Already asked for Ira Johnson's building."

Cindy moved up beside Hannibal and took his hand. A glance over his shoulder told him Everyone else was moving back toward the main house.

"Sorry to interrupt," Cindy said, "But those women are pretty torn up. This is all pretty confusing, and Young is making it sound like Cawfee went crazy and tried to kill you. Is there anything I can tell them?"

"I'll come in and bring them up to speed in a couple minutes," Hannibal said. "Go sit with them, okay?"

"And tell them not to tell a soul that Cawfee's in the hospital in a coma," Rissik added in stern tones. "If his accomplice hears that somebody here hurt her man, she might decide to retaliate and take it out on Mr. Brown."

Cindy nodded, gave Hannibal a soft kiss on the cheek and went to follow the others. Rissik took a couple steps in the same direction, but Hannibal stopped him.

"So that's it? A one-way briefing? What's up at your end? Did you check out that farmhouse where they held me?"

Rissik waved him off. "Low priority. They're all gone from there by now and they'd be crazy to go back. Besides, we got this Fridge's ID and need to hunt him down." Rissik started walking again and Hannibal had to speed walk to keep up.

"Hey, hold up, Orson. We got a problem, you and me?"

Rissik stopped suddenly and spun to face Hannibal. "To tell you the truth I'm kind of pissed off. You knew you were stepping on my investigation when I saw you in the Brazos Cantina. Then you just disappear, and I don't hear from you until it's all over. And now this. You couldn't call and tell me you had something on this Cawfee character? It would've been nice to be able to question him. The case might be over now if he could talk."

"Hey," Hannibal said, "I didn't bust him over the head."

"No, If you did I could be standing on your murder site instead. All because you can't learn to let police do police business." This time Rissik took four steps away before Hannibal spoke again.

"Okay, I can give you some real police business now. It's not really about the kidnapping but I'd bet it will result in a slew of arrests."

Rissik stopped, fists on hips, eyes to the ground. After a huff of air, he turned and walked back to Hannibal.

"Okay, what you got? And don't screw with me."

"There was this other puzzle bugging me," Hannibal said. "I kept seeing Amazon delivery trucks. I started to think Nelson was running a fleet of them, or at least that make and model of van, painted like Amazon vans. The plates were always obscured."

Hannibal started walking, just to get away from the spot where Cawfee got his head bashed in. Rissik stayed beside him.

"Vans painted like Amazon delivery vehicles? A slick way to move stuff unnoticed. We see those things so much they're pretty much invisible. But real Amazon might catch wise. They must track sales of those things."

"How?" Hannibal asked. "I looked it up. Amazon uses three different kinds of vans. The ones I saw every time were Ford Transits. Ford sells about a hundred and fifty thousand of those things every year. Amazon's fleet is only about thirty thousand. So it's really just a matter of buying a few used vans and getting the paint job right."

"And I'm not even sure copying the paint job is illegal, in and of itself."

"Unless you're moving illegal goods," Hannibal said.

"Yeah, but what?" Rissik asked.

They found themselves beside the swimming pool. In a moment of unspoken agreement, they dropped into side-by-side lounge chairs. Hannibal felt the wave of fatigue that meant his body was washing the adrenaline rush away.

"I have an idea," he said.

"It would have to be a good one," Rissik said. "We've been watching that Cantina for a long time, and my friends in Maryland have been watching the Indigo. I can say for sure there's no drugs moved in either place. No human trafficking, although there are some girls that work out of one or the other independently. Also, neither is a place that sells stolen items, so not a fencing operation. If Nelson's got bogus delivery vans, what's he delivering?"

Rissik sat forward when Hannibal said, "Well, here's what you don't know. Samantha Tucker looks to be connected with Nelson."

"The singer, right?"

"That's the one," Hannibal said. "And I stumbled over something unexpected in her house. It was a box like an Amazon box, but it was full of money. I mean cash in small, used bills. At the time I figured it was some kind of payoff but now I think her house was just a drop-off point."

A smile blossomed on Rissik's face. "Bars are cash businesses, and we know he's got at least two of them. Did you see those vans at the Optilorus building?"

"Sure did," Hannibal said. "Around back by the big, empty warehouse."

Rissik's smile grew bigger, as if he could see a series of arrests lined up in front of him. "You're thinking Nelson's laundering money. He collects money from other criminals' activities, in various places, and has it delivered to his clubs where he washes it with the bar's receipts. With the delivery vans, Nelson could move a whole lot of cash with no one having any reason to even suspect it's happening. And he never gets his hands dirty."

Hannibal slid his glasses off. "Check out the big brain on Orson."

"If we're right this gets pretty easy. We're already watching those two clubs and I'll do some research to see what else he might own. Then we just wait for an Amazon van to pull up and intercept the boxes being delivered. Fish in a barrel, and I'm betting those drivers will be glad to talk about their boss."

"Glad I could help," Hannibal said. "Does that make us even?"

Rissik got to his feet and stared off at his car, parked in front of the house. He looked down at Hannibal with his familiar smirk. "Yeah, I guess it does. Now I need to go get things in motion to, you know, round up the usual suspects. One of them will likely lead us to the missing man. And I'll tell you, I think this family needs you right now. Their whole world is falling apart and there's stuff that no amount of money can fix."

Hannibal walked with Rissik to his car and watched it recede down the long drive before going into the house. At the end of the hall, he saw Cindy waving him into the sitting room. Charlotte sat at one end of the fancy couch, hands in her lap, staring at something a thousand yards away. Beside her, Frankie stared at her mother's face, one hand resting on her mother's leg. Then came Gene Young, the last man in their lives. He had one hand on Frankie's shoulder, but he looked lost, unsure what to do. Frozen in place they were a medieval fresco, perhaps a lost da Vinci called The Victims or maybe Portrait of Suffering.

Charlotte broke the spell when she noticed Hannibal in the room. Her head turned toward him, her body still motionless.

"Is it true? Did Cawfee really try to kill you? I've known that man as long as I've known. Zander. Why would he want to hurt you?"

"I'm afraid Cawfee was involved with Zander's disappearance," Hannibal said. "As it turns out, he was the inside man."

"What?" The blood drained from Charlotte's face. "No. I trusted him. He was part of the family. Why would… wait. How long have you known it was him? Did you suspect him from the beginning?"

"No, it only came together this morning. And it was only a suspicion until he confirmed it all when we talked."

That broke Charlotte's tears loose. "He admitted it? Then why the hell didn't you call for help. You should have called the police before you confronted him. Now he's so hurt. He might not ever be able to tell us anything. He could die, and then we'll never find out what happened to Zander. It might already be too late."

Hannibal let her talk until she ran down. When she stopped he said, "Cawfee confronted me, not the other way around. And he did tell me one important thing. Zander is alive."

"But what now?" Frankie asked. Tears welled up in her eyes and her lower lip quivered. "Where's my daddy?"

"I don't know," Hannibal said. "But I'm going to go find him."

Hannibal moved out of the room. He heard the footsteps behind him but kept going. In the kitchen he found Sarge, draining a tall glass of juice.

"Bad times, brother," Sarge said. "You okay?"

Behind him, Hannibal heard Frankie say, "Well of course he's okay, thanks to Gene. Cawfee's the one who's not okay."

Hannibal turned to face her. "I really am sorry about all that. I think I could have handled it without the help, and Gene did go a little overboard. He could have hit Cawfee's arm or just called to him to stop."

"You kidding?" she said. "I'm proud of my man."

"But I know Cawfee was important to you too. He thought of you as a niece."

"Yeah, well I never saw him as my uncle," Frankie said. "He was, what's the word? An artifact. He was an artifact of Daddy's past. He's the past. Gene is the future. In the end, Cawfee moved like a thug. Gene moved like a boss."

Without looking up, Sarge said, "Cawfee ain't past tense yet, girl. And I'm glad he helped Hannibal and all but clubbing a guy from behind ain't moving like a boss."

To Sarge Frankie said, "Whatever." To Hannibal she said, "Find my daddy." Then she turned on her heel and stomped out of the room.

"Spoiled brat," Sarge said. "Sorry, man. I know I'm on the wrong side of that. Cawfee turned out to be a shit, but we kind of connected, you know? Worked out together and talked a bit about how the world works for guys like us."

"Really? Did you get him? Do you get why a guy whose whole life is built on his friend's would do this?"

Sarge nodded. "Maybe I do. Maybe I get how a man can get bitter, sitting so close to the grownup table for so long and only getting the scraps they throw him. Even if they're really great scraps. Jealousy can eat a man alive when he's got nothing of his own. And I know I'm just the hired help but Gene Young ain't no better than Cawfee, he's just dressed better and talks like a college boy."

"I see where you're coming from," Hannibal said. "And you're not just hired help to me. I'm glad I can get a client to put a few hundred in your pocket but that's got nothing to do with you being my friend."

Then, a memory arose unbidden, as they so often do. Hannibal glanced over both shoulders to be sure no one else would hear, then leaned closer to Sarge.

"Tell me something," Hannibal said. "Are you in my posse?"

Sarge's brow furrowed. "Now there's a word I ain't heard in a minute. Am I? I suppose. Maybe. I mean, I hang with you, and you know I'll do whatever to support you. I'll always back your play, brother."

Hannibal closed his eyes and clenched his lips together. He really had no idea.

But then Sarge continued. "But then, I don't know. You're a natural leader, Hannibal. I learned to spot them in the Corps and it's good to have a shot caller around when stuff needs to get done. But I do what I do cause I know you'll back my play, and you'll always be there if I'm ever up against it. I can count on you to have my back and you ain't never let me down. So maybe we are a posse, you, me, Quaker, Virgil and Ray. But I don't know if it's your gang. It's all of ours, right?"

Hannibal smiled. "Yeah, I think you got it, Sarge."

"So, all that said, what you need me to do today?"

Hannibal slapped Sarge on the back. "You're the best, brother. And yeah, I do have an idea for the day. I think Rissik missed a bet on this case. He thinks it's low priority, but I think he might be wrong. So, I want to go check it out and I can use some backup on this one."

CHAPTER 31

The Mercedes Benz Maybach S-Class Sedan was a car Hannibal could get used to. Whoever heard of a car seat that would give you a warm massage? Virginia's two-lane country roads wound beneath him without him feeling a single bump while Peter Gabriel sang about being Big Time. He followed his progress on the map in the oversized display in the center column and thought about how Cawfee came to believe he deserved the life that went along with this car. He also thought about Zander Brown, a man who gave his old friend a damned good life and trusted him so solidly that he never suspected the man might betray him for money.

Hannibal had wasted twenty minutes pushing buttons and flipping switches in that car before he gave up and pulled out the owner's manual. That's how he learned that there was a refrigerator in the back seat, as well as how to work the on-board GPS. He was able to view the last few trips the car had made and set the farmhouse he was held in as his destination.

He had never actually seen the area, having only been to the house at night. He had no idea how beautiful a drive he had missed out on. Vibrant green pines held the fiery maples and sycamores in check. Houses were alternately modest and ostentatious, with the occasional mobile home mixed in for leavening. He wondered if these neighbors ever talked to one another.

The little farmhouse turned out to be white with blue shutters and trim. It was rather cute sitting behind its deep unmown lawn. He was there because he thought he might find some clue to Zander's location. His captors were careless and who knows? A stray note, a message on the phone, a book of matches or a store receipt might give him a trail to follow. He started to turn into the driveway but at the last second, he parked in front of the rustic wooden fence. He had not expected to find a car in the driveway.

It was not a fake Amazon van, or a high-performance sports car, or a four-wheeler like the one that ran Hannibal into a tree. It was a little red Chevy Spark, high on gas mileage, short on leg room. Not a car Fridge would ride in. In fact, it ruled out almost everyone he had met in connection with this case. He had one reasonable guess as to the driver.

Hannibal backed up and pulled into the dirt driveway to park beside the compact. He had no reason to sneak about. He thought he might find some physical evidence in the house but now he just wanted some conversation and with any luck some useful information. He rapped on the front door with a knuckle, then stepped back. He put on his non-threatening face and waited. Twenty long seconds passed before she unlocked the door and opened it a crack.

"Yes?" she said. "Can I help you?"

He knew that voice. When he heard it last she was talking to Fridge. Then she was being brash and grating. This day she sounded soft and polite.

"Good morning," he said. "We haven't met, but I know you. My name is Hannibal Jones, and I'm a private detective. You're in trouble but you don't know it yet. I'm here to help you out of it."

Fear shone in her eyes and her respiration doubled. "You don't know me." She pushed the door, but Hannibal quickly jammed his toe into it.

"Leigh."

She pulled the door back an inch. "How?"

"Is that short for Quinnleigh? It's a pretty name."

Now she pulled the door all the way open. "Who are you?"

He saw her heritage in the high cheekbones and long, straight black hair. And the long legs must have been a family trait.

"I just told you. I'm private, not a cop. You are Quinnleigh Rogers. You've been trying to find your sister Katie."

"You know where Katie is?"

Hannibal smiled and looked left, then right. Leigh got the message, took three steps back and waved him inside. Then her eyes widened and she pulled her phone out of a pocket of her plain yellow frock. She looked at it long enough to identify a caller, then shoved it back into her pocket. After a flash moment of confusion, she marched through the front room to the kitchen. Hannibal closed the door and followed.

He could see the facial and physical resemblance between the sisters. Leigh was attractive too and nature had given her a nicely shaped behind. Sadly, she had received a second butt and this one was on the front. That, and the tiny lines around her eyes made him think she was the older sister. She was worried about Katie in a protective way.

Leigh settled onto a kitchen chair, sipped from a glass on the table and asked, "So what do you know about Katie?"

Hannibal sat facing her. "I know she got involved in a kidnapping. I need to know if you are too. I don't want you to go to jail for such a serious crime."

For a moment Leigh forgot to breathe. She put down her glass and went still. Her eyes darted from side to side. Hannibal waited.

After a few seconds she cleared her throat and managed to say, "I don't know what you're talking about."

"Look, you have information I need. I have the information you need. We can trade."

With a huff Leigh pulled her phone out again, shot the screen a dirty look and slapped it down on the table. "Look, I've got to get going. But you need to tell me where my sister is. I'm afraid she's in trouble."

"First, the kidnapping. I need the victim's location."

Leigh slipped the phone back in her pocket and stood up. "We're done. You don't know nothing. I got to go."

She had reached the door when Hannibal said, "Katie is dead."

She froze, one hand on the doorknob. "Bullshit."

Hannibal stood and walked slowly toward her. "She landed in the morgue day before yesterday. I'm not certain who put her there, but it had to be someone who knew all about the kidnapping plan. If I had to guess, I'd put my money on her girlfriend, the rapper. Do you know her?"

"Kronik." She breathed the name out in a pained whisper.

"Do you know where she is?"

Leigh took three deep breaths as if she was choking back a rush of tears. Then she turned just enough to see Hannibal's face.

"You're lying! Fuck you!"

On the verge of hyperventilating, she yanked the door open and ran out to her car. Hannibal stood in the doorway and watched her start the little car, slam it into gear and race down the long driveway. He pulled out his phone while he walked to his car.

"You got her?"

"On it," Sarge replied. "You guessed the direction right. She shot right past me. It'll be easy to keep her in sight. The hamster under the hood of that little toy car don't have a prayer of pulling away from me."

Hannibal had no doubt of that. She was too rattled to be looking for a tail and even if she was, she'd be looking for Hannibal's black luxury sedan, not Sarge's blue Ford Ranger.

"What did you say to light such a fire under her ass?" Sarge asked. "She's barely keeping that thing on the road."

"It wasn't me," Hannibal said. "She was getting calls or text messages. I think she was summoned. Which is cool with me. Maybe a meeting to discuss next steps. If we get lucky, we just might catch all the fish in the same net."

193

CHAPTER 32

Hannibal had paired his phone to the Mercedes so he could talk hands free. He kept the line open with Sarge, hanging back far enough to rarely catch sight of his friend's truck. Leigh led them on a long, winding path. They never got on a road bigger than Route 7, and even that was only a few minutes. They stayed on what Hannibal thought of as country roads with little traffic. Overcast skies combined with overhanging trees on many of the roads made it feel later than it was. He had no idea where they were but figured they were moving generally westward, deeper into Virginia.

It was an easy afternoon drive, but Hannibal was too keyed up to relax. He felt like Leigh Rogers was a missing piece in his puzzle and finding her pushed him closer to the answers he needed. He never lost focus on his mission. He needed to find Zander Brown, beloved sports star, party lover, hustler's mark, husband, father, betrayed friend. Victim.

His stomach rumbled, reminding him that he had missed lunch. Over the last couple of days his normal eating schedule, and his sleep schedule, had been badly disrupted. He didn't feel as mentally sharp as usual. Plus, some of his spiritual energy was being drained by the effort to ignore a spectrum of new aches. His face and his ribs had absorbed some abuse in the last couple of days. Even his arms ached, mostly from blocking punches from Fridge who, he now admitted to himself, was a whole lot bigger and stronger than he was. Of course, his hands hurt too, from slamming his fists into that walking side of beef. People who have never been in the ring don't understand how much you hurt even when you win.

"We're here H," Sarge said over the phone. "Brick front, two stories on your right. Drive on past and I'm maybe fifty yards on."

Hannibal slowed to pass the house and pulled up behind Sarge. There he was, in sight of another farmhouse in the middle of nowhere. This one was bigger than the last with more land surrounding it, but he was sure its purpose was the same. A safe place for wanted men to hide, far enough from its nearest neighbors that no one would hear you if you were inside screaming your lungs out.

Hannibal got out and walked to Sarge's truck. Sarge rolled down his window.

"I don't suppose you got binoculars in there?" Hannibal asked.

To his surprise, Sarge reached into his glove compartment, pulled out a small pair of field glasses and handed them to him.

"I take these to games to follow the action."

Hannibal thanked him and leaned over the back of the truck to focus on the house or, more specifically, the car in the wide, paved driveway. Leigh sat behind the wheel. Was she waiting for someone? Maybe she was just taking some time to wrap her head around what Hannibal told her. He wasn't sure how much she really knew. News of her sister's death clearly shook her, more than he expected. In the life she was stuck in, a person should always be prepared for surprises.

That applied to Hannibal's life too, but things could still take him by surprise. His jaw dropped open when a little white Mazda MX-5 Miata pulled into the driveway and rolled up beside Leigh's car. Here was one fish he didn't expect to be swimming in this school.

Samantha Tucker climbed out of her car and walked over to the driver's side of Leigh's car. Nelson slipped out of the passenger's seat, stretched and straightened his suit coat. Even his body language gave Hannibal a chill. Some men just give off a vibe, even at a distance, that makes you want to go the other way. Like walking up on a snake in your path. Some you'll step over, others somehow make you give them a wide berth. Nelson was that snake.

Nelson walked past the two girls, snapped his head toward the house and moved on. Leigh hopped out of her car. She and Samantha followed Nelson inside. Hannibal returned to Sarge's window and handed over the glasses.

"Time for the cops?" Sarge asked.

"I don't think so," Hannibal said. "We don't know who's inside, and we have no evidence of a crime. No point tipping our hand to Nelson. Besides, what if this is where they've stashed Zander? If we scare them, they might kill him, or at best we end up with a hostage situation." Hannibal stared at the house wishing for x-ray vision. "Need to know who's in there and what's happening."

Sarge looked out his opposite window, then back at Hannibal. "I known you too long, brother. Please tell me you ain't thinking what I think you thinking."

"I don't see any security," Hannibal said. "That would be conspicuous out here. Its remote location is what makes this place safe. And on that side, there's a blind approach. I can…"

"You can get your ass killed," Sarge said. "You got lucky once doing that."

"And this time should be even easier."

Sarge sighed. "Okay, if you made your mind up, let's do this."

"Hold up," Hannibal said as Sarge popped his door open. "I'll do this alone, okay? I'd feel a lot better if you're out here ready to call in the cavalry if things go sideways. Okay?"

Sarge clenched his fists, huffed, muttered "Okay," and slammed his door shut.

Facing the right front corner of the house Hannibal had no clear view of a window, which meant no one inside would be likely to see him. Still, he moved in a low crouch toward the building. He considered drawing his pistol but thought that might be inviting trouble. This should just be a recon mission.

When he reached the house he turned his back to the bricks and eased toward the back of the house. He stopped when his face was even with the bottom of a window. It was open a couple of inches and sheer curtains were drawn inside. He knew he could see through them. The question was whether he should risk being seen if anyone was in that room. The decision was made for him by the familiar voice, slightly slurred by liquor, that boomed out at him.

"You know you done, right?" Fridge said. "The bell for the last round. The shot clock done run out on your ass."

Hannibal's pulse jumped. Was he talking to Zander Brown? Was the gang about to finish him? If so, was there time to get police there? Could Hannibal burst in with his one pistol and manage a rescue without getting them both killed? He had to know how many were in the room. The newcomers might be in another room. But if someone saw him, his hopes for saving Zander would be over.

Maybe if Sarge drove into the driveway it would be enough of a distraction. If they all turned toward the front of the house he could risk looking inside. Hannibal pulled out his phone to call his friend but before he pushed the button to dial another idea struck him. Maybe he could use his phone a different way.

Hannibal crouched so that he was beneath the window. He held just the top right corner of his phone up over the edge of the windowsill. He tilted the phone downward, just a little, and pushed buttons like he wanted to take a picture. Now his phone was a view finder. He could see the whole room and he was confident no one inside would notice that one square inch of black plastic peeking in.

What he saw turned his fear into relief. Fridge sat in a wooden chair to his right. But Zander was not in the matching chair on his left. That chair was occupied by Veronica Jean Walker, better known by her stage name, Kronik. Thick bands of duct tape held her arms and ankles to the chair. Her expression was defiant, but he could see layers of terror beneath that thin top coat.

She jumped, to the extent her bonds would allow, when Nelson walked into the room. He and the two women behind him were dragging folding chairs. Nelson set his up in front of Kronik, just close enough that if he leaned forward, he could touch her knee. He ignored everyone but Kronik and his focus on her was chilling. The room was silent for ten long seconds. Nelson tilted his head to the side in the universal body language for a lack of understanding.

"Have you lost your mind?" Nelson said. "Did you really think you could get away with betraying me? Me?"

Kronik met his gaze, teeth bared. "I ain't do nothing to you."

Nelson sat back still looking at her like she was some alien animal he had never seen before. "Are you serious right now? Did you really think it was okay to go into business for yourself while you were working as part of my organization? Do you not understand who I am? What we do?"

"What you do?" Kronik said. "Oh, you think you the whole game, huh? You ain't no criminal mastermind, nigga. You a small-time crook, just like the rest of us."

On an impulse Hannibal pulled his phone down and pushed the button to record video. After the phone made its soft ping indicating it was recording, he held it back up. It wouldn't be great video but the audio could be priceless. He willed Nelson to keep talking. The ego of the criminal inside forced him to comply.

"You really don't understand," Nelson said. "I'm not in the game, as you say. I'm the shot clock. I'm above the game. I'm not a criminal. I don't steal, deal drugs or traffic in human vices. Those are all dirty businesses. I am a businessman. I provide criminal service support. Safe hideouts like this one. Clean documents for identity exchanges. Crime scene sanitation when things get messy. And this latest enterprise, in which I partnered with Ira Johnson and Miss Tucker here, this was my greatest achievement. A few used vans painted with a logo that made them all but invisible and I was able to pick up cash from a variety of true criminal enterprises and deliver them to my clubs and Mr. Johnson's bogus business. Money laundering is a valued service."

"Okay so you keep your hands clean," Kronik said. "What's your point?"

"My point," Nelson snapped, leaning forward, "Is that I fly below the law enforcement radar. That is my real talent. I've been very successful at it. That is, until you decided to add kidnapping to your resume."

Hannibal's mind raced. So, Nelson had figured it all out. And, somehow, he had found Kronik who may well be the only remaining member of the kidnapping gang. He knew it could get real ugly in that room real soon. Kronik, however, didn't seem to get it.

"So what?" Kronik asked. "You was making bank and throwing me crumbs. Why shouldn't I get rich too?"

"Moron," Nelson said. His calm demeanor never changed, even when he swung a backhand slap hard across Kronik's face. "Thanks to you, now we are all under the microscope, wanted by the police in connection with an idiot crime we had nothing to do with. Plus, you pulled away the goose from whom Johnson and I were still milking a lot of golden eggs. So, not only did you betray my trust and put everyone on my payroll at risk, but you probably cost me a great deal of money. But even that was not your worst crime, was it?"

Leigh rose from her seat. "That's why I'm going to claw your eyes out, bitch."

Nelson blocked her forward motion with an outstretched arm. "Miss Rogers, I'll need you to sit still and be quiet."

Leigh stared her hatred at Kronik. Nelson focused on Leigh until she finally faced him. Once he had eye contact, he dropped the next four words in a slow, cold whisper. "Sit. Your. Ass. Down."

Leigh looked as if she were being choked. Hannibal was reminded of the scene in Star Wars where Darth Vader casually demonstrates his power, as if Nelson found her lack of faith disturbing. Leigh lowered herself into her seat. Samantha reached over and patted her hand. Nelson returned his attention to Kronik.

"You know her rage is quite justified," Nelson said. "You killed her, didn't you? Slit your own lover's throat. For money."

How could he know that? Hannibal wondered. Was Nelson so well connected he could get into the medical examiner's files?

Kronik's head was down, but she looked up with her eyes. "You wouldn't kill a bitch for a million dollars? This business is about money. It's a cold world. Niggas got to supply their own heat. And the girl was nothing to me."

Leigh screamed from her seat, "You were fucking her! You were fucking my sister!" Then the tears came.

"She fucked me," Kronik shouted back. "When that bitch got caught, she should've just done the time she owed. Instead, she ratted me out. She gave me up. She's the reason I did that time."

"Also part of this business," Nelson said in his still calm tones. "Thieves do time. You were a thief. You were going to be locked up, sooner or later."

"You ain't never been in the joint, have you?" Kronik asked.

Nelson shrugged. "True, I've been to jail, but never prison. And yes, I know the difference. But that's beside the point. You played Katie Rogers, strung her along for months and set her up so you could murder her."

Kronik fell back in the chair and actually smiled. "Yeah. You got to admit it was a good plan. What, you saying it's not fair to use sex to get people to do what you need them to do?"

Leigh started forward but Nelson stopped her with just a raised hand.

"Again, you are missing the point," Nelson said. "She was not simply your lover. She was your business partner. She was an essential part of your scheme. I don't care about the sex. You killed your own partner, a member of your team. A violation of basic thug etiquette. A certain level of honor among thieves is crucial to the system. Behavior like this would drag us all into chaos."

"You one crazy ass crook," Kronik said. "So now what? You gone let the sister beat my ass?"

"Oh, I'm sure you'll be hurt, but not by her," Nelson said, standing. "What happens now is you tell me where you left the million dollars. I recover the funds, I compensate these ladies fairly for their losses and we all disappear."

"I want at least ten percent," Kronik said. "Finder's fee. That's fair."

Nelson bent to press his face close to Kronik's. "This is not a negotiation, although you do have options. You tell me where the money is. Or, Fridge here breaks some things and you tell me where the money is."

Kronik looked up. "My plan. My work. I get a share."

Nelson stood and turned his back on his captive. "Fridge, loosen her tongue, won't you? Ladies, if you'd like to adjourn to the dining room. I don't think you want to watch this."

"The hell I don't," Leigh said.

Nelson shrugged and followed Samantha out the door. Hannibal's arm was starting to ache from holding his camera in the same position so long. He pulled his arm down and pondered his next move. As much as he hated the idea, he had to save Kronik. She was the only person who might know where Zander Brown was.

The sound of a fist slamming into a person's midsection is unmistakable. They never get it right in movies or on television, but a fighter knows that sound.

He heard Kronik say, "Wait." The next sound was knuckles on a face. The chair hit the floor. She wouldn't last long. He slid his gun out of its holster. Nelson might be the only person in the building armed. If he moved fast he might be able to put Fridge down and get Kronik out of there without a long battle.

"Wait," Kronik said again. The sound of wood on wood said the chair was on its legs again. A cry of pain said Fridge had punched her in the gut again. One quick shot in the window would stop the beating. He was in a good, safe position to take Nelson down if he ran into the room. But was he cold blooded enough to shoot a man without warning? Even the man who had sucker-punched him?

"Wait. Stop. I'll tell you." Kronik's words were slurred.

"You better not be bullshitting," Fridge said.

Hannibal imagined her head shaking. He heard heavy steps to the door. Fridge shouted "Yo! Boss." Then lighter steps. The rustle of a dress, a smaller impact, a pained grunt. And again. Leigh getting her licks in. Or more accurately, her kicks in.

Hannibal held his gun, with his back to the wall. He didn't think Kronik would give in so quickly.

Inside, Nelson asked, "So, are we done with this foolish display of bravado?" Silence. Perhaps a head nod. "Good. I'd hate to see your looks sustain any more damage. Now. Where is the money?"

"Back end of my truck," Kronik mumbled. "Black Jeep Renegade." She spit. Probably blood.

"That's good. And where is this vehicle?" Nelson asked.

"Parking lot." Cough. "Pentagon City. Second level."

"Not bad," Nelson said. "Hidden in plain sight. That lot is usually packed, and it's likely no one would notice a vehicle left overnight for days. Fridge, why don't you take Samantha to the Mall and fetch my money."

"Seriously?" Samantha asked. "I got to travel with this ape? Don't you trust me to get a bag of money and bring it back?"

"Darling I love you," Nelson said with a smile in his voice. "But it is a million dollars."

"Won't we need the ticket to drive out of there?" Fridge asked.

"Oh, we don't want the truck. Just the bag. But you will need the key. Which pocket, Kronik?"

Another pause. Hannibal could almost feel Nelson's stare. Then Kronik said, "Around my neck."

"Really?" Nelson said. "Fridge, you may do the honors."

Hannibal heard the rip of fabric. Buttons bounced on the floor. The soft pop of a chain snapped. He realized this act of the play was almost over. Plans had flowed around in his brain until he settled on what sounded the most rational. He holstered his weapon and sprinted for his car, pulling out his phone on the way.

"Sarge! No time to explain but I need you to move your truck and get ready for some serious action."

CHAPTER 33

Samantha Tucker's little white Mazda was perfect for tooling around the narrow, winding roads of Virginia's countryside. This late in the afternoon she couldn't drive too fast even though there was no traffic. When the road twisted westward the sun would stab into her eyes, causing an instant of blindness. Still, she was making good time until she rounded a tight curve just a couple miles down the road and came up on a blue Ford Ranger mostly in the opposing lane but skewed just enough to keep her from passing. She rolled to a stop.

"What the actual hell?" she said. "Do you believe this idiot?"

"He'll move," Fridge said. He popped the door and unfolded out of the car. The other driver climbed out too. Another Black guy, not as big as Fridge but big enough.

"You got a problem?" Fridge asked, approaching. "Get that raggedy thing off the road."

"Stalled out," Sarge said. "Real sorry to hold you up, but if you give me a hand, I think we can push her over to the side."

Fridge stopped to think for a second. No point wasting time arguing.

"Hey Samantha," he called. "Come steer this thing. Me and this guy can push it over to the side so we can get moving."

There was no shoulder, just an earthen bank held together by tree trunks. Samantha pulled over as far as she could without risking a scratch in her car's paint. She got out and walked to the truck, her heels clicking on the asphalt.

Without a word she pulled the driver's door open, hiked up her dress and pulled herself up into the seat.

"Don't just stand there," she said. "I got it in neutral. Get back there and push."

As the truck began to move, Hannibal jogged around the curve, gun drawn. He saw Samantha's eyes widen with recognition. He held the muzzle of his automatic pointed at her face while he drew his right hand across his mouth as if pulling a zipper. The truck's right side wheels slid off the road and she hit the brake.

"Put it in park," Hannibal said.

Fridge stepped from behind the truck. His eyes also widened but Hannibal sensed more anger than surprise.

"What the fuck?" Fridge said.

"I wouldn't mind shooting you," Hannibal said, "but I won't if you just get down on your knees right now."

"Like hell," Fridge spat, stepping forward.

Sarge came up on the bigger man's right, yanking back on Fridge's right arm, spinning him halfway around. Sarge swung a right hook deep into Fridge's stomach. Fridge's legs wobbled and he dropped to his knees. Sarge's left cross spun Fridge's head around and he fell forward, raising a small puff of dust where his chest hit the ground.

"Stay down," Hannibal said, aiming at Fridge's back now. "Sarge, you got something to hold this guy?"

"In the back of the truck," Sarge said. "What about the girl?"

"She won't run far in those heels."

Hannibal stepped back so that he could watch both his captives. Samantha glared at him. He ignored her. He just needed another couple of minutes with no one driving by. He didn't need to explain why he appeared to be abducting two people at gun point.

Sarge dropped a knee into Fridge's back and wrapped a jumper cable around his wrists, tying him tightly. Then he grabbed the back of Fridge's shirt collar and hauled him to his feet.

Fridge muttered, "Cut me loose you son of a…" before Sarge slammed his chest into the side of the truck. Then he crouched, wrapped his arms around Fridge's legs and hefted him up and into the back of the truck. Fridge groaned in pain when his bulk slammed onto the truck bed.

"Okay, Samantha," Hannibal said. "Get out of the truck and go stand at the back of your car."

"Why should I do anything you say?" she asked.

"Two reasons," Hannibal said. "I don't want to shoot you, and you don't want to get shot."

Samantha stepped to the road. "And to think I was ready to give it up to you."

"To be fair, you were drunk," Hannibal said.

"That's when they usually say yes to him," Sarge said with a chuckle, getting into his truck and starting it up.

"You're a riot," Hannibal said. "Now get going. You've got a delivery to make, and our package might get restless."

Sarge threw Hannibal a mock salute and drove off. Hannibal waved Samantha to her car and pulled the driver's door open.

"Get in. You're driving." He kept his pistol pointed at her as he walked around to the passenger side, sat down and strapped in.

"Now start her up," he said. "But leave your seat belt off. If you decide to slam on the brakes or run us into something for some reason, I don't want to be the one thrown into the windshield."

Samantha put her car into gear and pulled onto the road. "So, where we going? I don't get what your game is here." Her lower lip began to quiver. "You one of Nelson's boys? Is he done with me now? Is this where I get beaten and dumped somewhere? Raped and beaten? You know, you don't have to do that part. I can…"

"Stop," Hannibal said. "Just stop. I'm not going to hurt you as long as you do what you're told. Where we're going is back to the house you just left. And no, I'm not one of Nelson's boys. We're in a funny spot here. You don't know how much I know, and I don't know how much you know."

"Wait a minute," Samantha said. "If you're not Nelson's boy, but you stopped me and Fridge on our way out…it's the money, isn't it? You found out about the million dollars. Look, we don't need to go back there. I know where the money is."

"Yes, I know. You were going to fetch that big bag of cash. But you didn't even consider just taking off with it, did you? You were going to bring it all back to Nelson, weren't you?" Hannibal grinned and shook his head. "Of course you were. I get it now. You were never his woman. You're part of his posse. Well, I'll take that car key from you when we stop, but that's not why I'm here. I'm here for Zander Brown."

"Zander." For just a moment, Samantha's eyes became dreamy, her guard dropped, and Hannibal wondered if this was the real woman at last. "Such a sweet man. And a real fan of my work, you know?"

"Yeah, and a family man."

"Yeah, he's married," Samantha said. "But I never tried to take him from her. Just wanted to borrow him now and then."

"You were with him before Nelson?"

Samantha shook her head. "Nelson sent me to him. I had to introduce him to Ira Johnson. It was a hustle. He was such an easy man, so open and giving. I did feel bad about that part."

"And the kidnapping?"

Samantha downshifted and they rolled slowly into the driveway. "I didn't know nothing about that until today." Samantha bristled. "That bitch Kronik. I thought she was my friend. I used to tell her about him, where we went, things we did. Everybody wanted into his money. I never thought…didn't see…never meant for him to get hurt."

They parked beside Leigh's car, the same place as before. She turned to him. Her knitted brow and parted lips said she was sorry. He believed her. His business was digging into people's personal business. One thing it had taught him was that sometimes, good people do bad things.

"Okay, so now we get out of the car. When I walk around behind you, you go to the door and walk in like normal. If all goes well, we can do this smooth and easy and get Zander back from wherever they stuck him."

Samantha stood, squared her shoulders and raised her chin. For a moment she looked like the proud woman in the poster Hannibal found in Zander's apartment. He touched her back with a finger and she walked forward, up onto the porch and tried the door.

"It's locked."

Hannibal reached around her with his free hand and pushed the doorbell. He stepped to the side just enough so only Samantha's face would be visible through the small glass pane in the door. Footsteps approached, flat shoes not pumps. A short pause. Samantha forced a smile. A lock clicked. The door swung in.

"What are you doing here so soon?" Nelson asked.

Hannibal pushed Samantha's back hard, shoving her into Nelson. Before either of them could regain their balance, he was inside, pointing his Sig Sauer at Nelson's forehead, standing just out of reach. Samantha quickly stepped out of the way. Nelson held his hands low but palms forward and away from his body. He was appraising the situation, his eyes on Hannibal, not the gun.

"Don't give me the pleasure," Hannibal said. Nelson relaxed, nodded and smiled. Hannibal returned the smile and said what they both were thinking. "You knew this was eventually going to come down to you and me."

"Yeah," Nelson said. "But it's cool. Game recognizes game."

"We're not the same."

"No, we are not," Nelson said, pointing to the pistol. "You're not a shooter."

"Are you so sure? Think a minute. I intercepted your friends on their way out. I brought the girl back. Do you see Fridge around here?"

That drew a slower nod and a half step back. "Okay, so why are you here now? If you're looking for money…"

"No, I'm here for the girl, Kronik, Got to keep her in one piece so she can take me to Zander Brown."

"No!"

The scream from down the hall turned all three heads. Leigh stood trembling with hate in her eyes and a big kitchen knife in her hand. Hannibal turned and took a step toward her. Nelson grabbed Hannibal's gun hand. Hannibal pumped a hard right into Nelson's ribs and slammed a stamp kick into his solar plexus. That backed him up just enough for Hannibal to swing his gun into the side of Nelson's head and take off. Hannibal was halfway down the hall before Nelson hit the floor.

Hannibal burst into the end room in a dead run. Leigh was kneeling beside the overturned chair with her right arm raised, knife blade glistening. Her left hand was wrapped around Kronik's throat.

"Katie loved you and you cut her throat," Leigh said through a veil of tears. "Die bitch!"

Hannibal did not slow down. His momentum carried him, shoulder first, into Leigh's back. For a moment she lay sprawled across Kronik, still taped to the chair, with Hannibal on top of her. He slid his gun away, across the floor, to grip Leigh's arm with both hands. A hard twist forced her to drop the knife. She squirmed and struggled, screaming in Spanish. He got an arm around her throat and rolled off Kronik.

"Kill her," Kronik said.

"You need to shut the fuck up," Hannibal snarled from beneath Leigh. She was struggling and shouting incoherently. He flipped them over and straddled her. She turned under him and tried to claw his face. He did the only thing he could think of to do. He threw a hard right down into her chin. She lay still. Panting, Hannibal stood and recovered his gun. He stood Kronik's chair back up on its feet. He picked up the knife and returned to the chair.

Kronik, he saw, had had a bad day. Her left breast hung exposed, but modesty was the least of her worries right then. Her left eye was blackened and the whole right side of her face was turning purple. Her swollen lower lip was split, and her chest and previously white blouse were stained with her blood. Maybe this was the earned fate of a heartless murderer, but it still bothered him to see a woman like this. Her tired eyes stared up at him as if wondering what else he could do to her.

"Tell me you know where Zander Brown is," Hannibal said.

Kronik nodded.

"Then you need to take me there." He used the knife on the bands of duct tape and slid an arm under hers to pull her to her feet. She moaned but managed to stand. He felt her left side and she flinched. Two or three cracked ribs. He knew what that felt like.

"I can walk on my own," Kronik said, pulling away. She moved out of the room with Hannibal behind her, ready with gun and knife. In the front room Nelson was nowhere to be seen. Well, even when you get all the fish into one net, you can't always haul them all into the boat. Samantha, standing by the door, gasped when she saw Kronik. Kronik looked up, her attitude back in place.

"You happy?" Kronik asked.

Samantha pointed with a shaky hand. "You did a bad thing, girl. You are evil. But, God. No one deserves this."

Hannibal looked at the spot on the floor where Nelson landed, then up at Samantha. "Left you behind, eh?"

"He got up, heard the noise back there and just took off," Samantha said. "Didn't say a word."

"What a guy," Hannibal said. "Trust me, you don't want to be here alone when Leigh wakes up. She's kind of in a bad mood. How about you just drive us to my car."

"Wait," Samantha said as Hannibal opened the door. "I don't care what she done, she can't go out like that."

Samantha ran back into the house and returned in a few seconds clutching a brown knit pullover. "I knew Leigh and Katie had stayed here from time to time. Figured they'd leave a change of clothes."

While Hannibal watched the hall, gun still drawn, Samantha stepped into the bathroom and ran water in the sink. She came back with a small towel, wet but rung out. While Kronik stood silent, Samantha got her out of the remains of her torn blouse and began to wipe the blood off her chest and neck. When he saw that Kronik wore no bra and was fully exposed, Hannibal averted his eyes. Samantha noticed him and turned Kronik's back to him. Her moans of pain clenched his stomach. When they eased he watched Samantha wiping Kronik's face tenderly, like a mother cleaning her child's scraped knee. Sharp intakes of breath made it clear that Kronik was doing her best to be stoic, but it must have hurt like hell.

She gave a louder groan when Samantha prompted her to raise her arms, but she managed to get the sweater over her head and her arms in the sleeves. When it was all over, Kronik whispered "Thank you," almost too low to hear. Hannibal tapped Samantha's shoulder.

"Why?" he asked.

"She was my girl," Samantha said. "She looked out for me." Hannibal recalled the phone call he intercepted in Samantha's house. Kronik did try to look out for her, in her own way. He wondered how he would react if a close friend did something so very wrong. He prayed he would never find out.

"Time to go," Hannibal said, ushering them out the door. He dropped the knife on the porch, holstered his pistol, and helped Kronik into the tiny back seat of Samantha's car. Once he was inside they headed down the driveway and back out onto the road with Samantha at the wheel and Hannibal sitting beside her. He kept one eye on her and used the rearview mirror to check on Kronik.

As they drew away from the farmhouse he thought of Quinnleigh Rogers. She would awaken in the big farmhouse alone. She had arrived at this place, and probably this place in her life, thanks to Nelson. Now she would awaken with no man, no car, no sister, no revenge. Thug life is hard, even on the women.

Staring straight out the windshield, Samantha said, "I only did it for the money," as if it was the middle of an ongoing conversation. It was an internal discussion which Hannibal decided not to join.

When they pulled up behind Hannibal's borrowed car Samantha didn't move. He got out and eased Kronik out of the car. They moved slowly to the Mercedes and he lowered her into the back seat again so she could put her feet up, but with her head at the passenger side. She was hurt but he didn't want her directly behind him. Then he went back to talk to Samantha. She rolled her window down and held out her hand.

"Here. You ought to have this." She dropped a car key into his hand. "There's a million dollars in the back."

"I know," Hannibal said. "Thank you."

"What do I do now?"

"You've got options," Hannibal said. "The cleanest is probably to go to the county police and turn yourself in. I don't know all of what your part was in the dealings of Nelson and Johnson, but if you turn state's evidence, they'll probably go pretty easy on you."

"I never wanted to hurt anyone. I was just trying to make it."

"Sounds like the start of a good song," Hannibal said. Every possible way to end that conversation was awkward so Hannibal just turned and got into his car.

213

CHAPTER 34

Kronik was slumped against the door, working at breathing. She didn't move when Hannibal pushed the button to start the car and pulled away from the shoulder, still thinking about Samantha. Sometimes, in his business, you had to be hard with decent people who had gone astray. He glanced at Kronik thinking that sometimes you had to be easy with bad people, broken people who thought the righteous path was for suckers. Kronik was waiting, he figured, to learn what's next. She was at the mercy of the universe now, and just needed to know what current she would have to float with. He'd give her a clue.

"You okay?"

"Hurt like hell, everywhere," she said, "but I think I'm done bleeding and nothing's broken that won't heal. I'm breathing so…"

"I think you might owe me your life," he said.

"Probably," she said. "So far at least. What did you do with Fridge?"

"He's breathing too. But thanks for the reminder." Hannibal laid his phone on his lap, set it to speaker, hit a speed dial and waited for a response.

"Go for Rissik."

"Orson," Hannibal said, "Sorry to use your cell phone for official business but, you got a minute for some good news?"

"Could use some. What you got?"

"In a couple minutes you're going to get a delivery," Hannibal said. "A guy's going to be dumped in your parking lot, tied up with jumper cables. He won't be able to tell you who dropped him, and you don't want to know. But anyway, this is a guy you been looking for. Goes by Fridge."

"And I don't want to know who's bringing him here." Rissik said. "I'm going to guess that's because I might have to take action about the way he was brought in."

"You're a smart fellow," Hannibal said. "But wait. There's more. Remember that farmhouse I told you I got dragged to?'

"The place where this Fridge character worked you over?"

"Yeah, that's the place," Hannibal said. "If you hustle your butt over there you'll probably find one Quinnleigh Rogers, sister of Katerina Rogers of Wilmette, Illinois. If she's not there she's probably walking out cause she's got no wheels. I think she knows a lot about Nelson's operations and might be willing to share some of that info."

"And Nelson?"

Hannibal sighed. "Afraid he's in the wind. But between them, I bet Fridge and Leigh Rogers can tell you just about everywhere he might go."

"Not a bad day's work. What do you do for an encore?"

"I'll let you know later but, keep your phone on, okay?

"Twenty-four seven," Rissik said. "Later." That was Rissik for goodbye.

After Hannibal disconnected the call Kronik said, "Good."

Hannibal glanced at her and managed a smile. "That should keep all your former partners too busy to be looking for you, so, like I said…"

"Yeah, I guess you saved my life."

"So now the question is, what do we do with you?" Hannibal said. He was driving into the sun which was dipping low. He kept on, keeping to the smaller roads, staying at the speed limit, rolling generally north.

"You could turn me loose and give me an hour's head start," Kronik said.

"You'd have to repay that level of kindness."

"And I can. I can take you to a bag full of money. A million dollars. All for you if you let me go."

Hannibal chuckled. "Nice try. First of all, I already know where the cash is stashed, and I've got the key to your truck. But besides that, the money isn't what this is all about. You really don't know why I saved you, do you? You're going to take me to Zander Brown. He is still alive, right?"

Hannibal asked the question with a straight face, but he was holding his breath until she answered.

"For sure. We kept him breathing," Kronik said. "Cawfee wasn't about to let anything happen to his BFF. He worshiped that nigga." She shook her head.

"Yeah, I guess you and he had kind of different ideas about friendship. Did you really slit your girlfriend's throat?"

"Damn, you know it all, don't you?" Kronik adjusted her shoulder harness to ease the pressure on her ribs. "Look, that bitch cost me seven years of my life. There ain't no getting that time back. So yeah, I played her until I found a way she could be useful, at least give me partial payback."

"I guess it all fell together for you when you met Cawfee. How did you two get together?"

"He was doing a little DJ work on the side, just to keep his hand in," Kronik said. "I think it made him feel like his own man, you know? Well, he did a gig with me at the Indigo, and when we got to talking about his life, it was like I could see my future laid out."

Hannibal was in a residential area now. He stopped at a red light and turned to her.

"Cawfee and Zander go back a long ways. How the hell did you get him to turn on his friend?"

Kronik smiled, the sharp intake of breath told him how much that hurt. "Listen, that nigga was sprung for real. He would have stabbed his own mother for me. Besides, I showed him how he could get out from under being his friend's slave."

"And you could get away from Nelson."

"The thing with Nelson was just a side hustle," she said. "He had a sweet thing going there, money laundering. They'd pool the money at places like Samantha's and that fake warehouse and I was kind of his eyes and ears at the Indigo, one of the places they washed it through. But I was ready to hop. Me and my man, with a cool million, in Barbados or somewhere."

Hannibal found himself on Route 7. They were losing daylight, but he had to play this woman just right. And the tone of her last comment surprised him.

"You care about Cawfee"

After a pause, she said, "Yeah… yeah I do. I was waiting for him at the Indigo when Nelson and Fridge came and scooped me up. I don't know how Nelson figured out what we was doing but he is one smart nigga."

Hannibal was silent for a moment. "Too bad about Cawfee. He was…delayed."

Kronik turned toward him, wincing as the belt yanked on her ribs. "You know what happened to him? Where is he? Did that bastard Nelson kill him?"

Hannibal gave it five seconds, then asked, "Where is Zander Brown?"

Kronik slumped back against the seat. She stared out her side window, examining her options. It was all the currency she had, and he knew she'd hate to spend it all in one place. Had he guessed right about how much Cawfee mattered to her?

It was quieter in that car than in anything Hannibal had ever ridden in. As darkness crept up on them it was exaggerated by the tinted windows. Was she watching the scenery go past or looking at her own reflection in the window glass?

"You're going the wrong way," she said in the same tone she might have used to say, "fuck off and die." He let her hate wash over him and waited. She turned to face him again. That was tantamount to admitting defeat. After a sigh she said, "He's in a house out on Lake Manassas. Couple of Zander's new friends live there but they on vacation in the Bahamas. We figured we'd only need it for a couple days."

"Address?"

She gave it to him, and he punched buttons on the dashboard console to get the GPS going. He was about forty-five minutes away if traffic was nice to him. Then he pulled out his phone. Better for the police to break into someone's house than for him to. He pushed the speed dial for Rissik, then cut the connection before it was made. Rissik was a good man, but he was Fairfax County. The house Zander was stashed in had a Nokesville address. That meant Prince William County. Rissik would have to wade through the inter-agency BS and how-do-you-know and why-didn't-you-call-the-FBI and who's-getting-the-credit-for-this and so on.

Zander was closer to his home than Hannibal was to Zander right then. That reminded him of his real responsibilities. He really should at least let Zander's wife know he was alive. In fact, that might be the best move to get police to him. The victim's wife might be able to get the local police into action faster than a competing department looking for cooperation. Feeling Kronik's eyes on him, he pushed another button on his phone. While it rang, he said, "Cawfee's alive." That should hold her for a minute.

"Brown residence."

Hannibal had called the landline, so he expected a female voice to answer, Charlotte or Frankie if they were near a phone, or the housekeeper if they were not. This voice was a surprise.

"Young?"

"Yes. Is that you Jones?"

"That's right," Hannibal said. "Is Charlotte nearby?"

"Took a pill and went up to bed early. Frankie's with her. Is there any news?"

"Yes," Hannibal said. "I've confirmed Zander Brown's location. And I have every reason to believe he's alive."

"Wow, that's great," Young said. "Charlotte will want to hear this herself. I'll go wake her up."

"Hang on, before you do that," Hannibal said. "I don't know what kind of condition he's in, so we might want to hold off on the celebration. What I need you to do is call the Prince William County Police and get them moving to the house. If he needs first aid or an ambulance, they can expedite that. I'm heading there now but they should be able to get there a lot faster."

"Okay, give me the address. I'll call the police, and then I'll head that way myself."

Hannibal repeated the address, said goodbye and took the next turn prescribed by the GPS. He cursed the evening traffic that was beginning to fill the road. He totally focused on driving, wishing he had brought his I-Pod. The right music always made the drive feel faster.

"So where is he?' Kronik asked.

"Who?"

"Cawfee," she said, louder than he expected. "You said he's alive. Do the cops have him? Did he…did he mention me?"

"I rather doubt it," Hannibal said. "Right now I believe he's in the Reston Hospital Center."

"What? How'd he get there? Is he okay?"

"He's not okay." Hannibal swerved around a car going just five miles an hour over the limit. "He's in a coma. Another friend of Zander's whacked him upside the head with a golf club while he was trying to stab me."

Kronik again slumped against the door, arms crossed. "Well, I guess Zander's in better shape than my Cawfee is right now."

CHAPTER 35

From the air Lake Manassas looks as if it was designed for maximum income production. Instead of a natural circular shape, the lake is a shapeless blob with uncounted inlets and peninsulas around its wooded edges. Therefore, it offers an overabundance of lakefront property, which one might think would be perfect locations for expensive mini mansions, each with its own pier where the wealthy would dock their big, showy watercraft.

In fact, Lake Manassas is a man-made reservoir. Since 1970 it has provided drinking water for area residents. There is a marina on the lake, but it is closed. Based on fear of terrorists or invasive marine species contaminating the water, the city government passed an ordinance outlawing recreational use. No swimming or boating is allowed, even with a canoe or kayak. To enforce this ordinance, police boats patrol the lake all day long. It would seem that law enforcement officers are the only people who get to have any fun on the lake.

Still, it was a very nice suburban area. Kronik pointed Hannibal past two different golf courses, then through a housing development of what he guessed were fifteen-year-old, two-story homes with token yards and barely walking space between them. Wedged between the golf courses and the lake, they probably sold for a million dollars these days. Then she guided him back up onto Lee Highway.

"Do you know where you're going?" Hannibal asked.

"Got turned around," Kronik said. "I only been there twice."

That kicked off a new line of thought. "Well I know Cawfee hasn't had much freedom of movement since you snatched Zander. You took Katie out. So could be nobody's been out here for a couple days. Who else knows where he is?"

"Nobody but me," she said.

"So nobody's checking on him. You sure he's even still there?"

"He's there," Kronik said. "Unless he could Houdini himself out of those cuffs and leg irons."

"You kidding me?" Hannibal said. "He's chained up? How does he eat? Get to the bathroom?"

"Don't look at me," Kronik said. "If his wife had just done as she was told he'd have been home yesterday and I'd be in San Tropez or somewhere doing shots with Cawfee. Hey, turn off here."

Hannibal took the turn, his right arm quivering with frustration. He could not remember ever feeling the need to punch a woman in the face before. Whatever his faults, Nelson had the right idea this time. She had earned everything Fridge had given her, and a good deal more.

They rolled down a narrow lane, bordered by trees on one side and open ground on the other. A farm of some type. It was too dark to tell now, and the people who lived here didn't feel the need for streetlamps. She motioned him to slow down but now he wanted to hurry.

"Right here!" she blurted, and Hannibal slammed the brakes just past a road he would have never seen if she hadn't called out. She grunted and cursed as she snapped forward against the restraining belt. Hannibal didn't feel bad about that.

He backed up and turned slowly onto the side road. It was just wide enough for two cars if both drivers were very careful. Hannibal realized this wasn't an actual road but rather a long private driveway. What felt like an endless drive into an abyss at ten miles an hour was probably closer to two hundred yards. He could smell the lake when they turned into a loop and stopped in front of a darkened house. It was one level, but long and rambling, like parts had been added after the original construction. A row of bushes stood in front of the porch on either side of the steps. In the moonlight he could see that this was not one of the standardized development homes they passed before. This was a building left from the 1940s or 50s, long before the Lake was dug. Sitting so close to the lake he could hear the water lapping on the shore. It was surrounded by woods, private, almost isolated. It probably wasn't worth half of what the tract houses would go for, but Hannibal would live here.

Then his head snapped up and he looked around. Why were they alone?

"Something wrong?" Kronik asked.

"Yeah. Where are the police? They should have been here long before us."

"Well I ain't in no hurry to see no cops," Kronik said.

He should wait for them. They would be here soon. Would another few minutes really make any difference? He imagined himself chained in a darkened house for an entire week. Thirsty. Hungry. Sitting in his own filth. Yes, every minute mattered. His door was open before he knew he was going to get out of the car.

"Where is he in the house?"

"Basement," Kronik said.

"How do you get in?"

"Through the door," Kronik said. Hannibal jerked back into the car, pushing his face very close to hers, one fist gripping the front of her sweater. For the briefest instant he saw fear cross her eyes.

"Okay," she said, panting. "One of the rocks in front of the hedges is hollow. There's a key under it."

After a deep breath to regain control, Hannibal pulled back and stood outside the car. Before he closed the door he said, "You stay here."

"Where I'm gonna go?"

He slammed the door and went to the house. The second rock he turned over concealed the key. He unlocked the door, stepped inside and flipped the light switch by the door. The house was neither cluttered nor sparse, but it was clean. Furnishings were contemporary but not fancy. It looked comfortable. He liked these people already and hated that their home had been invaded and co-opted for such an evil purpose.

Across the living room he opened the door that led down the stairs. Again, he turned on the lights and stepped down. The basement was fully finished and the size of the original house. They'd put in a wet bar right near the stairs on his right, bright recessed lighting in the ceiling and beige shag carpet. The wall he faced held a door, probably out to the back yard, and a big screen TV. There were a couple of small tables, each accompanied by two or three chairs. Movie posters decorated the walls. They partied in here. Two support posts stood near the wall with the television. The post at the far end of the room was the horrific end of his quest.

A tall black man sat with his back to the post. His arms were handcuffed behind it. His head slumped forward. The dark stain around the crotch of his pants told a story, as did empty water bottles and the wrappers of energy bars scattered carelessly around the floor. Someone must have held water bottles to his mouth, and held bars for him to bite, but would not release him even to eat. How long since the last drink? Hannibal's horror eased when he saw the man's chest rise and fall with labored breathing.

"Zander?"

No response. Hannibal rushed over to the man, lifting his head. It was indeed Zander Brown. After studying his photo for a week it felt like finding an old friend.

The man's eyes opened. They were glazed over as he tried to focus on Hannibal.

"You're new," Zander said.

"Not one of them," Hannibal said. "I'm here to get you out."

Zander nodded and tried to croak out another word, but nothing came out.

"Hang on," Hannibal said. "You could use some water."

He raced back to the wet bar. The refrigerator behind the bar was half full of water bottles. He grabbed two and closed the refrigerator door with a foot.

Zander watched him returning. He seemed to be looking through Hannibal or maybe past him. He almost managed a smile, but then his eyes went wide in what appeared to be a look of surprise.

Hannibal was halfway back to Zander with the water when the lights went out. Hannibal dropped the bottle in his left hand and reached for his pistol. He had it out and pointed in the general direction of the stairs when something hard cracked against the left side of his head. He staggered right, his shoulder hitting the wall, fighting to cling to consciousness. He heard the whoosh just before the impact on the other side of his head. He dropped to his knees and tried once more to raise his gun before his attacker's weapon crashed into the back of his skull and the darkness became even blacker.

CHAPTER 36

"Jones! Jones are you okay?"

The sound of surf against a beach pounded in Hannibal's head. No, the water sound was soft. His head was pounding all on its own. He was lying on something hard, damp and crinkly, something that smelled sweet, the way new growth or decay can smell. He forced his eyes open. In the darkness he could see just enough to discern nearby trees. He was lying on a bed of grass and leaves. The water he heard was maybe fifty feet ahead. Then a cone of light wrapped him, and his head exploded with pain.

"You okay? You scared the hell out of me." That was Young's voice, coming from behind the light.

"I'm alive," Hannibal said. "Want to get that light out of my face?"

"Sorry." Young turned his flashlight away.

Hannibal pushed to his hands and knees and bit back a wave of nausea. He reached up with his left hand to check for blood on his head. No dampness but then the vertigo hit, and he nearly pitched forward before he got both hands on the ground again. He focused on a point on the ground to fight off the disorientation. He recognized this feeling, which he knew in and of itself was a bad thing. You only get so many concussions before you start talking like an old boxer.

One more sound, tires on pavement, drew him back into the moment. His head jerked up and his last few conscious minutes came flooding back. He started to stand, and Young took his arm, helping him to his feet. He checked his watch, realizing then that it wouldn't tell him what he wanted to know.

"How long was I out?" Hannibal asked.

"Don't know," Young said. "I just got here, a couple minutes ahead of the police."

Hannibal turned to see the back of the house, about as far away as the water now behind him. Someone must have dragged him out the back door and dumped him here in the yard. If Young just arrived and the cars he heard pulling up were the police, then whoever knocked him out must have taken him outside. Was his attacker hidden inside? Why move Hannibal?

"Zander!" Hannibal said, so loud it made Young snap back. Hannibal darted for the door into the basement and ran down the cement stairs. He charged through the door, eyes probing the darkness. He found a wall switch and turned on the overhead lights again.

He felt ice roll down his spine. Zander was still there, in the same place, head still slumped forward. His features were obscured by the white plastic bag pulled over his head. And his chest was not moving.

Five long steps, and Hannibal's knees thumped on the floor beside the seated man. He yanked the bag away and checked for a pulse. He couldn't lay Zander down to administer CPR. It was too late anyway. There was nothing Hannibal could do to bring Zander Brown back. Eyes clenched tight, he slammed his fists into the floor. He was as helpless as Zander had been. Half-starved and dehydrated, chained to a pole, Zander couldn't have had much fight in him. When that plastic bag was pulled over his head he couldn't fight. He couldn't move away. He couldn't scream. All he could do was die.

"The police are out front." Young was standing behind Hannibal. He rested a hand on Hannibal's shoulder. "We should go up and let them in, eh?"

Hannibal nodded and stood. It wasn't his first dead body, but this one hit him hard. "How much did you tell them? I don't feel like talking much."

"When I called, I told them they could contact Detective Rissik in Fairfax County for details about the case. I hope that was okay."

Hannibal nodded. "Let's get them down here. No need for them to break the door down. Besides, I have a prisoner to hand over to them, outside."

"Where?" Young asked, climbing the stairs behind Hannibal.

"In the car," Hannibal said, stepping out into the living room.

"What car?" Young asked. "I didn't see a car. I was wondering how you got here."

"What?" Hannibal snatched the front door open. Four uniformed cops and one in plain clothes were gathered around the door. The uniforms had guns drawn. Hannibal and Young quickly backed into the room, hands raised. Young sounded terrified when he spoke.

"Please don't shoot. I'm Gene Young. I'm the man who called you here. This is Hannibal Jones, the detective who's been looking for Mr. Brown. We found him. He's downstairs. I'm afraid we were too late."

The uniformed officers filed downstairs. The fifth man was beefy with jowls like a droopy hound dog. He pulled out a notebook and pen. Hannibal pushed his palms toward the detective.

"Hold on a second." He slid past the man to run down the stairs, looking around in front of the house. Then he reached into his pocket, feeling for the car key fob that, like the car, was not where it should be. His shoulders dropped. He stared up at the stars looking for answers, but the stars were silent. The fault, he remembered, is not in our stars, but in ourselves.

"Sir?" the detective said behind him. "Detective Sanderson, Prince William County Police. You are Hannibal Jones, correct? Did you know the deceased?"

Hannibal shook his head. "Working for his family."

"I see. Well, be assured that we're going to do everything we can to get to the bottom of all this. Can you just tell me what happened?"

"What happened?" Hannibal said, his back to the man. "Sure. I failed. He died. She got away."

After a moment the detective asked, "Sir, do you need a minute?"

"Yeah," Hannibal said. "I guess I do. Go see to your crime scene. I'm not going anywhere."

What happened. Hannibal wanted to know too. Standing there in the darkness he forced his mind to gather the pieces of information he had and force them into a pattern. The most obvious option was that Kronik had lied to him. There was one more person who knew where Zander was. He must have been hidden in the house. He had let her walk him into a trap. He was usually better at reading people, but she had fooled him. The mystery man knocked him out, dragged him out of the way, returned to the basement and did what kidnappers do. He got rid of the only witness.

His phone rang. Probably Cindy, or Sarge, or worse, Charlotte Brown calling to ask how Zander was doing. That should be a face-to-face conversation. But he couldn't just ignore them. He clenched his eyes, pulled out his phone and hit the button.

"Yes."

"Where are you racing off to?" Rissik asked.

Orson Rissik? That threw Hannibal completely off balance. "What? What are you…?"

"You just zoomed past me," Rissik said. "Did you think I didn't catch the plate number of that fancy car you're driving?"

"Orson! Oh my God. Orson, I'm not driving. Turn around."

"Oh, hell, I'd never catch them now," Orson said. "Who's got your car?"

"The kidnappers," Hannibal said. "Probably the last two. They took my keys. Where are you?"

"On my way to Nokesville. Is that where you are? I got a call from the Prince William boys that they were about to close my kidnapping case. Or that you were. Figured I'd come down and congratulate you. Hell of a job."

Something twisted in Hannibal's gut. "The picture's not nearly that pretty. But you can at least catch the kidnappers if you can run down that car."

"Okay," Rissik said. "I'll put out a BOLO and see if we can't pull a net around the Mercedes before they get too far. If they don't know we're looking for them they won't be trying to be evasive, just going for speed. I'll let you know when we got them."

Rissik hung up before Hannibal could say more. He was silently grateful that his friend had not asked any more questions. It was obvious that things had gone sideways, and he knew Hannibal would not want to talk about it now.

He turned to find Sanderson staring at him. The porch light was on. At one end of the porch, two policemen were listening to Young who spoke in an animated manner. Hannibal knew the detective would want to take him to the other end of the porch. There was no way around it. Like a boy heading in to get a whipping from his mother, Hannibal trudged back to the porch.

CHAPTER 37

A crime scene team arrived just as Hannibal reached the porch. They exchanged a few words with Sanderson, then filed through the door to take pictures and collect whatever forensics they might find. Hannibal ached to follow them, but that wasn't his role that night. He wasn't an investigator right then, just a witness. For the next thirty minutes the man who was the detective on scene asked questions and Hannibal answered as fully as he could. There would be no privacy for the family now. With Zander dead it would all come out.

His questioning was interrupted when the EMS team arrived. Again, there was talk with Sanderson before Hannibal watched the stretcher being rolled through the door. The interview was interrupted again minutes later when they came out. Everyone lapsed into silence as they watched the stretcher pass. The black bag was zipped closed, but Hannibal could still feel Zander Brown's eyes on him, not so much accusing as questioning. Where were you? Why weren't you paying attention? How could you let some dude sneak up on you like that?

Hannibal didn't say another word until the ambulance had disappeared into the distance. Then he answered every question the detective had for him. After being assured that there might be more questions and being asked not to leave the area he stepped down and headed for Young who was leaning back against his car. His interview didn't take as long, but then, he hadn't found the dead man.

"I would imagine this is as bad as a day gets for you," Young said. "Thought you could use a ride."

Hannibal nodded and got into the passenger seat. Young got in and drove carefully around the police cars to get them on the open road headed north and east. Like many professionals inside or near the Beltway, Young's radio was tuned to NPR twenty-four seven. Hannibal thought news radio was an unbroken story of bad things people do or bad things that happen to people. He wondered how long it would be before he heard his name flow out of those speakers.

"Hey Gene, thanks for coming out."

"Had to brother," Young said. "Headed out right after I talked to the police."

"So you didn't say anything to Charlotte or Frankie?"

Young signaled left and went through the intersection before answering. "Honestly, I didn't want them to get excited too soon. At the time I was just afraid Zander might be in bad shape. Or maybe the kidnappers would move him before you got there. I didn't think…"

Hannibal let that lie for a few seconds, then asked, "Have you called them since you got to the house?"

"No," Young replied. "I mean, what would I tell them? I didn't figure it was up to me to drop this kind of bad news."

No, Hannibal thought. That hateful job belongs to me. And it's not one that should be handled over the phone.

The car knifed through the darkness, hopping from streetlight to streetlight, its two occupants lost in their own private thoughts. Hannibal tried to compose a sane message to give to Zander's widow and daughter. His stomach clenched at the thought of delivering this news. There was no way around it, but he needed to hear a friendly voice. He would call Cindy. She could absorb the bad news and be discreet until he got there. She would understand his pain as she always did.

He pulled out his phone but before he could push a number it rang. This time he looked at the display. It was Rissik again.

"Hey, Orson. What news?"

"Good news I think," Rissik said. "Are you still at the house?"

"No, I got a ride. Headed toward the Browns' house. Seen their car?"

"Actually, one of my boys spotted the car you borrowed running like a bat out of hell up 66. He turned on lights and siren and it became a high-speed chase."

Hannibal sat up straighter. "He catch them?"

"Not quite yet, but we're tightening the net. They've dodged the roadblocks so far, but we've got them turned around. Headed back your way."

"Really?" Hannibal said. "Where?"

There was a pause, and some garbled chatter Hannibal didn't get. He glanced to the side to see Young staring at him. Hannibal put a palm toward him, asking him to wait a minute. Then Rissik came back on.

"They're headed south on Route 15."

Hannibal slapped Young's arm. "Where are we?"

"Who's that?" Young asked.

"It's Rissik. Where are we?"

"What's going on?" Young asked.

Hannibal put his phone on speaker, then gripped Young's sleeve. "They might be headed this way, the two kidnappers. Now damn it, where the hell are we?"

Young leaned right to be closer to the phone. Clearly, he wanted to be involved in the conversation. "Right now we're headed north on Lee Highway, just past the Stonewall Shops. There's a big Dick's there. You know, Sporting Goods."

"Route 15 merges with Lee Highway up ahead," Rissik said. "Well, not ahead for you. You're past the intersection. But I'm following the cars following your car. I'll let you know when we make the collar."

Rissik hung up before Hannibal said, "Like hell." Then to Young he snapped. "Turn around."

"What? Should we be getting involved with police business."

"This is my business," Hannibal said in a low, threatening voice. "Now turn this thing around."

Lee Highway is a divided road. A couple tense minutes passed before they came to an intersection where Young could make the left to turn onto the road heading west. That returned them to the intersection they passed while talking to Rissik. The light was red and Young stopped. There was not a car in sight on the crossroad.

"Run the light," Hannibal said.

"What? I can't…"

"Run the light, damn it!"

Young eased forward just as the light changed. As they approached the next light Hannibal saw three police cars turn onto the road from the right, lights flashing and sirens blaring. One more car, smaller than the others, followed them. This one had lights but no siren. That had to be Rissik and he was pulling away from them.

"Stay with him," Hannibal said. "He's after the pack that's chasing my stolen car."

"Look," Young said. "It's a Lexus not a Maserati. It's built for comfort, not for speed."

"Bullshit!" Hannibal pressed his foot down on top of Young's and the car leaped forward, snapping Young's head back.

"Quit that!" Young screamed, eyes widened in terror.

"Then keep up."

Hannibal was surprised by how little traffic they encountered. They did pass a few cars on the side of the road, pulled over to clear the way for the police. He and Young flowed in the slip stream behind the chase cars. Hannibal wished he was driving but at least Young was keeping Rissik's car in sight. He knew the driver they were chasing was desperate. He was facing kidnapping and murder charges. How far would he run before he realized there was no escape? Hannibal would at least be able to tell Zander's family that the killer had been brought to justice. It wouldn't make them whole, but it was something.

The driver leading the pack wasn't turning off on any of the side roads. He seemed determined to stay on the highway, as if the Mercedes could outrun the supercharged police cars. He was probably driving on pure emotion, not thinking much. Eventually he'd hit traffic or a roadblock he couldn't dodge. It was already over, and if Young could keep up with Rissik's car Hannibal would be on site to see the cuffs go on.

For five minutes Hannibal leaned forward, his whole body tense, his mind fully into the chase. Then Young slowed but was still closing on the car he was chasing. The smaller car pulled onto an exit ramp and rolled onto the shoulder. Young followed and parked behind it, took a deep breath and dropped his head onto the steering wheel. Hannibal jumped out of the car and ran to the front car. Rissik stepped out to meet him.

"They stopped him?" Hannibal asked.

"And good evening to you," Rissik said.

"Sorry. Hi. They stopped him?"

"He stopped himself," Rissik said. "Let's walk up and take a look."

There were plenty of overhead lights and more from the three cop cars. Hannibal forced himself to open his aperture a bit to take in the whole scene. Lee Highway and Routes 15 and 17 meet in an ugly mass of on ramps, off ramps and cloverleaves. Beyond that on Lee Highway you came into a busy commercial zone of Warrenton with businesses lining both sides of the highway. Even at night there would be ample traffic there to turn the high-speed chase into a crawl. So the felons had pulled off onto Route 17 but Hannibal saw only police cars on the long straightaway.

"Over here," Rissik called, waving Hannibal farther up the shoulder.

Four uniformed officers stood at the edge of a narrow dirt road branching off from the asphalt. The road began with a steep but short drop-off. Moonglow revealed that about twenty feet ahead the road took another sharp right turn. The second curve had been too much for the driver and the car had rolled. Hannibal's borrowed Mercedes lay on its side in the grass maybe fifteen feet past the edge of the road. The woods were pretty dense there. The underside of the car rested against a stand of trees.

The rolling car must have disturbed the local insects because the scene held an eerie quiet. Rissik signaled the uniforms to precede him and they marched forward, weapons drawn and aimed at the car. Rissik scanned it with his flashlight. The cone of light zeroed in on the open sunroof. Rissik pointed with his hand and the officers moved to flank the car, two to their left, the others to the right. Rissik marched right up the middle, squatted and waved his light around the inside of the car.

"Unconscious?" Hannibal asked. "Or dead?"

Rissik stood, shaking his head. "Gone. The boys let them get out."

"Sorry, sir," one of the cops said. "We didn't think we should rush down here in case there was a fire or something. Besides, who gets up and walks away after something like this?"

Rissik sighed. "Cars don't burst into flames after a crash, except in movies. They just crumple. And people pumped with adrenaline can keep moving under some pretty extreme circumstances. You lost the suspects. Don't lose the lesson." Then he carefully scanned the woods in all direction. When he finished, he turned to Hannibal and raised an eyebrow.

"Nope," Hannibal said. "No signs they broke through the trees. Down this dirt road, then. Won't get too far. One of them was hurt pretty bad before the crash."

Rissik nodded and waved his men forward. They moved slowly down the trail that was barely wide enough for a car, with the trees moving closer as they went. The night insects were back to full volume. After a few steps Rissik drew his weapon, so Hannibal did too. The two of them walked side by side a few feet behind Rissik's men, moving from telephone pole to pole.

"I was on the phone with a Detective Sanderson in the car," Rissik said. "He pretty much brought me up to speed. You found him, huh?"

"Yeah," Hannibal said. "Badly treated but still breathing when I got there. Not now."

"Not your fault," Rissik said. "You know that, right?" Hannibal's response was silence. Rissik gave it a few seconds, then said, "Okay, tell me about this person you had locked in your car. You don't get to detain prisoners, you know."

"Actually, I rescued her," Hannibal said. "She had the ransom money and Nelson wanted it. Did you get a look at this guy they call Fridge?"

"You mean the thug I found mysteriously dumped in the parking lot outside my office?" Rissik asked. "Of course, I don't know who illegally detained and transported that guy. But for the record, you do know we've got cameras covering that whole parking area, right?"

Hannibal suppressed a laugh. "I appreciate your momentary blindness. That guy put a serious hurting on the woman in question. I got her loose. In return she directed me to where they were holding Zander. I thought she was making a play for leniency until somebody knocked me out."

"You sure it wasn't her?"

More and more grass and weeds showed in the center of the road. At first Hannibal thought it was an access road for people who wanted to avoid the highway. Now it looked as if it was cleared to give access to the telephone poles and no one ever came this far.

"I don't think this woman could muscle me out the door and halfway across the back yard. Definitely not in the shape she was in with a couple of cracked ribs. No, this was a man. He tossed me outside, took my car keys, murdered Zander Brown, jumped in my whip and took off. Pure luck they happened to drive past you. Otherwise, they'd be a couple state away by now."

The road petered out to a foot trail, and it was easy to see someone had broken through recently. They all pushed forward, between trees that grabbed at their clothes and limbs like the angry forest in The Wizard of Oz. He was happy to have cops for trail blazers and really hoped their quarry wasn't smart enough to lay in wait and start shooting when they got close. It was a lot darker and a bit claustrophobic on this trail.

After a couple hundred feet they broke into a clearing. Now the moon highlighted them, and Hannibal was feeling like a target. He knew he wasn't the only one on edge as they reoriented to the changed environment. A low, L-shaped building stood at the other end of the clearing. Two white dishes stood guard in front of it, facing different directions. They were tipped upward about forty-five degrees as if they were scanning the skies for alien invaders.

Rissik asked, "What do you think? Radio studio maybe?"

"Sure," Hannibal said. "A little a.m. station. Jazz or gospel programming. Guess we check it out."

The men relaxed as they approached the building that looked much like a private home from the outside. As they got closer Hannibal realized he was looking at the back of the building. He could see a real road beyond it. The paved road went right up to the front of the house.

"Dollars to donuts our runners hit that road and took off," Rissik said.

"May as well see if there's anybody home," Hannibal said. "They might have seen something."

"Or our killers could be holed up inside waiting for us. Why don't you head around front with the boys? I'll check it out."

"Come on, man," Hannibal said, one hand on the backdoor knob. "If you're right, they're probably down the road. If not, it's safer for me to lead. Kronik knows me, knows I saved her life. She won't let her partner shoot me. But most likely nobody's in here. Or if there is it's just a DJ."

"And if that DJ sees an intruder and pulls up a shotgun? What are you going to do? Show him your badge?" When Hannibal had no quick answer, Rissik said, "Together."

Hannibal shrugged and twisted the knob. The unlocked door opened inward. Taking Rissik's point about being seen as an intruder, he holstered his weapon. He entered a dark hallway and found a light switch on the wall. Mentally flipping a coin, he moved off to his left with Rissik following. The door at the end of the hall had a red lightbulb mounted above it, but the light was not on. This would be the broadcast studio and the light would be lit when someone was live on the air. Hannibal pushed inside, took two steps and froze.

A white-haired woman looked at him over half lens reading glasses. She was wide enough for Kronik to hide behind her. It didn't matter where Kronik had gotten the big kitchen knife, he just wished she wasn't holding it against the other woman's throat. Despite the fear on the hostage's face, the woman was still and unnaturally calm. Hannibal lowered his hands, palm forward.

"Kronik. Veronica Jean. You don't want to do this."

Kronik's face went from anger to stunned surprise. It must have been a long time since she heard her real name. "You don't know me. You don't know shit about me. But you my ticket out of here. At least, if you want this bitch to live."

The knife twitched and the white-haired woman gasped. Hannibal asked, "What are you doing? I can't get you out of here. The building is surrounded by police."

"I don't care. You getting me out."

The room was silent except for Kronik's labored breathing–a cracked rib was probably poking into a lung– and the very low-level sound of impassioned speech leaking from headphones lying on the sound board where the older woman had been sitting. Hannibal could hear just enough to confirm this was a gospel station. He dropped his shoulders.

"What are you doing, girl? There's no win for you here. There's only surrender and begging the mercy of a court. Hurting this poor woman won't do anything good for you. You're done. It's over."

They locked eyes and just for a moment Hannibal saw a wistful softness there. Then the hardness returned. He recognized it. He had seen it in the mirror. She tensed and her chin came up.

"You think I got no options? No, nigga. I choose."

Kronik shoved the other woman to the side, crashing her into the control panel. With a growl of rage she raised the knife and rushed forward. Hannibal had time to take one step back before he felt Rissik's arm stretched around his right side. The two shots sounded flat and dull in the small, soundproofed room. One hole at center mass, the other a couple inches to the left and higher. Then her body crumbled like a marionette with its strings cut. Her head thumped onto the carpet an inch in front of Hannibal's shoes, and he was staring down at the exit wounds, so much bigger and uglier than the tiny holes in her chest.

It felt cold in there. Hannibal said, "She didn't want to kill me."

Behind him, Rissik said, "No, but she would have. What she wanted was to end her story on her terms."

CHAPTER 38

The Prince William County crime scene technicians must have been getting some serious overtime. They had worked the scene of Zander Brown's death and now here they were at the overturned black Mercedes-Maybach sedan. Four huge spotlights set up around the vehicle created artificial daylight within a small circle.

Before this, they had worked the broadcast control room in the radio studio that was not far if you walked through the woods but turned out to be a pretty long drive from the crash. They had bagged the knife Kronik snatched from the studio building's kitchen, collected Rissik's brass and bullets and marked their locations. They had photographed the room from every conceivable angle and confirmed Hannibal's and Rissik's positions at the moment of the shooting. They had collected Rissik's service weapon. Two detectives neither Hannibal nor Rissik knew took statements from them both, and from the woman who called herself an announcer rather than a disc jockey. She was sure that poor black woman would not have hurt her. The Lord protected her. And she would pray for the woman's soul.

At the car they followed the routine that Hannibal was so familiar with. First, photographs of everything, inside and out. Close-up flashlight searches for hairs and fibers. Dusting for prints, a little tricky in the dark with one man holding a flashlight while the other worked. The only thing Hannibal saw them take out of the car was the key fob. About ten minutes into the process Hannibal's head jerked around, pulled by Gene Young's voice.

"Holy shit!"

Young stood ten feet behind the lights, staring at the car. Hannibal walked back to him.

"Is that Zander's car?"

"Yep," Hannibal said.

"It looks dead."

"I imagine it's totaled," Hannibal said. "Tried to take the curve too fast."

"And the driver?"

"Hard to say," Hannibal replied. "No corpses in the car. The girl I had in the car ran a ways, and ended up committing suicide by cop. My unknown assailant is in the wind. Those guys are looking for clues now. I figure this guy's probably been in trouble in the past, so maybe fingerprints or some other forensic magic will point us to him."

Young put a hand on Hannibal's shoulder. "This all must be pretty rough. But I don't think there's much more you can do here, and I'm kind of tired. How about we go back to the house and let Charlotte and Frankie know what's happened. They deserve to know. These cops aren't what you'd call tight-lipped. This will all probably be on the news by noon tomorrow."

They started back up the dirt road, but Rissik caught up to them just as they reached the pavement. He tugged Hannibal's arm, then slid his hands into his pockets.

"Listen, you want me to come along? You know a law enforcement official is going to have to deliver the news to the family. It's me or one of the Price William fellows."

Hannibal smiled his thanks. "I appreciate you, Orson. I really do. But this is for me to do. If we get moving, I can give it to them easy before the official notification. Okay?"

Rissik nodded. Hannibal followed Young back to his car and soon they were motoring back down Lee Highway at fifty-five miles per hour. Neither man had anything to say. Both stared straight ahead out the windshield. Hannibal spent the time silently rehearsing what he was about to do. He knew the words, he just wasn't sure how to deliver them.

As Young drove through the gate the house loomed in front of them. Hannibal considered how much bigger and emptier it would feel now. Young parked in the smaller garage just left of the house and they walked back to the front door together. Inside Hannibal found Sarge and Cindy in the sitting room. Cindy stood when she saw him. Sarge just looked up expectantly. Hannibal shook his head. Cindy rushed into his arms, hugging him tightly, feeling his tension, maybe feeling his pain. After a long moment he pushed her out to arms' length.

"Please go wake up Charlotte and Frankie," Hannibal said. "Need to talk to them now. We'll do it right here, where it all started."

Hannibal took one of the chairs and stared down into the rug until he was sure everyone was assembled. Charlotte, Frankie and Young resumed their familiar positions on the sofa, the two women in matching silk pajamas. Sarge chose to stand behind the other chair rather than sit as long as Cindy was standing. She was beside Hannibal, a hand on his shoulder. Silence wrapped the room like a shroud until Hannibal couldn't stand the tension anymore.

"Police won't be far behind me, so we probably don't have a lot of time," Hannibal said, finding Charlottes eyes with his own and holding them. "I'm sure you've already guessed I have bad news. I'm afraid Zander Brown is gone."

Charlotte let out one loud howl, her body shook, and tears flowed freely. She hugged Frankie to her until the daughter needed to free herself to get a breath. Charlotte covered her face with her hands. Frankie was able to speak through her tears.

"Were you there?" Frankie asked. "Did you see it? Can you tell us what happened?"

Hannibal took a deep breath. "I found Zander in a house in Nokesville Virginia, less than an hour from here. He was bound but had not been beaten or physically abused.

Someone knocked me out and when I came to, Zander Brown was…the man who hit me murdered him."

Shock moved Frankie closer to anger than grief. "What the hell? Why weren't there any police there? Didn't you call them?"

"I did," Young said, gathering one of Frankie's hands in both of his own. "Hannibal called me, and I called the authorities. Sometimes things just take too long."

Hannibal was prepared for more questions, but Young raised a hand, signaling that a moment of quiet might be best. Then he looked into Frankie's eyes, then Charlotte's, and turned to Hannibal once more.

"If I may, I think the ladies need some time to get their arms around their grief. It's late, we're all tired, and there will be much to do and many decisions to deal with tomorrow. How about we all retire for the night? We appreciate the help you and your team have offered, but perhaps you can leave in the morning, yes?"

Charlotte smiled on Young as she would on a son and Frankie squeezed his hand harder. Hannibal opened his mouth to speak, but Cindy stepped in front of him, turning to stop him with a raised palm, then turned back to the family.

"I don't think you understand," she said. "Law enforcement officials will be here soon to officially notify you of Zander's death. Zander's murder."

"Oh, no," Charlotte said. "I really can't. I'm so tired. Can't it wait until morning?"

"This is not an optional exercise," Cindy said. "If you really were asleep, they would simply wake you. You need to hear me. These people are not coming to offer condolences. They are now launching a murder investigation. And they're not going to be gentle, or kind. They will be watching you very closely. They'll be disappointed that you already know Zander is dead, but they will still want to see your reaction."

"What? Why would they be watching me?" Charlotte turned to her daughter.

"Because, Mama, you're a suspect," Frankie said. She stared at her mother and for a brief moment they seemed to exchange positions, the daughter sounding like a mother talking to her child. "Whenever a man dies the police see his wife as suspect number one. I guess most of the time they're right."

"Well, I guess. As long as Hannibal is here."

"No," Cindy said. "Hannibal shouldn't be in the room. They'd fear him polluting your testimony. In fact, I'm going to need all the men to clear the room."

"But…but…I'm not sure I can deal with this alone."

"Don't worry. You'll have your daughter for support, and it will be good for you to have an attorney in the room. That would be me, if you agree."

"Oh, yes," Charlotte said. "Yes. Thank you."

Cindy gave Hannibal an expectant look. He nodded and stood, said, "Let's go, fellas," and led the way out. "We'll be on our way in the morning." They all followed except Young. He shook his head, but Cindy fixed him with a hard stare and did not move until he finally sighed, stood and left.

In the guest room Hannibal showered longer than usual and once he was dry, slipped into bed. He was exhausted but sleep was elusive. Lying in the dark he pictured the scene below, a scene he had witnessed in person more than once. Detectives would waste little time on "sorry for your loss" before going into interrogation mode, asking all the questions Hannibal didn't ask at the start of this case when they all thought Zander might have been playing someplace and simply lost track of time. They'd make Charlotte and Frankie repeat things, re-examine the timeline since Friday, question their not knowing where Zander went when he went out. Cindy would annoy the cops, protecting the Browns from saying anything that might incriminate one of them.

He dozed in that twilight space where reality was foggy, but dreams stood off at arm's length. After what felt like hours, he heard the door open, and Cindy slipped into the room. She pulled the curtain, allowing just enough moonlight inside to let her navigate. He heard the rustle of clothing, watched her move in silhouette. More time passed, and then she lifted the covers and slipped in beside him. She wore the red nightgown she knew was his favorite but that night it had no effect on him. He sat back against two pillows and stared at the foot of the bed. Cindy snuggled up under his arm and also looked down, as if she was trying to see what he saw.

"You're trying to put this on yourself, aren't you?" she asked.

"No effort involved, babe." He kissed her forehead. "I missed something. Let my guard down at exactly the wrong time. Let a man come up on me from behind. That's why Zander is dead."

"No," she patted his thigh. "He's dead because evil, greedy men prey on good people."

"Men and women."

"True enough in this case," Cindy said. "But that's not your fault. That's just the way it is. Honey, you worked this case as hard as any you've had. You've hardly had any sleep in a week. You've been beaten, threatened, shot at and damn near stabbed. And for what? If they were going to kill him, they'd have killed him whether you found the house or not. If not for you he'd have lain there for who knows how long until the house owners came home. And thanks to you we know who the kidnappers were."

"Not all of them," Hannibal said.

"Maybe," Cindy said, "but they didn't get away with the money, did they? Two are dead and one's in the hospital. That's got to count for something."

"You are persuasive, counselor. But none of that changes the fact that a woman lost her husband, and a daughter lost her father, and I was there. I was right there."

Cindy took a deep breath. "I know you're hurting, honey. Maybe it will all look different in the morning."

Hannibal hugged her tight, wishing he believed that.

CHAPTER 39

Hannibal dressed in silence, slipped out of the room and jogged down the curved staircase. He paused at the door to verify that no one else was moving in the house. In the pre-dawn stillness, he heard what sounded like crowd noise, but very low. Then it rewound. He followed the sound to the big entertainment room and looked inside. An area filled the giant screen, fans cheering at a basketball game. Zander Brown moving across the court with an animal power and grace Hannibal would not have guessed. This was what moved so many people. Zander navigated around five moving human barriers, seeing where they were going and consistently being somewhere else until he was close enough to take flight and slam the ball down into the hoop.

Frankie sat on the big couch, alone in her white terry bathrobe. Her eyes were riveted on the screen while she worked the remote control. He realized that this was all she had left of her father, amateur video that she may have shot herself. He should leave her alone with him, with her grief. But then she raised her free hand and, without moving her head, waved him inside. Shouldering his guilt, Hannibal quietly moved in and sat beside her.

"He was so damned good," she said. "He said he was born to play this game. But he always told me it wasn't just about talent. He said it was about finding out what your talent was, and then working like hell to get better." Her face was dry, but Hannibal figured that was just because the reservoir was dry. He turned to the screen and tried to see what she saw.

After a moment of silence Frankie smiled and said, "So smooth. There! Right there! Did you see that?"

He had missed something important. Again. He looked at Frankie. Her smile was genuine as she rewound the video and started it again.

"There," she said, pausing at the right moment. "See how he's reaching around, pulling that other player off balance. And he's looking the other way, almost as if he didn't know he was doing it. So smooth."

"That should have been a foul," Hannibal said.

"Right! But the refs were distracted. He's watching the ball across court, but he managed that. He used to say basketball is a game of subtle felonies. It's about what you can get away with when nobody's watching."

"I see," Hannibal said. "It's not just about making shots. It's about the set up. Keeping your opponents off balance. And misdirection. Like a magic trick."

"Exactly. And he was good," Frankie said, turning to Hannibal. "That's how he could go out of here, go drinking, entertain other women, but at the same time, take care of the home, handle his business and keep Mama happy. I know he was a player. But he was so damned good at it."

"I think," Hannibal said, "I think he did the very best he could for you. He wasn't perfect, but he did his best."

She nodded. "Just like you did." She gave him a hug, then turned back to the screen. Hannibal nodded, stood, and turned to go. She had returned to her private time with her father. He thought about his own father, killed in Vietnam in the last days of the war before Hannibal could really know him. He envied her for the video.

A moment later he was on the front steps, staring up at an unforgiving moon. The sun was just staring over the tops of the tall trees, but the moon was unwilling to surrender the sky. Not yet. Too bad. Sometimes, no matter how hard you try, you just can't hang on.

Hannibal sat on the cold front steps and pulled out his phone. Nobody was in their office at 6:30 in the morning. Nobody normal is that dedicated to getting things done.

Certainly, no civil servant or government employee. Hannibal pushed the button and heard it ring twice.

"Go for Rissik."

"Good morning, Chief," Hannibal said. "Did you get any sleep?"

"The usual. You?"

"Not so much," Hannibal said.

"Well, I experience failure more often, so I'm used to it. What's on your mind?"

"Wanted to hear some good news," Hannibal said. "Did you ever get that bag of money?"

Rissik's smile came through the phone. "Oh, yeah, and brother, you did me a serious solid there. Not saying it's a time to celebrate, but the good news is all there. I mean, first I got this repeat offender who calls himself Fridge. Handed him off to get processed and he was already singing, looking for a plea deal. Then I hopped in my car and took a detail over to the Pentagon City parking garage. Guess who showed up just a few minutes later. Your friend Nelson. I watched him break into the Jeep and pop the trunk. Let him pull the bag out of the back before we moved in on him. That felt damn good."

"Well, that is good news,"

"Yeah, but that's not the end of it," Rissik said. "While I was there, I got a call that a singer named Samantha Tucker turned herself in, and she had the goods on Nelson and the grifter Ira Johnson. Oh, and another unit picked up Quinnleigh Rogers, on foot about a mile from the house you were held in. I owe you, buddy,"

The moon had disappeared, the sun was flexing its muscles and birds got busy with their daily chorus. The serenity level just felt unfair.

"That's all good," Hannibal said, "But nothing that will cheer up the Browns. Anything off the rolled car?"

"Sorry, man. The techs did their job well and sent reports to me as soon as they finished, but there was nothing to indicate anybody being in that vehicle but Kronik and you."

Hannibal shook his head. "What about the real crime scene? The basement where…"

"Just went through that report too. And again, a big fat goose egg. This guy that hit you and did the murder, he was way more of a pro than the known gang members. No hairs, no fibers, no prints after we screened out yours, Young's and the owners. Glad you're all on file but that just allowed us to hurry to the sad conclusion."

Hannibal stared at the wall of shrubs past the driveway. Something was hiding from him, not in the bushes but in his head.

"Well, I guess I should be happy you were on the road when you were, on your way to the crime scene. If the local boys hadn't made that courtesy call to you about Zander's location, Kronik might have gotten clean away."

"Yep, and honestly, I was thinking my workday was done when I got that call," Rissik said. "A lot happened in that hour or so between your call and theirs."

"Wait. An hour? Are you sure?"

"Well, I can check on my cell. Hang on a sec."

A fox poked its nose out of the hedges, looked around and scooted across the lawn into the woods. The puzzle pieces Hannibal had been pushing around in his mind for a week settled into a new pattern. While he waited Hannibal checked his own phone. He looked through his calls, moving backward, focused on the last few calls to and from Rissik. There was his call to Young. And there was his previous call to Rissik. He had driven around with Kronik for twenty-two minutes in between.

"Hannibal? Yeah, I'm looking at it now. Actually, the call from Prince William County came in an hour and seven minutes after I talked to you. See? Got a lot done in a little time."

Hannibal sat back, took a deep breath and let it out very slowly. His empty hand curled into a fist, and he slammed it down on the brick steps once, twice, a third time. He needed another breath to speak to Rissik calmly.

"Listen, Orson, I'm going to need you to check one more thing. But after that phone call I'll need you to come out here one more time. We need to end this."

CHAPTER 40

Hannibal had moved a chair to sit beneath the huge flat screen in the big lounge room. Sarge stood beside the door, arms crossed. Virgil, Ray and Quaker sat on one end of the big, L-shaped sofa. Charlotte was at the other end, legs straight out on the chaise lounge. Beside her, Frankie and Young sat, more focused on each other than Hannibal. Across the room, Cindy fidgeted in the recliner beside the short end of the sofa.

When Rissik walked in he looked around, nodded solemnly, and took the easy chair off the longer end of the sofa. Hannibal interlaced his fingers and looked down at them resting on his thighs. When he looked up he focused only on Charlotte Brown.

"My friends and I will be out of your life in an hour, but before we left, I wanted you to know exactly what has happened, how it all went down, and most importantly, how your husband died."

Charlotte returned his gaze, her eyes red from a night of crying but her face surprisingly passive. "Yes. I'm ready."

"To start, Monday morning when you called me Zander Brown had already been kidnapped. We just didn't know it. I was pursuing a missing person who may have run off on his own or been hurt in an accident. I tried to get a close look at his life outside his home, but as it turned out my tour guide was one of the kidnappers. Now he's comatose at Reston Hospital Center. It may give you some small comfort to know that the two women involved in planning and executing Zander's kidnapping are dead. I actually saved one of them from a beating and she's the one who led me to

Zander. Drove her there with me. But she later decided to commit suicide by cop. I was on the scene one way or another when three people died this week. Only one of those deaths was planned.

"So, they have all paid a price," Young said, "Except for the man who actually killed Zander." He turned to Rissik. "Are you on his trail?"

Rissik's face was passive.

Hannibal answered. "We will bring that murderer to justice. But first I want you all to know that Zander was a victim before the kidnapping. He was being hustled by a grifter who was siphoning off hundreds of thousands of dollars. He's in custody now too. And I want it to be clear that Zander's death was not due to poor police work or my lack of diligence. It was due to a blind spot I had, beginning with Cawfee. Had we been able to question him, I believe we could have saved Zander. He would have given us Zander's location, probably that same afternoon while the police were here."

Young's head snapped back in indignation. "Hold on. You're not going to put this on me. Maybe you don't remember how that all went down but let me remind you that I saved your life. Cawfee was going to stab you."

"Maybe," Hannibal said. "I might not have been able to beat Cawfee, but I'd have taken those odds. But that's not the point, is it? When you saw me wrestling with Cawfee he was on top of me, and you were behind us. No way you could have seen the knife he was pushing down at me."

Young looked around for support. He got it from Frankie, squeezing his hand. "He's being crazy. You did see it, right?"

Hannibal continued. "Most people, seeing two men in a fight, would have shouted. But I didn't hear, 'Stop' or 'let him go.' And even if your reflex was to grab a club and move quietly up on us, you could have swung that club into his arm to make him drop the knife. Hell, you could have just kicked him off me for that matter. But no. You took a real golf swing only instead of a little white ball you aimed for his temple. You tried to kill him."

Young stared at Hannibal in disbelief. "What? Cawfee and I were friends. Why would I want to kill him?"

Hannibal looked down, shaking his head. "I've been thinking about that a lot for the last couple of hours. My blind spot. You and Cawfee weren't friends. You were both part of Zander's posse but more rivals than partners, competing to be top dog in that little club of Zander's followers."

"Okay, that's wack," Frankie said, coming to her man's defense. "Cawfee was down on me and Gene getting together but it wasn't like he hated him."

"Oh, I didn't say Cawfee hated Young," Hannibal said. "They had too much in common. Both jealous of the man they served, despite all he'd done for them. Both seeking a lazy path to a better life. Both driven by greed."

"Fuck you," Young said, standing up. "You're just a gun for hire yourself. And none of that is a reason to try to kill a man."

"Sit your ass down," Hannibal said, getting to his feet. "The reason is simple. Crazy but simple. You knew Cawfee could lead us to Zander. Zander wasn't crazy about you marrying his little girl. It might have taken you months, years to close the deal. But if we never found him, well then, Frankie's ready to tie that knot right now. And since you handle all the finances, I'm sure you're looking at total control of that huge trust fund."

"Actually, Gene Young is the executor of that trust," Rissik said. "Not to mention what turns out to be a ten-million-dollar life insurance policy."

"Yep," Hannibal said. "Mister Young gets his hands on a whole lot of money right away, once he marries Frankie and a whole lot more now that Zander's gone for good."

Charlotte turned to her daughter. "Honestly, honey, you didn't seem too sure about this marriage until this week. Maybe…"

"No!" Frankie said. Then to Hannibal, "This is bullshit. Why are you doing this?"

"And anyway, I didn't kill Cawfee," Young said. "And I don't care about what happened to a bunch of kidnappers and criminals. You need to stop trying to distract us from the point. This is about you failing to save Zander. You and the police. You was all too late."

Hannibal took two slow steps toward Young, who was pointing a finger at him. "I told you to sit back down."

Young backed away from Hannibal's icy stare, looked around the room again for support, and slowly lowered into the sofa.

Hannibal turned to Frankie and his eyes softened. "Before I do this, I want to answer a question you asked me a couple days ago. You see, life, like basketball, is a game of subtle felonies. We show our dark side when we commit those felonies while the world is looking the other way. You can tell the bad guys by the size of the felonies they try to slip past the judges." Then he turned back to Young. "Now, let's talk about those cops being late. Those lazy, unresponsive, country cops, right? Give me your phone."

"What?" Young stared up, trying to look tough. "No. I'm not giving you my…"

Hannibal interrupted him with a slap across his face that turned his head and rattled his brain. Hannibal pulled Young's jacket open, snatched the phone out of his inside jacket pocket and tossed it to Rissik.

"Give me that back you…"

Hannibal leaned in until his nose nearly touched Young's and his voice dropped to a guttural growl. "If you say one more word before I tell you to talk, I will slap the taste right out of your mouth." Then he turned to Rissik. "Chief? Do you see the recent calls?"

Rissik looked back at Hannibal with a half-smile. "Jones, are you unfamiliar with the term illegal search and seizure? I can't look in this man's phone." Then he handed the phone off to Virgil. "But I am curious."

Virgil pushed buttons and looked up. "It's locked."

"Password?" Hannibal asked, cocking his arm back to deliver a backhand slap.

"You don't have to do that," Frankie said. "It's his thumbprint." Hannibal smiled and grabbed Young's right arm. He squeezed Young's forearm and his hand opened. Virgil leaned over and pressed the phone against the upraised thumb. Then he sat back and nodded that he had the phone open. Hannibal pulled out his own phone and handed it to Virgil.

"Okay, Virgil, in Young's phone do you see a call to the Prince William County police?" Virgil nodded.

"So what?" Young asked. "You know I called them."

"Yeah," Hannibal said, looking at Frankie instead of Young. "But why from your cell phone? When I called you and told you to send the police you answered on the landline here. I mean, you already had the phone in your hand. So, Virgil. Look in my phone. Do you see my call to this house?"

"Got it," Virgil replied in his low, slow, Eeyore voice.

"Okay. How much time between me talking to Young here and him talking to the police?"

Virgil's brow knit, then one eyebrow rose. "Hmph. I make it forty-two minutes between calls."

"Forty-two minutes," Hannibal repeated. "Why wait so long to call?"

Frankie frowned. She turned to look at Young, then slid a few inches away from him, sudden doubt in her eyes. "Yeah, why so long? You knew where Daddy was. You knew he could be in danger."

"Let me give it a try," Hannibal said, pacing in front of the sofa. "Gene, you can stop me when I go wrong. All alone in the parlor, he was thinking about that trust fund. I've learned enough about Zander to know that he loved his little girl and wanted the best for her. I'm betting he already told Gene he wasn't the right guy. Maybe that he was too smooth, but one way or another, that he wasn't man enough to handle Frankie. Am I right?"

Young's eyes blazed at Hannibal, a burst of hate energy that Hannibal brushed off and ignored.

"But you know, persistence and persuasion are the very essence of Gene's business and his success," Hannibal said. "He knew he would close the deal eventually, so he hung in. Then Zander disappeared. He knew if Zander never came home, eventually could be much, much sooner. Even if Cawfee woke up, he'd go to jail. Young would be the only man Charlotte or Frankie trusted and he handled all the finances. Plus there was that life insurance policy. He'd handle the proceeds. It must have seemed like fate had handed him a golden opportunity that he just couldn't waste."

"This can't be real," Charlotte said at last. "Gene please tell me he's got it wrong. You went to try to save Zander."

Hannibal shook his head. "Your boy jumped in his whip and raced to the address I gave him. But he didn't call the County police until he was almost there. He was probably a little bummed when he saw I beat him to the house but no biggie. He saw the car and I'm sure the woman inside, one of the kidnappers remember? I'm sure she was happy to tell Young I was inside with Zander. That was the moment. That's when he got brave."

Frankie looked at Gene, her face constricted with pain. "You went in to help him, right?"

"He went in all right," Hannibal said. "But first I'll bet he grabbed the tire iron from his trunk, or maybe he had his golf clubs in there. He's got a mean swing."

"Don't listen to him," Young said, turning again to Frankie. "I told you I got there after Zander was dead."

"Seriously?" Hannibal asked, staring Young down. "You saying you arrived at some stranger's darkened house, there's no car, nobody in sight, and you just ran inside? You assumed the door was open, that no bad guys were inside, and just went in looking for Zander on your own. And then you found him, dead, tied to a pole, and you didn't even pull the bag off his head? Good luck getting a jury to buy that story."

Charlotte sat upright and softly muttered, "Bag off his head?"

Hannibal regretted his outburst, but he couldn't pull his words back. "I'm sorry, Charlotte, but yes. When I went back inside There was a plastic bag, like a small trash bag, pulled over his head. If he hadn't been so weak from thirst and hunger, no one could have killed him that way, but as it was..."

Young's eyes wandered wildly now from Hannibal to Rissik to Frankie. "Wait. I never said I went inside first. I found you first."

"What?" Now Frankie stared at him in disbelief. "You got to the house where you knew Daddy was, and instead of going inside you walked around to the backyard? In the dark? For what? What the hell were you looking for?"

"Wait," Young said. "You don't understand."

"Yeah we do," Hannibal said, backing away. "You ran in there, knocked me out, and dragged me outside. Then went back in the house and suffocated your friend while he was helpless. Now I get why he didn't look scared when he saw somebody behind me, just surprised. And I get why you were quick to feed me the idea of another kidnapper. That was after you gave Kronik my keys and told her she was going down for murder if she got caught. That's why she lit out like a bat out of hell. And now I get why she chose death over getting arrested. She thought she was facing the death penalty and if that was the deal, she wanted to go out on her own terms, to literally go down fighting."

Hannibal closed his eyes for just a second to shake that ugly image out of this mind. Then he stared at Young again. "What I don't get is how you could kill a man who was your biggest client and helped you build your business. Why do it when, in a couple years you'd have probably been a member of his family. Why?"

Young sprang to his feet and for a brief moment his face betrayed him. It was just a second of hate, frustration and rage, as if a literal spirit of evil had possessed him.

"You got no idea what it's like," Young said to Hannibal as if they were in the room alone. "What it's like to cater to men with huge fortunes they don't deserve, to work your ass off for a tiny sliver of what you earn for them. To have a woman who held it all out to you but kept it just out of reach. Fate gave me a shot and I rolled the dice."

Then the demon released him, and he seemed to remember his entire audience. Hannibal wanted badly to break this murderous asshole's jaw, but he held it in. Young must have seen Hannibal's urge in his face because he turned to scan the others in the room. Sarge, Virgil, Quaker, and Ray all had fire in their eyes but none of them moved. Rissik's face was impassive as he slowly stood and pulled handcuffs from the back of his waistband.

"I figure this is where I say you're under arrest for the murder of Alexander Brown and advise you that you have the right to remain silent."

Rissik stopped as Frankie stood up, shaking with fury, fists held at her sides. Her breathing was fast and deep. When she finally found words, they were steel hard and razor sharp.

"You …little…BITCH!"

As it turned out, Frankie had a respectable right cross. Her one vicious swing was enough to not just spin Young's head but to drop him to the floor. She stood over him, like Ali had over Foreman so many years ago. When Young sat up blood dribbled from his mouth. Rissik knelt behind him, pulling his hands together.

"Too bad you tripped and fell on your face like that," he said. "Oh, and anything you say can and will be used against you in a court of law."

Frankie spun slowly, like a boat set adrift in a strong current. Her mother had screamed and fallen into Cindy's arms. She was sobbing while Cindy patted her back and whispered something in her ear. Frankie looked at Hannibal. He nodded. She rushed into his arms and began to dampen his shoulder with her tears.

CHAPTER 41

An hour crawled past. Rissik was long gone with his prisoner. Everyone was packed up. Hannibal's friends were outside waiting. Hannibal and Cindy sat in the kitchen, hands locked together on the island. The case was over, but the wound was still fresh.

"You did as much as anyone could," Cindy said.

"They did nothing to deserve this," Hannibal said. "Zander had his faults but nothing that earned him a painful death. I should have seen more, sooner. And now they have no one. All the men in their lives are gone, everyone they trusted."

"They're not helpless," Cindy said. "They are strong, intelligent women with bottomless money and now a razor-sharp eye for con men or cheats. They'll make out."

A deep breath. "They came to me for help."

From the doorway came, "It ain't on you." Frankie walked in and stood a foot away from them, looking at Hannibal but every few seconds, shifting her gaze to Cindy.

"You the best thing that's happened here in a week," Frankie said. "Mama, she's broken right now but she'll heal. The truth is we got lazy. We knew Daddy would protect us, and we didn't even see how the two men we trusted with our home and our money really felt about him. We took Cawfee in like family. And I nearly..." This needed a deep breath, but Hannibal and Cindy waited. "I was ready to be all in with Gene."

"I'm sorry things went down like they did," Hannibal said.

"Don't do that," Frankie said. "If I never met you, Daddy would still be dead. You gave me more than you know. You gave me the only reason I have to think any man can be trusted." She hugged him tight and held it for a long moment. Then she backed away, and nodded thanks to Cindy for allowing the momentary intimacy.

"You need to go get back to your life. And we need to find ours. We get a new normal, maybe with love cut out of it, but some of the poison cut out too."

- END –

AUTHOR BIO

Austin S. Camacho

Author • Publisher • Writing Instructor

Austin S. Camacho is the author of the Hannibal Jones mystery series about Washington DC-based private eye Hannibal Jones. He is also the author of the Stark and O'Brien International Adventure-Thriller series, and the stand-alone detective novel, Beyond Blue. His short stories have been featured in several anthologies including Dying in a Winter Wonderland—an Independent Mystery Booksellers Association Top Ten Bestseller. He is featured in the Edgar nominated African American Mystery Writers: A Historical and Thematic Study by Frankie Y. Bailey. Camacho is also the editorial director for Intrigue Publishing, a Maryland small press.

To My Readers…

First, THANK YOU for going on this Hannibal Jones journey with me. I hope you enjoyed the trip and will investigate all of Hannibal's adventures.

I love to hear from my readers! After you've read my novel please send me some feedback. Your opinions and reactions will help me with shaping future novels. You can write to me at ascamacho@hotmail.com and I will always respond. You can also reach me through my website—www.ascamacho.com and see my latest news on Facebook at austin.camacho.author.

The only thing better than hearing from my readers is meeting them! So, if you're a member of a book club, and your group decides to read one of my books, I would be most happy to attend the meeting when you discuss it. That way I can answer any questions you have and fill you in on the background of how that particular book came to be. I might even bring along some special gifts for your group!

I would also be happy to do a Zoom meeting with any book club, bookstore or any other group that would like to discuss my novels.

Thanks again for reading my work, and I hope I get the chance to meet you or hear from you in the future.

Ciao, for niao,
Austin